SATTLER'S WOODS

A NOVEL

SEAN THOMAS

Caleb,
Thanks for your support in during
answer in English this year.
Hope you enjoy!

N.T

For Meaghan

Prologue

The man watched the house that night just as he'd done countless nights before. His breath escaped from his chapped lips in a steady plume before freezing on the windshield. The soft glow from the bay window seemed almost alluring from where he watched on the dark, shadowy street. Occasionally, a car passed by, and he'd duck down in his seat as the headlights would sweep across his dashboard. He had to, just in case someone noticed his silhouette and wondered what he was doing there, parked on this quiet street in the dead of a cold night. Watching.

He'd been watching the house for four years, but this was the first night he planned on actually going up to it, on feeling the floorboards of its front porch shift beneath his boots, on hearing the screech of its screen door as he opened it, on breathing its old woman-smell deep into his lungs.

She would be going to bed soon: he had to do it now. He wanted it to keep her up, to give her nightmares like the ones he'd been having.

He fumbled for the handle of the car door with trembling fingers. The envelope was in his back pocket, the pistol in his right hand. He gripped it tightly. Too tightly. His fingers tingled before going numb. He left the car door slightly ajar after stumbling out of it.

The gravel crunched beneath his boots as he stalked up the driveway. The light was still on in the bay window, but he didn't pay it any mind. His gaze was lower. The basement windows. He knew what they hid behind their dark, impenetrable surfaces. He knew what lay buried beneath the darkness.

His grip on the pistol didn't relax until he'd slid the envelope under the front door and plunged back into the shadows of the street.

He watched the house for another hour, until the light in the bay window went out and the light in the upstairs bedroom came on.

His mouth was a thin, hard smile. Maybe the dreams of the boxes—the dozens of cardboard boxes—bursting from the depths and floating on the surface of the darkness, like body parts from a dismembered corpse, would finally stop now.

One

As Rory Callahan drove east over the Walt Whitman Bridge, the Philadelphia skyline slowly vanished from the corner of his rearview mirror. The early summer haze bled the edges of the skyscrapers into the gray sheet of sky, rendering the city a mere smudge on the horizon. And then it was gone.

"Fuck," he grumbled to himself. "That was anticlimactic."

He glanced over again at the rearview mirror as the towers and cables of the bridge shifted into view, replacing the vanished city skyline, which were replaced in turn by walls of trees and gunflint sky as he turned south onto the expressway. Irritated the classic rock station was airing the same Led Zeppelin song they played five times a day, he jabbed at a button on the radio to silence it. He had swallowed down two cups of coffee that morning, his only breakfast, and could taste the jagged edge of acid reflux at the back of his throat.

He had only a suitcase, a laptop case, and a few duffle bags piled in the backseat of his used Ford Focus. Most of his possessions were, by choice, left with his ex-wife at their row home in Queen Village. He never really liked the idea of owning a bunch of junk anyway. He'd secretly hated it whenever she'd buy something he considered particularly useless, like the coffee table books or the driftwood sign etched with *Welcome to Paradise* that hung above the sliding glass door leading to the backyard. It seemed a betrayal of her former idealism about living simply and rejecting consumerism. Rory had resented the perceived betrayal and harbored it, along with a plethora of others, deep inside, where it remained for years, unspoken and festering.

Maybe turning his back on Philly, the only place he'd ever called home, and making the drive deep into the heart of South Jersey would be a liberating, even cathartic, experience.

After all, he'd wanted the divorce just as much as Marie did. They both knew what they had become: roommates who shared a house, bills, a bed, and little else. The passionate, sometimes raucous discussions they used to have about the rise of the American plutocracy and the forces at work to create a permanent underclass in places like North Philly—discussions they constantly had when they first started dating as students at Temple, and into the infancy of their marriage—had evaporated. Every once in a while, when they'd go out to dinner on a rare occasion, one of them would attempt to recapture those early years by bringing up the latest corruption in city hall or bemoaning the rapid gentrification of places like Fishtown and Fairmount. But the attempt always felt halfhearted and insincere, and a strained silence would quickly settle over the dinner table once again.

Occasionally, a random memory from the good years would unexpectedly resurface in Rory's mind. Just that morning, as he was carrying his bags down the narrow staircase of the quiet house, he'd suddenly thought of the countless Friday nights they once spent together, getting buzzed off cold Yuenglings and talking about politics, work, books. Both of them exhausted, both of them releasing a week's worth of tension and stress. The crowd at the Phillies game would always be murmuring from the old TV in the living room. And then, during a lull in the conversation, they would kiss: slowly at first, then passionately. They would strew their clothes all along that narrow staircase as they'd make their way up to the bedroom, only to muffle their moans and panting once they got there so as not to wake their son Kevin in the next room over. The futile attempt at quiet sex, along with the tiredness and the beer, would cause them both to burst out laughing—which, of course, they then had to stifle as best they could, often unsuccessfully.

Rory had even smiled at the memory before the newer ones, the ones that felt more real, came flooding back. The way he would dread the impending weekend and its empty hours. The way he would feel more alone with Marie than he would by himself, even turning away in tacit disgust whenever his hand accidently brushed against hers in bed. Then, the buyout at *The Inquirer* two years ago—when the drinking, and therefore the divorce, became inevitable. What had Marie told him about Oedipus and Greek tragedy? The more you struggle against your fate, the more rapidly your fate launches downfield, just outside your peripheral vision, to clothesline you when you least expect it. Something like that.

Rory also understood the logic of moving to Hollingford. His mother was the strongest person he knew—teaching in a Philadelphia elementary school for thirty-five years, she had to be—but he'd become officially worried after receiving a call from the police a week after New Year's. She had apparently walked to the post office in the morning and couldn't remember how to get home. The officer who'd picked her up late that afternoon said she was near-hypothermic: she had also forgotten her scarf and hat back at the house. She had been wandering by the edge of a blueberry field nearly five miles from home when the officer spotted her.

Still, as much sense as the move made, an anxiety bordering on home sickness sat intractably in his intestines. He loved and hated the city, but he needed it, and he presumed the city needed him, too. The city needed him for his institutional knowledge of the paper, his familiarity with city hall, his dozens of relationships with council members and staff. In his mind, it was a co-dependent relationship.

What the hell am I going to do out here? he couldn't help thinking. *What the hell am I going to do?*

Even though late June was prime beach season, traffic on the Atlantic City Expressway was light. In a mere forty-eight hours, the highway would be a solid grid of SUVs and minivans snaking, slowly and agonizingly, toward crowded shore towns, but at 11 AM on a Wednesday, Rory was flying through the endless miles of farmland and pine forests of South Jersey. He took the exit for Hollingford forty minutes after he'd crossed the Walt Whitman and muttered a final "fuck" just for good measure as he cruised through the E-Z Pass lane.

Two

Winding down the exit ramp, Rory watched them from the corner of his eye as he always did when he came to visit. Cresting from the deep woods in a far corner of town, like a lonely cluster of white caps in an otherwise placid ocean, were the pale gables of a colossal mansion. They were conspicuous, even in the gray haze, as they jutted from the tree line like bone fragments poking up from a grassy, shallow grave. Just as quickly as they had surfaced, the gables sunk back into the thick woods as Rory turned into town, where they would remain submerged until the next time—whenever that might be—he'd stare at them again from the top of the eastbound exit ramp.

The mansion belonged to the Holling family, Rory remembered. His parents had told him about it once. Over a century ago, the town's founder personally designed the mansion and had the finest masonry work and stained glass imported from Europe for its construction. He died before seeing it completed, though his descendants have lived there ever since.

Rory knew little about the mansion's current owners besides their tremendous wealth. Not only was the town itself their namesake, but almost every business in town seemed to belong to them, too: blueberry farms, a real estate company, a sprawling car dealership. They all bore the Holling name. But Rory mostly knew them from the ghostly gables of their mansion that never failed to transfix him every time he exited off the highway.

Rory had actually never even heard of Hollingford at all until his parents decided to move there back in the 80s. They had both retired and wanted to get away from the city's taxes, noise, and ever-growing crime epidemic. They couldn't afford to buy a house down the shore

6

like they'd always dreamed of, but Hollingford was close enough for easy day trips to Avalon and Stone Harbor and for nice dinners in Atlantic City.

A few miles from the expressway exit was Route 30, known locally as the White Horse Pike. It cut through the center of town and was littered with fast food joints, convenience stores, and gas stations. Rory stopped at a Wawa to pick up an Italian hoagie for himself, a chicken salad sandwich for his mother, and a jug of peach iced tea for the both of them.

The drive to his mother's house brought him past Central Avenue, which had been Hollingford's primary thoroughfare before they built Route 30 in the early 50s. Scattered along it were the local library, a number of churches, and a handful of family-owned businesses: restaurants, bars, barber shops, a hardware store. A couple of them had foreclosed since Rory's last visit and were now marked by blank, sun-bleached signs, adrift in empty, weed-choked parking lots.

He came to a stop at the traffic light where Elm intersected with Central. On one corner was The Oasis bar, its once-white clapboard a decided gray now, and its letter board sign unchanged since Christmas: *Enjoy Our Fa-la-la-abulous Drink Specials This Holiday Season*, it still read. The Oasis still seemed open for business, however: the fluorescent beer signs in the windows were turned on for the lunch crowd, at least. It had been a favorite spot of Rory's father's for many years—the perfect place to catch a Phils game, throw back some PBRs, devour cheap buffalo wings, and curse at everything from the Dallas Cowboys to the "rat bastard politicians" on a mission to destroy Philadelphia's once-powerful and proud unions. Those memories were actually some of Rory's fondest of his father in the final years before his death.

Besides an old man sporting an incongruous fedora and a full, pinstripe suit, Central Avenue was practically abandoned. As he waited at the light, Rory watched the old man shuffle down Central, toward the Catholic Church at far end of the block. *Jesus, how can he stand wearing that suit in this heat?* When the light turned, Rory tried to catch a glimpse of the old man's face as he passed—maybe he was a church friend of his mother's?—but he was already too far down the block to get a good look.

His mother's house was a yellow Cape Cod with a small front porch and an attached single-car garage. Rory stood on the front porch, his suitcase in one hand and the Wawa bag in the other, inspecting the front yard and the planter bordering the porch. Both seemed well manicured and lovingly maintained.

Maybe she's doing better. Maybe she's doing ok here.

No one came to the door when he rang the doorbell, so he set his suitcase down, opened the screechy screen door, and knocked.

"Mom? You home?" he yelled. After a minute, he tried the door and found it unlocked. "Mom?" he repeated, poking his head into the hallway.

He heard swing music playing loudly from the back of the house, then a voice that burst with surprise, but also warmth. "Oh, Rory! Is that you? I wasn't expecting you today!"

We just talked about it this morning. God damn it. Rory began to let out a defeated sigh, and then caught himself. "Sorry to drop in on you like this, mom. Hope this is ok."

The volume of the music dropped and a gray-haired, diminutive woman emerged from the darkness of the hallway. She was wearing a blue, flower-print dress and dark leather moccasins. She flashed that same beaming smile that had melted the hearts, and won over the trust, of some of her toughest students back in Philly.

"Hey, mom. It's good to see you," Rory said, reaching his arm over her shoulder and inelegantly dangling the Wawa bag behind her back as he hugged her.

She kissed his cheek. "I'm sorry I didn't hear you. I had some music playing back in the kitchen while I was making lunch. Hungry? It's she-crab soup."

Rory held out the Wawa bag. *She forgot I had asked her about the sandwiches this morning, too. But she's active. She's in good spirits.* "That sounds great. We can save these sandwiches for supper."

She gently nudged past him to grab his suitcase from the porch and carried it off into the first-floor bedroom.

"Thanks, mom. I could have gotten that."

"No worries," she said, reemerging before taking the Wawa bag from his hand. "Lunch will be ready in ten minutes if you want to settle in a bit."

"Let me know if you need help." She dismissed the offer with a curt, backwards wave and disappeared back into the kitchen.

Rory placed a hand on his rumbling stomach as the rich, creamy smell of the she-crab soup drifted into the hallway. He was about to go unpack to take his mind off his hunger when he noticed something under his sneaker: a letter in a sealed envelope. It had obviously been slid under the door.

He reached down for it, wondering why it had been left there and not in the mailbox at the end of the driveway. *Kathleen* was written on the envelope in cursive. And inside was a single sheet of paper with a message written in neat, print handwriting:

> *I am still watching and always will. Through the bay window. In your bedroom. Young blood was spilled once. I will spill old blood and bathe in its righteousness should the time come. When will the time come? We both know the answer to this question.*
>
> *-The Guardian*

Three

"I think we should talk to the police about this."

The letter lay in the middle of the small kitchen table. A bowl of she-crab soup and a plate of crackers sat in front of each of them, although only Kathleen was partaking at the moment.

"Oh, there's no need," she responded, dipping her spoon into the soup for another helping.

"I respect your brave face, mom. But this," he said, pointing at the note, "is stalking. And harassment. And I'm pretty sure a death threat, too. This is fu— "

Kathleen shot him a glance.

"Sorry. Screwed up. This is really screwed up."

"I know who's sending them, though. He's harmless," she said, swatting the air as if shooing away a fly.

"Them? You mean you've gotten more than one of these?" Rory felt a wave of guilt wash over him. *And where have I been? Where the fuck have I been? Getting drunk every afternoon while my wife was teaching and lesson planning and my mom was getting death threats.*

"Yeah, but they're from little Billy Dannucci. He's not gonna do anything," she said dismissively, chuckling to herself.

"Billy Dannucci? He lives here in town?"

"Nah, he's over on Christian street with his aunt and uncle."

Christian Street? Rory thought, confused. *Back in Philly?*

Kathleen slurped up another spoonful of soup. "Your father hated Billy all throughout high school. And I'm pretty sure Billy was terrified of your father. And who can blame him? Your father was starting linebacker and looked so tough in that varsity jacket of his. Once we started dating, Billy left me alone."

It took Rory a moment to realize that Kathleen must have been mixing up memories. *Billy Dannucci. Must have been a little shit-bird neighborhood kid back in South Philly who had a hard time dealing with rejection.* "But dad's not around anymore. What if Billy," he paused a moment, picking his words carefully, "tried something? More than just leave a note like this."

Kathleen reached across the table and patted Rory's hand. "I can take care of myself, sweetheart. Always have, always will."

Rory nodded as he tried to process the threatening letter. *Billy must have stalked her and left her threatening notes like this one in high school. Maybe this is triggering some long-forgotten memories for her, and she's getting confused. But would his notes have been as cryptic and disturbing as this one, though? I just hope this is the one and only note she's gotten and the not the latest in a fucking conga line of them.*

"Mom, do you still have the other letters you've gotten under the door like that?"

"I threw those away. Why hold onto them? They're just nonsense."

The thought occurred to Rory that maybe Billy Dannucci, all grown up, as lonely and pathetic as ever, had somehow discovered Kathleen's address—it's not very hard these days—and came out here to terrorize her once again. *Maybe he watches her every night, standing out in the dark, staring into the brightly lit windows of the house.*

A second thought, dark and enraging, then occurred to him: perhaps Billy even knew about her failing mental health and was planning to take advantage of it to exact some horrifying, long-festering revenge? But—is anyone really that twisted, to harass a girl he'd known from high school fifty years ago? It seemed improbable. But that, then, presented the deeper and more troubling question: if Billy hadn't written the note and surreptitiously slid it under the door in the quiet hours of the night, who did—and why?

Four

Rory tried to take his mind off the "Guardian" letter and simply enjoy lunch with his mother, but certain phrases kept intruding in his mind the more he tried to ignore them. *In your bedroom...I will spill old blood...When will the time come? We both know the answer to this question.*

After doing the lunch dishes, he announced his intention to take the note to the police.

"It's simply not necessary. They have much more important things to do with their time," Kathleen protested.

"I know. But I'd at least like to run this by them. Maybe other people in town have been getting similar notes. I just want to see if they know anything."

"If you insist," she said absently, sitting back down at the kitchen table with a Virginia Woolf novel.

The Hollingford Police Department was housed in a nondescript, two-story office building on Central Avenue, between the public library and town hall. Rory parked on the street and stepped out into the dead air which had all the weight and grayness of a corpse in *rigor mortis*.

Upon entering the building, he was directed over to Officer Matthew Ackermann, who sat at an island of desks divided by opaque, plastic partitions in the center of a small, freshly carpeted room. There was a small number of other police officers in the room, either passing through on their way out for patrol or seated at their desks typing away on computers. Ackermann looked up from his own computer as Rory approached, letter in hand.

"Officer Ackermann? Rory Callahan."

Ackermann stood up tentatively to shake Rory's out-stretched hand. "Good to meet you. What can I do for you?"

"The lady at reception sent me over. Said you could help me with a threatening letter my mother received."

"Sure. Of course. Have a seat," Ackermann said, dragging over a chair from an adjacent, unoccupied desk.

Officer Ackerman looked to be in his late 20s. He had dark, close-cut hair and equally dark, practically black, eyes. His skin was colorless and clammy to the touch. He was thinly built, even scrawny—his blue uniform hung loosely from his narrow shoulders.

"Now, what is this letter your mother received?" he asked, dutifully turning to a fresh page in his notepad and withdrawing a pen from a mug filled with them.

Rory showed him the letter and explained how he couldn't be sure if this was the latest of many or the first and only, given his mother's condition. He also mentioned the name Billy Dannucci and his history of threatening behavior—at least, the strong possibility that he acted threateningly many decades ago—while admitting that the odds of Billy being responsible were pretty low.

"It certainly is unsettling," Ackermann said, scanning over the note.

"A good way to describe it."

"You say you found the letter earlier today, when you arrived at your mother's house?" Ackermann asked quizzically, looking up at Rory with those coal-dark eyes.

"Yes. It had clearly been slid under the door."

"Is it possible the note had been lying there for a while—perhaps days, even weeks, before you discovered it today?"

Rory recoiled at this suggestion about his mother's mental state, but acknowledged to himself that it might be possible. "It seems unlikely. You don't know my mom—she keeps the house spotless. I doubt she would have stepped over an envelope sitting there on the floor for days or weeks."

Ackermann raised his eyebrows and twisted his lips in a strange attempt to convey concern. "Right. But still…possible?"

"Possible," Rory said begrudgingly.

"The only reason I ask is that we picked up a drifter last Tuesday. He had been hanging around town for at least a few weeks. Bothering people on the street, knocking on doors late at night. He even barged into the McDonald's on Route 30, spouting off some Biblical quotes about the rapture and the resurrection of the dead. Reminds me a little of the language in this," he said, tapping the note with a long, bony finger.

"What happened to him?" Rory asked.

"We brought him in after the McDonald's incident, tried to help him. Found out he has family in Vineland—or at least he claimed he did. But we couldn't find anyone who knew him. He's now up at a mental health facility in Trenton."

Rory was immediately skeptical that this drifter was responsible. "Did he slide notes like this one under anyone else's door?"

Ackermann frowned. "No. No one's reported anything, at least."

"So why, of the 35,000 people in town, would he specifically target my mom with an explicit threat?"

"I can't be sure, sir. The man *was* quite mentally ill."

Rory sighed and ran his fingers over his stubble. "Would it be too much to ask to have an officer stationed outside the house tonight? Maybe the next couple nights?"

A brief, wheezy laugh escaped Ackermann's lips. "I don't think that's necessary, sir. A patrol car will roll through your mother's neighborhood twice tonight to check up on everything. It's part of our normal, nightly procedure."

"That's great, but nobody was there last night—"

"If it was last night."

"If it was last night," Rory responded calmly, "when someone crept up to the front door and left this for her."

"I don't think it's an appropriate course of action at the moment."

"Really? Just for a few nights. Let's say, midnight through five AM. I plan on staying up anyway, but it would be easy for the guy to disappear before a cop shows up."

Ackermann sighed. "I would love to say yes, but we have limited resources in the department." His tone became gradually patronizing. "We had two armed robberies, at the Rite Aid and the CVS on Route

30, in the past month. Prescription drugs. There've been a rash of burglaries up in Northwest Estates recently. Real crimes. Real victims. And for all we know, this," he said, gesturing toward the note again, "could be a harmless practical joke."

Rory had to deploy every ounce of energy in his body not to fly into an expletive-laced tirade at the useless, empty suit sitting before him. "Not sure I would call a promise to 'spill old blood' a harmless practical joke. I'm not asking for much here."

Ackermann flipped his notepad shut, returned the pen to its proper place in the mug, and sat back in his office chair. "I'm afraid until something else happens, there's nothing much I can do. We can't expend all that time and manpower for every unusual message people in town receive. Especially when the man who most likely wrote it is being cared for in Trenton as we speak."

Rory grabbed the note off the desk, folded it, and shoved it in his pocket. As he got up to go, he smiled and said, "Thank you so much for your time. You've truly demonstrated your tireless efforts to protect the most vulnerable members of the community—job well done," before marching out of the building.

Just as he was about to get into the car, he heard someone cry, "Wait!" from behind him.

He turned around to see another young officer—possibly younger than Ackermann—jogging up the sidewalk toward him. She was short, fair-skinned, with ink-black hair tied into a tight bun. Thick clouds of freckles covered each of her cheeks and the bridge of her nose.

"Mr. Callahan?" she asked.

"Rory," he said, shaking her hand.

"Jess Daniels," she introduced herself. Her voice had a hint of gravel to it. "I may have overheard some of your conversation with Officer Dickface back there. I can't decide if he's flat-out incompetent or just obsessed with kissing ass."

Rory laughed. "Don't worry about it. I'm sure he's just following orders."

Daniels rolled her eyes. "It's true," she said, lowering her voice and shooting a glance back at the station before continuing. "We've been under a lot of pressure from the mayor and town council to make some ridiculous drops in crime stats in a ridiculously short amount of time. They're trying to maintain this image of Hollingford as an unspoiled, *Leave It to Beaver*-type utopia. Meanwhile, we broke the record for heroin overdoses last year. I'm not saying that's a problem we could, or should, try to arrest ourselves out of, but it does show how out of touch with reality they are."

"As politicians and police commissioners tend to be."

"For us, that means brushing off as many 'minor,'" she explained, adding air quotes, "crimes as we can."

"I guess they've finally exported that little tactic from city policing out into the suburbs."

"Personally, I wouldn't call death threats to a senior citizen 'minor.' Do you mind if I see the note?" she asked.

"Not at all." He pulled the letter out from his pocket and handed it to her.

"Shit," she said as she read it over. "Scary stuff."

"I know. And with my mom's situation, I just can't be sure how long this has been going on."

She looked up at him with warm brown eyes and smiled. "Kathleen, over on Stockton, right?"

"You know her?" Rory asked, surprised.

"I gave her a lift back into town last winter."

The memory of that cold, January day—when Kathleen had gotten lost on her way home from the post office—stung, but Rory smiled anyway. "That's right. Thank you for doing that."

"She's an incredibly kind woman. Anytime I drive by on patrol and she's out working in the yard, she'll wave and ask if I need coffee or a slice of pie."

Rory nodded. "That's my mom all right."

Daniels glanced down at the paper in her hand before looking back up at Rory. "Listen, it won't be easy—I'll have to do some serious string-pulling and call in a bunch of favors—but I'm going to find a way to get someone out there for the next few nights."

Rory was taken aback not just by the generosity, but by her willingness to undermine Ackermann, her fellow officer. "Are you sure? You won't get shit for that?"

"I'll be fine: I've covered plenty of overtimes for plenty of people. They owe me some big favors. And yes, I'm sure. I'll get them to park down the block in an unmarked car so we don't scare this guy off if he comes back."

"That would be perfect. Thank you so much for your help." Rory smiled and shook her hand again.

"Of course. Here's my card, in case you need anything else. Mind if I hold onto the note?"

"Be my guest," Rory said, scanning over her card before tucking it into his wallet. "Thanks again."

"Give my best to your mom," Daniels said before turning around and heading back to the station.

So there is hope for humanity after all, Rory thought as climbed into the car and started back for his mother's house.

Five

As dark descended that evening, Rory pulled a chair up to his first-floor bedroom window and sat down with a tumbler of Jameson in one hand and that morning's *Philadelphia Inquirer* in the other. He rested the whiskey on the window sill and propped his feet up on a wooden chest that sat beneath the window. Sounds from the TV in the living room, where his mother had settled after dinner, drifted into the front bedroom. From the sound of it, she was switching back and forth between the Phillies game and a rerun of *Modern Family*.

From the bedroom window, he had a clear view of the front yard and the street—and if he leaned forward just a few inches, the porch and the driveway, too. He took a sip of whiskey, unfolded the paper in his lap, and began flipping through it. *Typical steaming pile of horse shit. The Eagles, who don't start their season for three months, have a front page story while the triple-shooting in Kensington gets barely a mention on page three. And of course: the ubiquitous ads.* He refolded the paper and dropped it back in his lap.

Outside, the sky was dark purple and cloudless; the haze from earlier in the day had finally lifted around suppertime to reveal a clear twilight sky. Fireflies blinked across the front yard and in a stand of pine trees across the street like distant stars in the void. A group of teenagers rode by on bikes, speaking in loud, echoey, voices. A couple walking a black dog came into view only to exit seconds later.

Rory tipped forward in his chair again and scanned both directions down the street. He noticed a gray sedan parked under a streetlight a few houses down and thought it might be the cop car Officer Daniels had promised, but then swore he could remember seeing it parked there earlier in the afternoon.

His gaze shifted to the stand of trees across the street. It wasn't very wide—maybe twenty feet—but it provided a sizeable buffer between the two houses on either side. It was also thick. He wondered if there was someone standing in there right now, hidden by darkness, watching the house as he'd promised in the note. But the more he thought it about, the more ridiculous it seemed—maybe the note actually was left by that drifter Ackermann had mentioned? Despite the medication, Kathleen was gradually getting worse; perhaps she really hadn't noticed the envelope lying there on the foyer floor for days or weeks. Or maybe it was some kind of sick joke. High school kids egging each other on and gloating about it on Twitter and Snapchat.

He also realized the longer he stared into those dark trees, the more his eyes played tricks on him. It had actually started already: there was a human figure standing there, motionless, ten feet back from the curb. A bit to the left was a big, grinning, white face. Rory shook his head, reopened the paper, and began working on the crossword puzzle, taking another sip of whiskey as he did.

By the time Rory fell asleep in his chair at two in the morning, he had finished two Sudokus in the paper and nearly completed the crossword puzzle. At around 10:30, Kathleen had come in to kiss him goodnight and to tell him he should stop worrying and go to bed.

"I will soon. Just want to keep a lookout a little while longer."

"Seen anything yet?"

"A few cars go by, but none of them stopped."

"It's just Billy. I told you already: he's harmless." She kissed his forehead again before quietly making her way upstairs to her bedroom.

At around midnight, and on his third tumbler of Jameson, Rory sat in the dark—he had turned the bedroom light off to reduce the glare on the window—and started to think about his ex-wife Marie and their son Kevin. It was almost three years ago to the day that he and Marie had driven Kevin to the airport: he was starting a new job at a tech startup in Palo Alto after graduating from Bucknell a month earlier. They had stopped at Jim's on South Street for lunch—"When's the next time you're going to be able to have a real Philly cheesesteak?"

he remembered Marie saying with a sad smile—and still managed to get to the airport over an hour early. Marie bawled when she'd hugged him goodbye. Rory had tried to remain stoic, so he rattled off movie reference to deflect his growing despondency—everything from *Indiana Jones* to *American Graffiti*—but he'd still struggled to keep from welling up. Kevin, who never liked attention, had seemed embarrassed as they hugged him, but also excited to start his new adventure.

Rory vividly recollected the drive home from the airport. The silence. The sinking, queasy feeling of an impending, inevitable conversation: a conversation that would lead to a pathetic, whimpering end to their once impervious marriage. There wouldn't be any fighting or screaming. Just a somber acknowledgement that their lives were now, for all intents and purposes, separate, so why not make it official and at least sleep better at night? They had succeeded in this one great task together—raising a decent, happy, well-adjusted son—and now there was nothing left to do.

By about one in the morning, Rory had downed his fourth tumbler of Jameson and was feeling his eyelids get heavy. "Marie," he stammered to the dark window, the silent front yard, the mysterious pine trees across the street. "I'm sorry. I know I stopped trying. When I lost the job…I let that affect everything. Your suggestions were good. They were really good. The blog was a brilliant idea. Maybe if I didn't get discouraged and give up, people would have started reading that shit. Grad school was a good idea, too. And I fucked it all up. I stopped trying and eventually caring, and I know everything was my fucking fault."

Just before two, Rory stood up and peered through the window. His head was swimming, and he nearly fell back into his chair. "Fuck," he grumbled. He stared outside for a moment, squinting into the darkness, and froze—was that movement in the trees? Someone was pacing back and forth, just beyond the first line of pines. But maybe not. This was the effect of tiredness, and boredom, and whiskey. He still saw the dark, stationary figure and the grinning face as well. He watched for a few more seconds and then collapsed into the chair, the empty tumbler spilling from his hand and rolling across the hardwood floor until it collided with the baseboard. When sleep came suddenly and deeply seconds later, Rory's eyes were wet with tears.

Rory awoke sore and partially drunk at daybreak. "God damn it," he whispered hoarsely to himself. He was repulsed by the taste of his own breath. He staggered out of the bedroom and into the front hallway where he half expected to see another envelope on the floor by the front door. But there was nothing.

He pulled sneakers onto his bare feet and trudged down the gravel driveway, crossed the quiet street, and stood at the edge of the pine trees opposite his mother's house. He took a cursory look for any signs of human presence—cigarette butts, food wrappers, footprints—anything to confirm or refute his nighttime visions. But there was only a carpet of brown, fallen pine needles and the tangled underbrush. The motionless figure he had seen was a stunted, nearly branchless tree mixed in with the others. The grinning face was a circular wound left where a thick, heavy branch had snapped from a huge pine tree and fallen to the forest floor.

On his way back to the house, he grabbed the newspaper off the dewy front lawn and brought it inside, placing it on the kitchen table for Kathleen to read while she drank her coffee. Before returning to bed to sleep off the whiskey, he took two aspirin and chugged a large glass of cool water.

He slept fitfully for the next few hours, dreaming of the house down in Ocean City he and Marie would rent every summer when Kevin was young. Except in his dream, the house was isolated, surrounded by empty, gray beach rather than row upon row of duplexes and streets busy with bicyclists and families on their way to the boardwalk. The three of them were huddled on the floor of the living room. The ocean, which they could see beyond the railing of the balcony, was black and boiling. Rain lashed the windows and the wind mercilessly, if not maliciously, pummeled the entire house. They could hear sand whipping at the walls and the roof and the doors like unending rounds of birdshot from dozens of shotguns. Just before the house shuddered and groaned and yawned as the roof was torn off the rafters and carried into the maddeningly swirling black vortex of sky, Rory looked into the eyes of his ex-wife and son and saw utter dread—dread of some unavoidable, unspeakable horror.

Six

That afternoon, while Kathleen napped on the living room couch, Rory walked the half mile to The Oasis bar to have a few beers and catch the early innings of the Phils game. The day was blindingly bright and warm; Rory worked up a sweat on the short walk to Central Avenue. But the exercise—however brief—felt good.

As soon as he pushed open the door, Rory was greeted by the familiar, distinct smell of the bar he and his father had frequented for years: it was some peculiar combination of stale beer, fried crab cakes, and long-dormant dust. He was also greeted by Al, the taciturn, seemingly ageless bartender who was just as much a fixture of the bar as the TVs, the beer signs, and that unique combination of smells. He had been unpacking cases of beer and loading them into a small fridge beneath the counter when Rory walked in, but he popped up when he heard the bell on the door jingle.

"The prodigal son returns," Al said. He wore the same yellow golf shirt he seemed to always have on while his slicked back hair and thick moustache completed the timeless ensemble.

"That's a truer characterization than you know," Rory said.

Al tossed a cardboard coaster onto the counter and whirled around to pour a Guinness as Rory claimed a stool under one of the two TVs screwed into the wall behind the bar. Other than a young couple seated in a booth by the window and a middle-aged man with full sleeve tattoos on both arms at the very end of the bar, The Oasis was deserted.

"Visiting Kathleen for a few days?" Al asked flatly as he placed the perfectly poured Guinness in front of Rory.

"Visiting, but longer than a few days." Rory took a sip of the beer. "I'm actually going to move in for a while."

"That's good of you. I'm sure she'll really appreciate that," Al said as he returned to unpacking the beer.

"I'm doing it as much for me as I am for her, to be honest with you." He took a longer sip of beer. "Marie and I are done."

Al stood back up from his crouch and gave Rory a look of genuine sympathy and concern. "Gee, I'm sorry to hear that." He patted Rory on the shoulder and then turned around toward the liquor shelves. In a matter of seconds he returned with a shot of Jim Beam and placed it next to the Guinness. "Well, you came to the right place."

"Thanks, Al," Rory said as he downed the bourbon. He let it burn down his throat rather than chase it with the beer.

Sensing an end to the conversation, Rory looked up at the TV. The game was only in the second inning, and the Phillies were already down three to nothing. The crowd noise and inane conversation of the commentators served as white noise for Rory, and he felt himself relax for the first time since finding the strange, threatening note on his mother's floor.

By the end of his second beer, Rory had the bar to himself. When Al finished loading up the fridge, he stood with his back leaning on the counter to watch the game as well.

"Gonna be a long season," Al lamented.

"One day, looking back on it, we'll truly get a sense of just how big a shit Rueben Amaro actually took on this team."

"Pretty sizable, I'd imagine." Al glanced over at Rory's glass. "Another?"

"Why not?" As Al was drawing the beer, Rory asked him, "How are things going for you here?"

His back turned, Al gave a noncommittal shrug and said, "Not too bad. Business's been steady." He replaced the empty glass with the fresh one. "How about you? What'll you be up to while you're in town?"

You're seeing it, Rory thought. He sighed and said, "Not much it seems. I'm going to stop in to the *Hollingford Herald* office tomorrow, see if they need help. Maybe I can do some freelance for them."

"Doesn't hurt to ask," Al said conclusively, before leaning back on the bar and looking up at the game again.

When the bell on the door jingled and an evanescent beam of bright afternoon light shot into the dim bar, Rory didn't even bother to turn around. He was watching the game—even though the Phillies were predictably getting slaughtered—and enjoying both the soothing white noise from the TV as well as the slight buzz from the beers and the shot. It wasn't until Al turned his head, a look of utter frustration in his typically placid eyes, that Rory did the same.

An elderly woman, her stringy, white hair coarse-looking and tangled, her worn-out blue jeans far too baggy for her emaciated figure, was affixing a flyer to a corkboard on the wall beside the door. The board typically featured badly outdated advertisements for school plays, notices about yard sales, and information on missing pets.

"Cindy," Al said with a surprising amount of force and volume. "Don't make me call the cops again. You know I will."

The woman turned around and approached the bar. She didn't respond to the threat, but rather slid one of her fliers onto the counter toward Rory. "Telling the truth isn't a crime, is it?" she asked. She smiled at Rory, revealing yellow smokers' teeth, and then was gone, the bell tinkling behind her.

"God damn crazy woman," Al muttered.

Rory looked down at the piece of paper on the counter. There was a series of pictures, some in black and white, others in color, all of the same man at various ages. There was a picture of him as a toddler on a miniature horse, another of him surrounded by presents and blowing out birthday candles. A high school graduation photo. One of him at a bowling alley, his arm around a much younger version of the woman who'd been hanging up the flyer.

The top of the flyer, in all caps, screamed, *MY SON IS INNOCENT!!!* Beneath the photos was more information: *On January 9th, 1994, Randall Thompson III, was WRONGLY convicted for murder. The police aggressively pursued and charged Randy not based on any evidence but because of PREJUDICE and HATRED. I will continue to spread the word of Randy's sweet-nature and kindness until he comes home. Even if that never happens, I will NOT allow his character to continue to get assassinated by the police, lawyers, and media. Randy is INNOCENT.*

Al seemed to expect Rory's confused expression when he looked up from the flyer. "I can take care of that right now for you. My apologies," he said, crumpling the flyer into a ball and flinging it into a trashcan behind the counter.

"What's this all about?" Rory asked.

"You remember the Blueberry Hill murders, maybe twenty years ago now?"

"I think so. It was pretty big news, even back in the city. And it's all my parents could talk about for months." Rory paused to think. "Three kids, wasn't it?"

"Attacked in the woods behind the middle school. Bodies were found months later, right at the edge of the state park."

"That's right," Rory said, remembering more details. "My parents were actually pretty close with the grandmother of one of the kids."

"Well that whacky old biddy," Al said, pointing toward the door, "is the mother of the guy who did it. She's been on her pain-in-the-ass, one woman crusade for years now. Don't mind her."

"So the guy's indisputably guilty? I guess a mother's love is unwavering."

"Oh, he was always creepy. Whenever you ran into him around town, he made you feel…" Al searched for the right word. "Off. Even before the murders he'd been in jail for molesting kids, or something like that. Just an absolute monster."

Rory spun around on his stool and examined the flier now hanging on the corkboard. Randy looked like a typical, if not slightly awkward, but genuinely happy high school kid in his graduation photo. He had shaggy blond hair, patches of mild acne on his forehead and chin, peach fuzz on his upper-lip. His eyes were bright blue, practically sparkling. And his smile was shy and sweet. It was hard to imagine that same kid going on to commit an appalling triple-murder—Rory remembered reading the murderer likely beat in the skulls of the children with a stick or a rock.

Looking at those sparkling blue eyes, that shy smile, Rory wondered if they were as disarming and kind as they seemed. Or if, perhaps, they were part of a carefully cultivated disguise to keep dark secrets and heinous predilections hidden deep inside.

Seven

As the sun set and Kathleen settled into the living room to watch her nightly round of sitcoms, Rory once again seated himself by the bedroom window and rested a tumbler of whiskey on the sill. But unlike the previous night, he wasn't staring intently out the window, but rather at his laptop screen as he eagerly searched for information on Randall Thompson and the Blueberry Hill murders. He could remember the basics of the case, Thompson's arrest, and the conviction, but the specific details escaped him these many years later. It wasn't long, however, before he unearthed archived stories from *The Philadelphia Inquirer*, *The Press of Atlantic City*, *The Courier Post*, and *The Hollingford Herald* which helped him piece the story together.

Around nightfall on April 13th, 1992, three boys were on their way home from the Blueberry Hill Middle School, a single-story, brick building in the northwest corner of town. Just as they had done hundreds of times before, they cut through Sattler's Woods, a dense, 12-acre forest behind the school, on a wide, well-trodden trail.

It's unclear if all three boys were walking together, but almost certain two of them were: Nathaniel Foster and Christopher Fitzgerald, both 7th graders, were close friends and were leaving school late that night because of rehearsal for the spring musical. The show was *Grease* and was supposed to premiere after Easter in a couple of weeks. The third boy, Andrew Skelly, was an 8th grader and was purportedly not close with the two 7th graders, if he even knew them at all. It's unknown why Andrew had been at school as late as he was. He was on the baseball team, but practice ended at 5:30, and he was typically

SEAN THOMAS

home 15 minutes later. His parents later said he planned on getting pizza with teammates that night and would be back later than usual, but no one on the team could remember plans to get dinner that particular evening. In fact, no one on the team could remember seeing him after 5:30 when practice ended.

The boys most likely left school around dusk. All three of them lived in the Laurel Acres neighborhood just beyond Sattler's Woods, so the trail would have been familiar and comfortable to them, even in the fading light. By about 9:30, after no sign or word from their son, Christopher's parents started to worry. They called the police. When the police received a call 15 minutes later from Andrew's concerned parents, they sent two officers over to the school to check the athletic fields, playground, and courtyard. When Nathaniel's grandmother, his sole guardian, called the police station shortly after 10 PM, they sent two more officers to the school to comb the woods and the trail between school grounds and Laurel Acres.

Even in the dark, police found obvious signs of a struggle at the midpoint of the trail. A wild cluster of footprints disturbed the sandy topsoil. A cushion of fallen pine needles along the trailside had been kicked and scattered. Several heavy objects had clearly been dragged through the dirt, back toward the school. And most alarming, fresh blood was both spattered across the soil and pooled in two larger patches. Flecks of brain matter were later identified flung across the disturbed ground as well. Two of the officers tried to retrace the footsteps back to the start of the trail behind the school to get a sense if the boys had been followed, but they got only a few feet when the footprints ended: someone had covered the tracks with a rake or a shovel.

Meanwhile, the two other officers waded into the woods alongside the disturbed soil, their flashlights piercing through the dark trees and heavy underbrush. It wasn't long before they found the fist-sized rock and the thick, heavy, birch log—both were spattered with blood, still warm and sticky to the touch. They also found a smaller, sharply pointed stick coated with blood as well.

Soon, Sattler's Woods was crawling with flashlight-wielding cops. Nearby residents, including the parents of the three boys, stood at the

28

edge of the forest, watching the numerous, ghostly beams of light float through the darkness, waiting to hear that dreadful, imminent cry that would surely go up when the bodies were discovered. But no cry went up that long night.

By morning, Sattler's Woods was roped off and a full-fledged search effort was underway. Schools closed. Families stayed inside and watched wave after wave of search party members—both police and citizens—move through the streets, yards, and woods. The numerous blueberry fields were scoured. Crystal Lake, just off Route 30, was dredged. But no bodies were found.

That wouldn't happen until late September, after a full, nightmarish summer of anguish and false hope for the families, friends, teachers, and neighbors of the three boys. Two hikers, a husband and wife, got lost on the Batona Trail in a state park about ten miles from town. Already off-course, the husband delved deeper into the woods to take a leak when he literally stumbled over the badly decomposed bodies of the middle school students behind a large, fallen, cedar tree. They had been buried in the shallowest of graves. Alongside the corpses were all three of the boys' backpacks, seemingly untouched; the back pocket of Andrew Skelly's bag still contained his beloved Game Boy with the *Super Mario Land* cartridge inserted.

The area was so remote, it took the two hikers nearly a full day to find it again with police in tow. The police briefly considered the hikers suspects due to the pure randomness of their discovery, before quickly clearing them: they lived in West Chester, a western suburb of Philadelphia, had solid alibis for April 13th, and, most saliently, would have no reason to call attention to self-damning evidence.

Upon examination, all three bodies were discovered to have their cheap, Velcro, wallets with them, also apparently untouched, with each containing small amounts of cash. This, along with the backpacks, allowed police to rule out a popular theory: the boys were victims of a robbery gone bad. It also gave the police cause to search the home of suspect Randall Thompson III. An anonymous tip only a day or two into the disappearance had put him on their radar. When they realized he was a registered sex offender, they questioned him and concluded his alibi for the night of April 13th was weak: he was out taking a walk, like he did every night, around town. He couldn't recall bumping into anyone who could identify him or stopping at any of the stores on Central or Route 30 where a clerk or customer might be able to identify him. His mother—he still lived with her—couldn't remember what time he returned home that night: she was asleep in bed by nine.

They had no direct evidence linking him to the murders: DNA pulled from the bodies, clothing, and the supposed murder weapons did not match Randall's. The bodies themselves were too badly decomposed to reveal evidence of sexual assault. One of the footprints from the trail through Sattler's Woods, while nearly indistinguishable, appeared to be the same size as Thompson's: a size seven. Abnormally small. But there was no way to prove the footprint was left by Thompson and not one of the boys.

The biggest problem for Thompson came in the form of a paper grocery bag buried at the bottom of his closet. The police discovered it when they searched his mother's house. It contained dozens of tapes of child pornography, some of them featuring horrifically violent footage. The investigators who watched the tapes reportedly required therapy after witnessing the unconscionable horrors inflicted on children—the majority of them, middle school-aged boys. The police arrested, and formally charged Thompson with the murders, shortly after viewing the tapes.

When Randall was charged in early 1993, his mother Cindy put a second mortgage on the house to hire well-regarded defense attorney Clive Romero. The trial was long and drawn-out, but Romero seemed to be successfully illustrating that the shadow of a doubt about Thompson's guilt was really a black hole. He highlighted the immense pressure the police were under from the community, the families of the victims, and the media to make an arrest as quickly as possible. He argued that they zeroed in on Randall early in the investigation, spinning a false narrative of a man controlled by inner-demons, who was so ashamed of accosting and assaulting the three middle school students, he had to destroy both the witnesses and objects of his cruel lust. As a result, investigators put up blinders to other potential suspects and motivations.

Any momentum Romero was building with the jury suddenly died in late summer when the judge accepted the prosecutor's request to show the nightmarish video tapes found in Thompson's closet. Upon watching them, over half of the jury broke down in tears at the footage; several members became nauseated and had to excuse themselves from the courtroom. After that, they didn't seem so bothered by the lack of physical evidence. Apparently, when the prosecutor argued that Thompson hid the bodies so well because he knew any sign of sexual assault would be erased by time, they believed it.

Unsurprisingly and understandably, the jury was unmoved when Romero stated that Thompson never meant to purchase the ghastliest of the video tapes and that he wasn't even aware they were included in the bag when he picked it up from an anonymous dealer at an expressway rest stop. Because of Thompson's quiet, sullen demeanor, Romero decided not to have him take the stand in his own defense. While perhaps it seemed like a wise gambit at the time, the jury's inability to consider Randall anything but a lying, sociopathic, pedophile sealed his fate: in the early fall of 1993, he was quickly convicted and sentenced to life in prison with no chance of parole.

Romero filed for an appeal after sentencing, but it was quickly denied. Thompson spent three years at Southern State before being transferred to South Woods State Prison when it opened in 1997, where he has been incarcerated ever since.

In the years since those agonizing weeks and months in 1992, when every nighttime shadow was that of a child-stalking killer, when every unfounded rumor sparked panicked school lockdowns and early dismissals, Hollingford has slowly recovered, moved on, and even started to forget. The recovery began with Thompson's arrest, when parents all over town were able to breathe a collective sigh of relief, continued with his conviction and sentencing, and was realized a year later when Sattler's Woods was razed and a new baseball field, dedicated to the memories of Nathaniel, Christopher, and Andrew, was built in its place.

As many of the children who had known the three boys, or even just had clear recollections of the heartache and terror surrounding their vicious murders, grew up and moved away to college, never to return, the collective memory of that long, painful time, and the deep bruise it left on the entire community, began to fade. The details of the murders, the investigation, and the trial—once vividly ingrained in the brains of every citizen of Hollingford over the age of five—have become hazy and vague.

Among present day elementary and middle school children, the killings have even taken on the dimensions of folklore or campfire stories: many sleepovers and campouts feature a telling of "The Hollingford Cannibal," about the demented, backwoods piney who emerged from the deep forest one night and began preying on the children of Hollingford in their sleep. He would sneak into their bedrooms at night, incapacitate them with a chloroform-soaked rag, and drag them off to his torture chamber in the basement of a remote house. There he would have his way with the children before eating them, piece by piece, while they were still alive and sentient, aware of everything happening to them.

Perhaps in an effort to reclaim even just a tiny slice of her son's dignity from grossly inaccurate characterizations, Cindy Thompson began her quest to spread the word about Randall's innocence a few years after his conviction. Her bluntness—or tactlessness, depending on who you ask—initially reopened old wounds and was met with anger and, in a few cases, violence: she received dozens of death threats and even emerged one morning to find the windows of her station wagon smashed in and *die lying cunt* painted on the hood in blood-red. In the summer of 1999, her small home was set ablaze while she slept in an upstairs bedroom; firefighters arrived quickly but were unable to salvage it. Since then, the outright hostility toward Mrs. Thompson has drifted to mild irritation or, mostly, lack of any kind of interest at all. Most town residents view her as a harmless, mild curiosity or local oddity. They pay her little to no mind when they see her distributing flyers or even approaching them to discuss a cover-up in the police department.

But the apathy hasn't dissuaded her from trying. Every morning, she will sit in her efficiency apartment and prepare new campaigns—a flyer, a booklet, a blog—and new angles to win over even a single adherent to Randall's innocence—or at least his humanity. The attempt may all be for naught, of course—how could an admitted pedophile and convicted child-killer garner any sympathy?—but it would seem to have given the bottomless, hopeless pit of her existence a semblance of purpose or meaning. It might be worth it. At least for that.

Although there were dozens and dozens of articles, transcripts of court records, photographs—everything from Randall Thompson's mugshots to a haunting image of Mr. and Mrs. Skelly in the days after the disappearance, standing in the front yard, pleading for Andrew to come safely—available online, Rory kept coming back to just how quickly the police zeroed in on Randall Thompson, then how quickly he was convicted without a shred of physical evidence. It bothered him. He kept expecting to find news a of a breakthrough, even post-conviction, that would have vindicated Randall's guilt: DNA evidence that was finally tested, a witness who saw Thompson at the school that night finally coming forward, a signed confession from Randall himself after sitting in jail year after lonely year. But there was nothing. Just the strained, haunting silence of a community coming to terms with horror, of accepting it and moving on.

It was past four in the morning when Rory's eyes started to sting: he'd been staring at his computer screen, practically unblinking, for hours. He closed his laptop and glanced out the window for any sign of an intruder, but the street was empty. What he most noticed was his own tired reflection looking back at him in the glass.

He arose, stiffly, from the chair and crawled into bed. Although he was exhausted, when he closed his eyes he couldn't help but see police tape across the entrance of the trail through Sattler's Woods, Mr. and Mrs. Skelly's desperate eyes and grim faces as they stood in front of their home, pleading for their son to be returned safely, and, most upsettingly, the school photos of the three boys—huge smiles, bowl cuts, wrinkled polo shirts—that had been plastered all over South Jersey in the days and weeks following the disappearance. Eventually the images and details of the case stopped swirling in his brain, and Rory was able to fall into a troubled sleep.

Eight

The Oasis was not yet open, and he didn't want to return home to his mother's just yet, so Rory drove aimlessly down Central Avenue. He was just leaving the one-room office of the *Hollingford Herald*, where he had stopped in with the faintest of hopes that they might be looking for a writer. They weren't, of course. He'd been told by the editor-in-chief—a bubbly, portly, and thoroughly pit-stained man—that they do accept freelance work (though they can't pay for it) and were putting an article written by a local high school student on the front page of the next issue. The comment had been made in passing, just a bit of congenial small talk, which only made the blade of self-pity and embarrassment that tore through Rory's abdomen all the sharper.

Rory drifted along Central until the houses and business disappeared and sprawling blueberry fields spread out from either side of the road. He'd reached the edge of town. He made a U-turn and then mindlessly drove down the first side-street he came across. He wove through a quiet neighborhood before pulling back out onto Central.

He had put on a suit and tie for his visit to the *Herald* office—the most dressed-up he'd gotten in months—which now felt suffocating. Even though he blasted the air conditioning, he still felt a patch of warm sweat between his shoulder blades simultaneously trickle down his lower back and spread up toward his neck.

As he coasted back into the heart of town, he once again saw the decrepit old man, wearing a full suit and a fedora, hobbling toward the Catholic Church, just as he had been two days earlier.

Still decked out like that in this goddamned heat?

Rory pulled up beside the sidewalk next to the old man and rolled down his passenger side window. "Excuse me, sir?"

The old man continued shuffling down the sidewalk, either not hearing or ignoring Rory.

"Excuse me, sir?" Rory repeated, louder this time, practically shouting. "Can I offer you a ride some place?"

This time the old man reacted. He stopped, slowly swiveled toward the car, and removed his hat. The man's face, while certainly wizened, still had a youthful, if not vibrant, look to it. He had a sharp jawline, a small, pointy nose, and full, ruddy cheeks. He smiled readily, almost mischievously, crinkling his narrow, bright blue eyes.

"I appreciate the offer, son. Just headin' to church over there, so not much more to go. Plus, the exercise keeps me young." He winked before replacing his hat and continuing on, slowly, toward the church at the end of the block.

With nowhere else to go, Rory drove around Central for a little while longer before deciding to change the scenery and head out to Route 30. He ended up stopping at Hollingford Bagels, a small breakfast place in the middle of a strip mall, where he ordered a large cup of coffee as well as pork roll, egg, and cheese on a bagel. He casually flipped through the latest *Hollingford Herald*, which he had purchased for 50 cents from a machine outside the restaurant.

None of the few articles in the paper—profiles of honors students, coverage of a charity walk a few weeks back, a calendar of community events this summer—was particularly engaging, so he closed it and gathered up his trash. He was just getting up to leave, prepared to spend a listless afternoon with his mother, when a familiar figure entered the restaurant. Same stringy gray hair, same worn, baggy jeans: Cindy Thompson, mother of the convicted child-killer.

She quickly affixed a piece of paper—the same flier she had slid along the bar toward Rory—to the community corkboard beside the front door, and was gone before anyone behind the counter had a chance to see her.

Not exactly sure why he was doing it, Rory took off after her into the early afternoon glare.

It took a minute to figure out which way she had gone: she was nowhere to be seen in the parking lot or on the sidewalk bordering the storefronts of the strip mall. Maybe she had gone into one of the other shops? The strip mall was not very large—there was a Chinese restaurant next to the bagel place, then a nail salon, a dollar store, and a vacant storefront on the end that looked like it had once been a Blockbuster Video—so there was a good chance Rory could catch her before she continued her mission elsewhere in town. He was about to go check the Chinese restaurant next door when he spotted her, waiting to cross at the intersection past the far end of the parking lot. *Damn, she's quick.* Rory jogged, in his suffocating shirt and tie, across the parking lot to get her attention before the light changed.

"Ms. Thompson," he gasped, bounding ungracefully onto the sidewalk. Beads of sweat rolled down his forehead, into his eyes. "Ms. Thompson," he repeated, breathily.

The light had turned. Cindy was beginning to cross Route 30, but stopped when she heard her name. "Yes?" she said hesitantly, turning to face Rory.

"Do you remember me? I was in The Oasis when you came in yesterday."

"Hmm." She squinted at him in the bright summer sunlight. Her gaunt face was dull gray and liver-spotted. She cradled a manila file folder in an insect-like arm. "Ah yes," she said after several seconds. "I think so."

"My name is Rory Callahan. And I was wondering if I might—" Rory paused, rewording his request in his head. "I'm a newspaperman. Or, I used to be at least. I believe in honest, fair journalism…and I don't think you, or your son, have ever gotten that."

Cindy nodded as she continued to squint at him.

"In other words, I want to hear your side of the story," Rory said.

Cindy's pale, blue eyes darted from left to right before landing back on Rory. "If we're gonna talk, best we go someplace private. Unless you like getting spat on and cursed at." She actually smiled at that, flashing her crooked, yellow teeth. "Wait fifteen or twenty minutes, then come to the Hollingford Arms Apartments, two blocks past Wawa. My apartment number is 303."

Without waiting for an acknowledgement, she turned and crossed the street at a brisk, but seemingly unhurried, pace. Seconds later, she disappeared behind the line of thick, slow-moving traffic that resumed when the light changed.

Nine

The Hollingford Arms was a utilitarian, three-story building off a section of Route 30 that, if not quite residential, was at least free from wall-to-wall chain restaurants and shopping centers. Law and dental offices, realtors and orthodontists, were scattered on either side of the apartments. Rory parked in an alleyway beside the building, pulled off his tie, rolled up his sleeves, and walked around to the front entryway to the hum of dozens of window air conditioners. While not expecting to get much use out of them, he brought a spiral notepad and pen with him, vestiges of his former life that he kept, from force of habit, in the center console of his Ford Focus.

The vestibule of the building smelled faintly of cat piss and cigarettes. The names and numbers on the intercom board were all faded, but he was able to decipher *"303 Thompson"* on the bottom row of buttons. He was quickly buzzed in to begin his ascent up a narrow, dim, moss-green carpeted stairwell to the third floor.

The door to Cindy Thompson's apartment was already cracked when Rory arrived, out of breath once again, on the landing of the third floor. For a moment, he hesitated: was it really such a wise move to crash blindly into a strange woman's apartment? After all, this was the mother of a convicted murderer. Who knows what kind of psychological, even physical, torture she had inflicted on her only son to transmogrify him from a sweet kid to a sinister child-killer? He shook away the rising doubt—was he really going to shit his pants over a woman who seemed frailer than his own mother?—although a certain, solid anxiety rested in his gut as he approached the apartment door.

The apartment itself was miniscule: a short counter separated the kitchen from the living room, which also served as the bedroom. A narrow, green-tiled bathroom jutted into the wall on the right. The kitchen cabinets, the wallpaper, the brown carpet, all seemed run-down—Rory wondered if any of it had been replaced since the apartments were built decades ago—but generally clean and well cared-for. Although the air conditioner was buzzing softly in a living room window, the apartment was warm, stale, and reeking of cigarettes.

Cindy Thompson sat on a dilapidated, orange loveseat beside a bright window in the living room. "Come in," she said, lighting a cigarette. "Don't be shy. Have a seat." She turned, popped open the window, and blew a cloud of smoke into the muggy afternoon. She smiled up at him. "Not supposed to smoke in here. You want any anything to drink?"

"I'm fine for now, thank you." Rory sank into the loveseat, noting the scissors, glue, markers, and stacks of paper and photographs spread out on the coffee table inches away from his knees. The manila folder she had been holding out on the sidewalk was there, too. Stacks of old newspapers and over-stuffed file folders were piled precariously beneath the table.

"So," Cindy began. "You want to know about Randy? I mean, really want to know about him?" She broke her intense stare at Rory every few moments to exhale a lungful of smoke out the window.

"Yeah, I do. I think the court of public opinion can be swift and cruel."

The corner of Cindy's withered lips lifted in a mild, perhaps defensive, sneer. "What do you think about him now?"

"I think a man is serving a life sentence because of some weak circumstantial evidence. It was some weak shit, but you march out a guy who's got child porn stashed in his closet—some of it torture porn for good measure—in front of a jury, and I think, weak shit or no, that guy is pretty much fucked."

Although it wasn't particularly bright in the apartment, even beside the unshaded window, Cindy squinted at Rory as she sat beside him, analyzing him. "And why should you care? Having me sit here and tell you 'my side of the story,' as you called—what's it all to you? Said you don't even write for the newspaper anymore."

Rory wasn't completely prepared for this question; he had half-expected Ms. Thompson, enthralled by the opportunity of finally having a willing, listening audience, to instantly launch into richly detailed accounts that were left out of the papers—of how her son was bullied by the police, how they neglected to pursue other, credible suspects. But being forced to reflect on that question helped him figure out, in his own head, why he was now sitting in this tiny, cigarette smoke-laced apartment, and even why he'd raced out of the bagel shop to talk to this woman in the first place.

"It's true: I may not be a writer anymore. And even if I were, and I believed everything you're saying about your son, I doubt I could do shit about it. But it seems to me that no one in this town is even willing to listen to you, to hear you out, even a little. That's for a reason. They all have a narrative of what happened, and why, and convicting your son put an ending on that narrative, a nice ribbon to wrap up their lingering doubts and fears and let them sleep at night without any more nightmares."

Cindy gave an almost imperceptible nod, more of a slight flinch, but kept her eyes fixed on Rory.

"I have no idea if your son is guilty or not," Rory said. "I thought about that as I stared at the flier you hung in the bar yesterday. One second I saw a sweet-natured mama's boy, the next, a stone-cold sociopath. And as much as I want to simply believe the latter like everyone else in town, to feel good knowing justice was served, the guilty man was caught and locked up, and then just move on to pondering the Flyers' roster moves, part of me—like an itch I just can't scratch—can't help thinking: what if that's not right? What if they pinned it on the sweet-natured kid—he's an easy target because of his past—and someone else killed those three boys that night?" Rory paused, realizing he was beginning to meander. "Anyway. I think you deserve to be listened to, at least. In my mind, there isn't any justice until I at least do that."

While none of what Rory said was bullshit, he also couldn't helping thinking as he spoke, *And if I weren't here talking to you right now, fuck knows what I'd be doing. Maybe writing family friendly movie reviews or recaps of neighborhood block parties.*

Cindy watched Rory intently for what felt like minutes. *Must be assessing me, figuring me out*, he thought. *Wondering if I'm someone she can trust or if this is just a joke…or worse, a scam of some kind. I'm sure it's happened before. Maybe multiple times.*

Finally, she leaned forward to tap her cigarette on the lip of a glass ashtray at the corner of the coffee table, and said, "Don't want or expect you, or anyone, to do anything for my son. To get him out of jail or any nonsense like that. This isn't about that." She paused, covered her mouth, and hacked up a deep, moist cough before continuing. "And that child porn you mentioned—the one they showed the jury? That was a set-up. Don't know who would set him up like that, but that's what it was."

Perhaps out of instinct, or because of some vague notion that he was actually hearing something important, Rory took out his notepad and pen and began writing. He stopped practically as soon as he had started and glanced up at the old woman seated beside him. "This ok?"

"Why not," she replied. "Couldn't hurt at this point."

"So you're saying that Randall never bought those tapes they showed at trial?"

Cindy shook her head sadly. "No, he bought the tapes. Hence why his situation is hopeless. But those horrible tapes—and I don't mean to imply that they weren't all horrible, because of course they were—but those *really* disgusting, evil ones, the ones that made folks on the jury sick, he would never, ever, in a million years wanted, or liked, something like that. I tried to tell his lawyer Romero that time and time again, but he didn't listen. Kind of an arrogant man if you ask me, God rest his soul. I don't mean to speak ill about the deceased."

"Romero's dead?"

She nodded slowly. "Four or five years ago. Aneurysm."

Who knows what he took with him, Rory thought. *Maybe he knew the truth.*

"But getting back to the tapes," he went on. "Randall still knowingly purchased them in the first place?"

Cindy took an exceptionally long drag on her cigarette before stubbing it out in the ashtray. "I don't mean to suggest my son didn't have problems—he certainly did. Plenty of them. But I swear to

God—and yes, I still somehow believe in God despite all this—that he would never dream of touching a child, let alone hurting one.

"I always knew Randy was different," she said wistfully. "When he started high school, I kept waiting for the day he'd bring home, or even bring up, a girl—or even a boy. I know what the Bible says, but it wouldn't have bothered me; I'd have loved him the same. But that day never came. Even if we were out for dinner or at church and there were pretty girls around, he never seemed awkward or even nervous, really.

"No," she said, pausing to sigh and, for the first time during their conversation, truly avert her gaze from Rory. "That happened when there were—" She hesitated again. Rory wondered if this were the first time she'd ever talked openly and honestly about her son to anyone. It might have been. "—little ones around." Her voice was softer than before. "First time I noticed was at a church picnic one Sunday afternoon. Cute little girl, couldn't have been older than five, was running around in her little sundress. When she ran over to our picnic table waving and smiling and laughing, Randy's cheeks went red and he looked away. Then he excused himself and went inside.

"Then I started to notice how he acted around his cousins. They were in elementary school when Randy was in high school. Same thing: he'd seem flustered and try his best to get away from them. I remember one time it was pouring out and we were watching some dumb TV show. His little cousin, the boy, went to go sit on Randy's lap—Randy couldn't of jumped up any faster if he had felt a snake slither by his ankle. At first I was mad at him. He seemed cold toward his cousins, and I guess I had always envisioned him being warm, caring—you know, a role model for the younger kids. This went on, this strangeness around little ones, for years. Practically all of high school. And as much as I didn't want to, I couldn't help having those thoughts sneak into my brain. What if? What if? What if? But we never talked about it. How could we?"

Rory began to feel sorry for Cindy Thompson, wondering what must have raced through her mind on quiet nights as she lay in bed trying to fall asleep: wild, insane suspicions about her son's sexual predilection. They'd have to be insane, right? Would they have smacked her in a sudden wave of panic or slowly but unstoppably opened beneath her feet like an unfathomable chasm? And of course she was right: they couldn't have talked about it. How would she broach that topic, and what would happen—what would possibly get better—if she did? Better to bury suspicions like that, about your own son, for Christ's sake, deep down inside. And then hope, and pray to God, that you're wrong and that one day you can forgive yourself for ever suspecting that in the first place.

"Was Randy's father around for any of this?" Rory asked delicately.

"Nah, he was gone before his first birthday." She snorted before lighting another cigarette. "I often wondered if he was following the story from somewhere far away, thanking his lucky stars he was such an asshole and didn't have to get tangled up in all of it."

"Seems like the world is unduly kind to assholes."

"From my experience, I'd have to agree with you." Cindy looked reflective as she sat there, ancient memories swimming to the surface of her mind. Maybe she was thinking about Randy as a young boy: how he loved catching fireflies in the summer, or how he cried when his goldfish died, or how he used to curl up in her arms when they watched TV, a tiny, soothing bundle of warmth and boyhood smells, and fall asleep. The countless months and years before that dark cloud of suspicion—*Could my son be—? Is it possible he—? How could this happen?*—settled over her existence. But Rory had no way of knowing what she was thinking as the two sat in silence on the beaten-up loveseat, Cindy taking long, deliberate drags from her cigarette, distance in her pale blue eyes, Rory waiting patiently for her to resume her story; he was eager now to know more.

"When he left for Rutgers," Cindy said, breaking the silence but still gazing into some hypnotizing, tantalizingly vivid memory, "I hoped the whole thing would somehow vanish. Maybe being away from home, out on his own, would help him figure things out—figure himself out. Or maybe I'd see there was nothing for him to figure out in the first place, that he just had low self-esteem in high school but would grow and flourish in college. And for a while, I thought that was happening. As the year went on and Randy was getting good grades, making friends, even telling me he wanted to go to med school after he graduated, I'd sometimes laugh at myself on the drive into work for being so dumb, so afraid. There were days, maybe even weeks, when those old thoughts didn't haunt me at all. When he came home for summer break as happy as I'd ever seen him, it was like waking up from a bad dream. It was like waking up from a bad dream and beginning to forget what the dream was even about."

Cindy's eyes refocused as she broke from whatever reverie she had fallen into, whatever memory she was replaying in her head. She looked deeply, but briefly, into Rory's eyes again before dropping her gaze and allowing a deep, heavy, pent-up—for years, perhaps—sigh rise from her smoky lungs. "I remember everything about the day I got the call. Was a warm, Indian summer type day in the middle of October. Elton John, 'Crocodile Rock,' playing from a radio we had on top of a file cabinet at work. He was calling from jail in New Brunswick. Crying. Ashamed. It had been a sting operation. Heard whispers of a guy selling child porn from an RV outside of town. Got into his car to go, only to talk himself out if about a hundred times. He told me later he had to get himself drunk to finally drive out there and see the man. And they arrested him on the spot."

She set her cigarette down on the table, leaning it against the ashtray, while she stared down at the shit-brown carpet. "Can't say I was completely shocked. Part of me was, just because he'd been doing so well recently. But part of me, deeper inside, knew it was inevitable. Like watching a sad movie the second time through and hoping, even though you know what's going to happen, the ending will still somehow be different. But it won't, of course. I guess I really had known all along."

"And that's what got Randy on the sex offender registry."

Cindy nodded. "Spent three years in jail, too. I remember feeling so furious, so ashamed. Betrayed is the best way I can describe it, like he did this to hurt me after I had given him my life. I didn't want to see his face. Didn't want to hear his voice ever again. There were times I even hoped he'd get his throat cut in jail, like they say sometimes happens to the pedophiles. Then I could start to distance myself from the shame, the underlying question no one actually wanted to ask me, that I didn't even want to ask myself: What kind of mother could raise a person like that? I know it was wrong to think that—wrong to think that about my son, my own son. I couldn't even bring myself to be there for his trial. It wasn't till I saw his picture in the paper—his mugshot and being led out of the courtroom, handcuffed, looking like a lost little boy, my lost little boy, not some horrible monster—that I decided I could, and should, I guess, visit him up in Rahway. The first time I saw him through those thick sheets of Plexiglas, full of fear and self-loathing and repentance, I knew I couldn't hate him. I knew I couldn't turn my back on him. I saw that God had given him a cross to bear, a crushing, heavy weight to carry, and he'd been shouldering it by himself his entire life."

She sighed again, shallower, less despairing, more peacefully resigned than before, and picked up her cigarette. "I'm glad I didn't turn my back on him either, in spite of everything that's happened since. I let him come home to live with me when he got released, which was tough at first. He was a changed man. Hardly ate or slept. He roamed the streets at night, sometimes for hours. Didn't laugh or smile anymore at his favorite TV shows. We never talked about prison or the arrest. All meaningless small talk all the time. But after a month or two, he started to see a shrink out in Cherry Hill once a week, and that was good for him. I started to see signs of the old Randy come back to life. Slowly, one piece at a time. He even told me the doctor was helping him redirect his attraction. Maybe a few days after that, when I came home from work, he told me, almost braggingly, about how he saw a stunning woman walk by the house that day, how he couldn't take her eyes off of her. He was doing real good.

"But I suppose with any deep-seated habit you're trying to break, you're bound to relapse. It can't be helped. I don't know when Randy bought that bag of videos that they found. And I would have thrown him out of the house if I'd known he had. But there's something he said to me when he was doing his therapy, something that's stuck with me all these years later. He said, 'Ma, I don't know why I was made the way I was. I don't know how those wires got weirdly crossed the way they did. It's nothing I'd want or ask for, and I still hate myself for it most of the time. But I know I'd never touch a child. Ever. I know I'd be destroying a life if I did. I know that. And I know you believe that about me, too. I know you believe that I am a good person. Because that's how you raised me.'"

They both let silence settle over the little apartment. Rory had scribbled some notes—about Randy, about Ms. Thompson's theory that he was set up in some way—which he looked over cursorily. Cindy was studying the creases in her baggy jeans and smoking steadily.

"Those words," Rory said finally, "what he said to you about being a good person. They must have been kind of an inner-refrain for you during the murder trial."

"Yes. They certainly were. Still are to this day. It's why I decided to start all this," she said, directing the tip of her cigarette toward the materials scattered across the coffee table. "My son will never see the outside of prison, I know that. But I'll be damned if I'm going to let a lie about who he is, what kind of man he is, go down as history for the people of this town, at least without fighting somehow. If I can convince even just one person before I lie down for eternal rest, then I've made a moral victory, however small."

"I understand that." Rory hesitated a moment. *There might not be a delicate way to phrase this. She won't be offended. And if she is, then what the fuck?* "Can I ask—I apologize in advance if this comes across as flippant."

"By all means: go ahead and ask. There's nothing I haven't heard from others, or thought about myself, these long years."

"Ok. Well. What if you're wrong? Maybe we can only know a person, even the people closest to us, so well. Maybe he was sitting at home every day while you were at work—did he usually stay home?"

"Yes. It was difficult finding a job after the conviction, but he took care of the house and the yard and the garden."

"So maybe he's sitting alone, or working on the lawn alone, day in and day out, for months and years, falling victim to forbidden fantasies and then beating himself up for it. An endless, obsessive cycle. That's a lot of psychological stress—torture, even. Maybe he eventually broke under the pressure and—," he paused, unsure of how to proceed with the question tactfully.

"Did what the prosecution said he did," Cindy finished the sentence for him.

"Yes. I'm sorry to ask it."

Rory felt a slight wave of relief when Ms. Thompson met the question with a toothy smile. "Meet him. Drive down to South Woods. He'd talk to you. I'm the only one who visits him, three times a week. He's sick of seeing me. But meet him. You'll know then."

Before talking to Cindy, Rory would have considered visiting a state prison to talk to the convicted murderer in poor taste, an ennui-driven act to satisfy a passing bit of morbid curiosity. But it was clear now that Ms. Thompson was not only lucid and vibrant, contrary to her appearance, but she was not deluded about her son: she honestly recognized his faults and struggles, yet still managed to believe in his innocence.

"Maybe I will. Things are a bit busy with taking care of my mom at the moment," Rory lied, unable to admit he was becoming increasingly fascinated with the 22-year-old murder case, that getting drawn into it has assuaged his fear of endless, meaningless days of sitting in the house, watching game shows in the middle of the day, waiting for his mother to take a turn for the worse. "But if I can find the time, I will."

"You know, I understand what you were saying about not knowing people. I get that. Everyone has their secrets. Everyone has their shadowy side, whether we want to admit it or not. But there are things you also just know about a person you love. Good things about them that aren't ever going to change, that outweigh the bad things and define that person's character.

"There was one day back when Randy was in elementary school. Must have been during Easter vacation. I took off work so we could spend the day whole together: the playground in the morning, lunch at McDonald's on the White Horse Pike, reading Roald Dahl books in the backyard all afternoon, homemade pizza for dinner. So, right after breakfast, I took him to that big, wooden playground on Zelley—it was brand new back then—and watched him run along the bridges and through those little forts, go down the slides and climb up the ladders. I remember smiling as his laughter echoed through the park; we were the only ones there. I looked down at the paperback I had in my lap for just a few seconds, but when I looked up, he was gone. I waited a minute or two, thinking he'd eventually pop his head up in one of the windows in the forts, laughing and yelling, 'Ma! I'm over here!' But no: I couldn't hear or see him from where I was sitting. I started getting nervous. I walked through the playground calling his name. I peeked into the corners of the little forts, thinking, fearing, I'd spot his little body collapsed in a heap. But still no sign of him. I wandered to the far end of the playground and started scanning that field next to it, right where the mulch ends and the grass begins.

"And then I saw him. He was over by some trees maybe thirty yards from the playground. And he was surrounded by older boys. As I got closer, I could see they were shoving him, laughing, saying nasty things. When they saw me coming, the boys took off like a herd of frightened deer. And there was my son, barely holding back tears, his hands clenched in tiny fists, standing with the sorriest little cat I have ever seen in my life in the grass at his feet.

"'Randy!' I screamed. 'What happened?'

"'They were being mean to him, ma,' he told me, pointing at the kitten. 'Kicking him, spitting on him, throwing rocks. I tried to get them to stop.'

"I knelt down to hug him, and then took a closer look at the cat. It was clearly near death. Blood was trickling from his ears. One eye was swollen shut. His fur was roughed up and damp with blood, and there was even a missing patch that was raw and blistered, like he'd been burnt. One of his legs looked badly mangled. He wasn't moving, but at least was mewling very, very softly, so we knew he was alive.

"'Randy, I don't think we can save him.'

"'Yes, we can,' he told me. And he scooped up the cat and carried him back to the house, bloodying up his little t-shirt. But he didn't care. He stayed with that kitten all day and night. I remember coming into his bedroom the next morning and seeing him sprawled out on the floor next to his new pet who was sleeping on one of his pillows. It was the same story for the next week or so, never leaving that cat's side, day or night. He fed him, washed him, put ointment on his burns and cuts. Named him Thumper, after the rabbit in *Bambi*, his favorite movie. And it wasn't long before Thumper was fully recovered. That cat loved Randy. Followed him from room to room, slept on his bed with him. Lived a long, full life, too. He was still alive when Randy—" Her voice broke, ending the steady stream of words that had come so effortlessly. "—got back from jail.

"And that's how I know, Mr. Callahan. That's how I know that the thought of stalking those boys into the woods, hurting them in any way, would never have even occurred to my son. Someone else followed those boys down that trail that night. Not my son. Never my son. And I know that to be truer than anything I've ever known."

Ten

The afternoon sun was blinding; at first, Rory didn't see Officer Daniels approaching the steamy vestibule of the apartment building just as he was pushing open the glass, handprint-smudged door to exit it.

"Mr. Callahan," she said. "What brings you to these parts?" Her freckled cheeks dimpled in a wide smile, though her warm, brown eyes were hidden behind the darkly tinted lenses of sunglasses.

For a moment, unsure of how "bonding with the town pariah over a possibly botched investigation into a decades-old murder case" would fly with a sworn officer, Rory scrambled for a lie: Looking into apartments for himself, or maybe his mother? Profiling a member of the community who happens to live in these apartments for the *Hollingford Herald*?

But Daniels, even in their brief conversation the other day, exuded not just intelligence, but also trustworthiness. His gut reaction was to tell her the truth, so he did.

"This might sound strange," he prefaced, "but a woman—Cindy Thompson—came into The Oasis yesterday."

"I know Ms. Thompson well. She piqued your interest, did she?"

"After doing some research last night, I thought she might be worth hearing out."

"And?" Daniels looked slightly bemused but also genuinely curious.

"And—she was worth hearing out."

"Fair enough. I guess we share a common hostess today: I'm visiting Ms. Thompson to remind her that she can approach anyone she wants to on the street, but actually going into Burger King and talking to paying customers is out-of-bounds."

"That's reasonable."

"It's a monthly meeting we have," she said, sounding surprisingly congenial rather than annoyed.

Daniels seemed about ready to continue speaking about Ms. Thompson, but she abruptly stopped herself, most likely wondering, just as Rory had seconds earlier, if she could trust a practical stranger with sensitive information that could blow back on her. She must be well aware, Rory thought, of the swift, cruel retaliation brought down upon Cindy Thompson when she began her doomed campaign to win back a modicum of respect for her son. And particularly in the police department, questioning an over-and-done case, the most significant in town history, would hardly win her any love from her bosses or colleagues. But there must have been something in Rory's haggard, whiskey-weary appearance she found genuine, or at least disarming, because she did continue, slowly, and with the slightest bit of doubt and caution at first: "I agree with you: she is worth hearing out."

"Really," Rory said, slightly surprised. "What makes you say that?"

Although only the occasional car passed by and the sidewalks were empty, Daniels took a step closer to Rory and lowered her voice. "Between you and me—I mean, if it got back to the chief or anyone—"

"Don't worry about that," Rory assured her. "Your brazen act of independent thought is safe with me."

"Thanks," Daniels chuckled. "People in this town don't exactly embrace dissenting opinions about Ms. Thompson. Or her son."

"I get that sense. I think I might be the one person in town who actually thinks the lady might be telling the truth."

"Well," Daniels said in a hushed tone, "that's actually two of us. Because between you and me—" She paused, waiting for one last reassurance from Rory.

"Of course."

"Between you and me, that was a shit investigation."

"Yeah?"

"Sadly, yes. And no one, cop or civilian, is interested in questioning it. Now, I'm not saying there's a guy in jail who shouldn't be in jail for obvious reasons."

"He bought that collection of videos."

"Right. But whatever happened that night did not go down the way the state said it did. I can barely remember when the murders happened: I was only six then. But as I got older, the whole thing—this dark town secret—became morbidly fascinating to me. I became kind of obsessed with it. I mean, I still think about it all the time. So needless to say, I've done a fair share of unsolicited research, to say the least. And it's just—there are some things that don't add up."

"Like what?"

"First of all." Daniels stopped to scan their surroundings again before continuing. "First of all, have you seen him? Randall Thompson?"

"Pictures," Rory replied.

"He's not exactly built. I find it difficult to imagine a puny, 27-year-old guy being able to attack, subdue, and brutalize three healthy, pre-teen boys, one of whom was an athlete."

This, of course, made complete sense to Rory. Up until now he had really only considered the character of the convicted murderer—is he the kind of person capable of beating in the skulls of three children, lifting up a rock, slick with blood, and striking over and over again until their bodies stopped twitching?—and hadn't yet mulled over the practicalities of the crime.

"So to me this means one of three things," Daniels said. "One, Thompson acted alone but premeditated the attack. He would've had to. He would have needed a weapon and restraints—zip ties or something—to overpower them. It seems like a stretch, but I guess it's possible. Then again, it would also undermine the prosecution's story—that he happened to cross paths with the boys, couldn't control his urges, and then was so ashamed of what he did, he had to remove any evidence of it from existence."

"Good point."

"Two, Thompson was there that night and is even complicit in the murders, but he didn't act alone. He might have even been pressured or blackmailed into helping an accomplice."

"Why wouldn't he say something about it then, if that's the case?" Rory asked.

"Maybe he's protecting the other person, or people, but out of fear or loyalty, who can say?"

"Right."

"Or three, Thompson didn't do it. He may have a weak-ass alibi and a shady past, but those factors also make him a perfect scapegoat for the police and D.A. Of course, that would mean he's telling the truth about his innocence and the entire thing—the investigation, the trial, conviction—are all bullshit."

"And whoever killed those kids is still out there, somewhere."

"And we have no idea who they might be or why they'd murder those children."

Rory smiled wryly. "I can see why you'd like to keep your theories just between you and me."

Daniels returned the smile. "If you don't mind. Despite evidence to the contrary, I actually do love my job and would prefer to keep it." She was about to continue past Rory to ring the intercom for Cindy Thompson, but stopped. "Oh, I almost forgot. Nothing suspicious the last two nights outside your mom's house. We'll have someone there through the weekend, but if you're still feeling uncomfortable, or something else happens, let me know; I'll see if I can extend it into next week."

Rory felt a slight twinge of embarrassment at receiving this news: with each passing uneventful night, he was becoming increasingly convinced that the threatening note was merely a nasty practical joke, perhaps even slipped under the wrong door of the wrong house, and that his request for police assistance had been an overreaction. "Actually, that's not even necessary," Rory said. "I'm starting to think I took that note a little too seriously."

"I don't think so. It's possible the guy who wrote it never comes back, but if having an officer out there a few more nights gives you and your mother some piece of mind, then we'll do it."

"Thank you. Again."

"Not a problem," Daniels said. After identifying herself to Cindy Thompson, she was quickly buzzed into the building and, seconds later, had disappeared through the glass doors.

Eleven

For dinner that night, Rory made fish tacos so his mother could sit in the cool living room and read with *Jeopardy* and *Wheel of Fortune* droning indistinctly in the background. Rory's unfamiliarity with his mother's kitchen, as well as his extended hiatus from cooking even a semi-elaborate meal, produced liberal utterances of "Jesus fucking Christ" and "Oh, for fuck's sake" as he fumbled for supplies in various drawers and cabinets, burnt himself on more than one occasion, and knocked over ingredients with flailing, unwieldy elbows and wayward hands. But he also managed to drink three Yards IPAs while he cooked, so by the time dinner was ready and set out on the table at dusk, his small bursts of kitchen-rage had long-since subsided, leaving a pleasant mellowness in their wake. When his mother claimed they were the best fish tacos she had ever tasted, Rory felt genuinely flattered by the compliment and satisfied to return his mother's generosity and hospitality, at least in part.

After a few minutes of small talk about the Phillies and the latest book Kathleen had started—a collection of Flannery O'Conner short stories—the conversation at the kitchen table fell silent.

Rory took a sip of his IPA and was starting on his third taco when Kathleen said, softly and haltingly, as if she'd been thinking about it for a while, "Are you sure you're happy here? I know it's very quiet compared to the city."

"It's not so bad," Rory said, after swallowing his bite of taco. "It's good being here with you." He reached over and patted her hand. "It's also nice to be away from the city for a bit—change of scenery after everything with Marie."

"And how is Marie?"

"She's good. Still working her butt off. Teaching summer courses out at Radnor."

"I don't know how she manages to corral those middle school kids, but she's so good with them. Always has been."

Rory winced at this: Marie hadn't taught middle school in five years, ever since the city flipped her school, the altar where she had sacrificed her own life for nearly two decades, into a charter, laying off all faculty and staff in the process to make room for an army of fresh-faced Teach for America twentysomethings. She was able to land a high school job out in the suburbs where she struggled for the first two years with the transition. Marie had often called up Kathleen, a fellow teacher and veteran of the Philly school system, as a sympathetic ear and mentor. The fact that Kathleen didn't seem to remember those long phone conversations with Marie from only five years ago frightened Rory, but he couldn't be sure if it was normal wear and tear on a seventy-five year-old mind, or an indication of his mother's worsening dementia.

"Marie is actually teaching high school now," Rory said. "But she still loves it. She'll be teaching her first AP class in the fall, actually."

"That's wonderful. Will she come down to visit this summer? You must miss each other."

Jesus. She doesn't remember the divorce? I guess I can't blame her for letting go of that one. Kathleen never understood why her only child was ending his 25-year marriage, a marriage to a wonderful woman he was lucky to land in the first place; Rory had tried explaining it to her over the phone, often three or four tumblers of Jameson deep, to mounting frustration and futility. "Your father and I had ups and downs, but we fought through them. Why can't you? Why are you just giving up?" Rory had tried to explain the shame of being unemployed, of how each wasted, useless day after another felt like drowning, or slow suffocation; how getting black-out drunk by three in the afternoon was the only way of forgetting his shame and humiliation; how Marie had given him an ultimatum: AA or you're moving out; how he tried three times to go to the meetings only to be lured back in by the siren song of the corner bars, of the absolute joy of escaping his sham of a life as the inkling of a buzz, that loosening of tension, the release from paralyzing self-hatred and dark thoughts, evolved into an all-out drunken stupor, and the sweet freedom of numbness that always followed. But Kathleen had no sympathy for a man willing to walk away from a marriage, and he didn't blame her.

Deciding not to explain the divorce again, fearing it could spiral into a repeat argument that had already played out during those long, maddening phone calls, Rory simply said, "Not sure, mom. She's really busy with her summer courses."

"I understand."

When most of the food was gone, Rory finished off his beer and was about to get up to clear the table, when Kathleen asked, "Are you finding ways to keep busy here?"

"So far. Yeah."

"What did you do today?"

"Nothing too wild. Looked into doing some writing for the *Hollingford Herald*."

"That's good, Rory. I'm glad to hear that."

"Thanks, mom. I went downtown and grabbed some coffee after that, read the paper for a while," Rory rambled while he considered the wisdom of divulging his subsequent visit with Ms. Thompson.

Ever since Cindy Thompson intruded into The Oasis with her flyers, Rory had been contemplating asking his mother what she remembered about the Blueberry Hill murders. If he could remember correctly, she had been close with Evelyn Chandler, grandmother and legal guardian of Nathanial Foster, youngest of the three victims. But part of him remained reluctant; he felt preemptive guilt for dumping another macabre weight, on top of the enigmatic death threat, upon the fragile structure of her mind. Then again, she seemed more irritated by the note than terrified by it. Perhaps Rory was, as he had often done, underestimating his mother's toughness. Even more so, however, his burning curiosity about the murder case and the impulsiveness fomented by the beer pushed him to ask, "What do you remember about the Blueberry Hill murders, back from '92?"

Kathleen's eyes simultaneously narrowed while taking on a clarity and depth Rory hadn't seen in months, maybe years. "More than I'd care to." Her voice was soft but smoldering, like gently crackling kindling moments before bursting into flame. "Every day I seem to lose more and more good memories, but I still carry those with me. A cruelty, without a doubt. Those poor children. And that poor, poor woman."

"Evelyn Chandler—Nathaniel's grandmother?"

She nodded. Her dark blue eyes, even in the deepening night and the light from the dim bulb hanging above the kitchen table, were somehow luminous.

"You were friends with her?"

"I was. When your father and I moved out here after living in the neighborhood for—forty years?—it was a little overwhelming. Don't get me wrong, it was nice leaving the city after so much time. I remember how strangely quiet it was our first night here: seeing light from the stars illuminate practically the whole yard, hearing cicadas in the trees. It felt otherworldly, but peaceful.

"But then, there was the loneliness. We missed you and Marie and Kevin. And we didn't know anyone in town, of course. The neighbors mostly kept to themselves; there were a few we never even saw at all. For a while, we felt like outsiders looking in on a separate little world we didn't belong to, even when we'd go shopping or out to one of the restaurants on Central. And then, one Sunday at church, Evelyn came up to us after Mass and introduced herself. Said she'd noticed our new faces for a few weeks and had been meaning to welcome us. She invited us to donuts and coffee over in the rectory where we met more nice people, even some couples who had moved out from the city, just like us, when they retired.

"From then on, there wasn't a book group meeting, potluck dinner, canasta game, or church function Evelyn didn't invite us to. She's the one who helped us finally feel at home here. She was warm and comforting to us when we needed it. She had that rare ability to know exactly what you were feeling and to say, or do, the exact right thing to make you feel better. I don't know what we would have done without her."

Rory, both eager to learn more about Evelyn Chandler and pleasantly surprised by Kathleen's sharpness and lucidity, had let his mother speak uninterrupted. But she stopped here. She took a small sip of water and gently placed the glass back on the table. Rory watched her closely as her eyes became glossy with tears and her withered lips began to tremble.

Shit. Exactly what I thought might happen.

"Sorry for bringing this up," Rory said, genuinely contrite. "Let me take care of these dishes, then we can see if there's a movie on HBO or something."

The corners of Kathleen's lips turned up for a moment in a slight smile. She looked into Rory's eyes. "I'm fine. It's not bad to remember. Helps honor memories of the dead."

Rory nodded. "When did Evelyn pass away?"

"A week before Christmas the year Nathaniel died. Before they even convicted that man of killing Nathaniel. They said it was heart failure."

"I'm sorry, mom. I remember you telling me about her, about the funeral. I guess I never realized how close you were."

"The worst part was how much she had changed that year. At first, she tried to stay so optimistic when the boys went missing. She told me, over and over again, not to worry. Three middle school boys? They took off on some adventure—maybe into the Pine Barrens to look for the Jersey Devil—and got turned around and lost in the woods. On days when she was in a darker mood, she thought Nathaniel had run away, that the other two boys were helping him. Apparently, a few weeks before that awful night when those children never came home, she and Nathaniel had gotten into a terrible argument and had barely spoken to each other since. After he went missing, she would get a call every so often, usually late at night, but when she'd pick up, no one would answer. She was convinced it was Nathaniel wanting to come home, but too afraid he'd get in trouble."

"Did she ever tell you what the argument was about?" Rory asked gently.

"She never did. I remember staying after Mass with her one Sunday a month or two after the disappearance. We were kneeling, praying to the Blessed Mother like we did every week for Nathaniel to get home safe, when Evelyn started weeping. I put my arm around her, and she started saying, 'It's my fault. It's my fault. It's all my fault.' I told her it wasn't, that she shouldn't blame herself for anything—and that's when she told me about the argument. I tried asking her more about it, thought that I could reassure her if I knew what they had fought about. But she got quiet, shook her head, and just sobbed for a while. I told her that fighting with preteens was normal, that your father and I had some raucous fights with you when you were Nathaniel's age. That seemed to comfort her a bit. But we never talked about the argument again."

"Do you remember anything about Nathaniel—what kind of kid he was?" *Maybe peppering her with these questions isn't a great idea. She's not a Philly council member for Christ's sake.* "Sorry for all the questions, mom. If you don't want to talk to talk about this anymore, I understand."

"I don't mind," she said. "Like I said, it's good to remember." She sighed deeply, pinched her eyes shut, and rubbed her chin as she reached back for the memories. "Nathaniel was a good boy. Extremely smart. Polite. He would always say hello to me and your father in church. He was a voracious reader. I can hardly remember his face now, but I have a clear memory of him curled up on the couch in Evelyn's living room—we were in the kitchen, playing cards and drinking gin and tonics—and seeing him in the yellow light of the table lamp with a massive Stephen King novel in his hands.

"And he was very quiet, very shy. At least around me. Maybe he was different with his friends at school. But I don't think he had very many. I remember Evelyn once telling me she was afraid he was lonely, maybe even getting picked on by some neighborhood boys. But I got the sense he never really talked to Evelyn about it. Maybe he didn't want to burden her with his school problems."

"Sounds like a nice kid," Rory said.

"He was. Very sweet."

"Were his parents completely MIA?"

"The father—Evelyn's son—yes. Never saw or heard from him, and she never talked about him. The mother had drug problems. She lived out in California and always made plans to visit but broke them at the last minute. One time Nathaniel and Evelyn even went to the airport to pick her up. The flight she was supposed to be on arrived, but she was nowhere to be seen. She was at his funeral though. She came to that. When they—" She stopped herself again and did her best to blink away the incipient tears. "Poor child. And his poor grand-mother. She lived for that boy, so when they found him…" Her voice trailed off.

"She must have been inconsolable."

"An understatement, if there ever was one." She looked down, studying the sun spots and bulging blue veins of her hands. For a moment, the only sound in the kitchen was that of the house settling and the clock on the wall ticking incessantly. Then, suddenly, Kathleen slid her chair back from under the table, gathering up dirty plates and cups from dinner in the process. "Anyway, enough talk of those times." She marched the dishes over to the sink and came back to the table for a second armful. "But if you're curious, Evelyn did leave me a bunch of things: clothes, books, kitchen knick-knacks. They're boxed up in the basement."

Rory turned in his chair as Kathleen stacked the dishes in the sink and began running the water. "You've kept them this long?"

"We were never sure what to do with them," she answered, her back to Rory as she leaned over to scrape leftover scraps of food into the compost bin. "And we never seemed to have the heart to give those things away, or even go through them and sort everything. But feel free to take a look if you want."

"Thanks," Rory said, getting up. He came over to her and kissed the top of her gray head. "And thanks for talking." He gently nudged her away from the sink full of dishes. "I've got this. You go relax."

She flashed him an ostensibly annoyed looked, but then smiled as she dried her hands. She kissed his cheek. "Thanks for dinner, sweetheart. I'll go find a movie for tonight. Something light."

Shortly after their movie, *The Way, Way Back*, ended and his mother was in bed, Rory crept down the creaky basement steps to examine the contents of the boxes Evelyn Chandler had left for his mother. After winding past a dusty, unplugged treadmill, a wall of shelves containing everything from unopened rolls of wrapping paper to cobwebby beach toys, and plastic bins stuffed with old Christmas decorations, Rory came to a collection of 16 cardboard boxes, stacked in even columns, in a far corner of the basement. The single lightbulb hanging near the bottom of the steps barely illuminated that corner of the basement, so Rory dragged the boxes over into the pool of light that spilled across the cold, concrete floor.

None of the boxes were labelled, so Rory randomly began opening and rifling through them. Most of them were stuffed with clothes; he gave those boxes a cursory look, just enough to assess which of them contained Evelyn's wardrobe and which held Nathaniel's. Several boxes were filled to the brim with books. Another held a variety of ballerina figurines of different sizes and shapes, carefully bubble-wrapped and fit together like *Tetris* pieces. One contained toys and action figures while a separate one featured several stacks of VHS tapes.

Then there was one containing picture frames and photo albums. Most of the photo albums were empty; Rory guessed Evelyn had bought them dreaming of future pictures of graduations, a first car, a wedding reception, great-grandchildren—pictures that never were to be. The pictures in the frames were almost entirely of Nathaniel at various ages: squinting into the camera on a bright day down the shore, baring a big gap-toothed grin while opening presents Christmas morning, blowing out birthday candles, the elastic band from his cone-shaped party hat loose under his chin.

Rory picked out one particular picture that caught his eye and sat down on the cool floor, his back leaning against the newel base of the staircase. The picture was of Nathaniel on his First Communion. He stood on the bottom step in front of St. Rose, the Catholic Church on Central Avenue, with his hands folded piously. His bright green eyes glinted in the springtime sun; his blonde hair was perfectly combed and parted. He looked cherubic. Rory tried to imagine that platinum blonde hair turned dark, and damp, with blood. He tried to imagine the startled shriek that quiet, book-loving child made when he was violently accosted in Sattler's Woods that April evening. Did he scream when his skull was bashed in with a rock, or was his mouth covered with duct tape? Did he struggle, did he fight back, or were his arms and legs bound with zip ties?

SATTLER'S WOODS

As he sat there staring at the photograph, a wave of anger suddenly washed over him. The more he thought about the empty photo albums that would never be filled, the more he thought about his mother's eyes filling with tears at the memory of her friend getting dragged through hell for eight torturous months, the angrier he got. After today, the story told by the state about Randall Thompson was not sitting well with him. His gut was telling him—practically yelling now—that whoever followed those three boys into the woods that night, whoever beat them senseless and crushed their skulls in, whoever callously dumped their bodies in a shallow grave in the middle of nowhere, was still out there, free to follow another Nathaniel Foster onto a different dark trail through a different forest, free to leave another family broken and shattered with grief.

He decided that tomorrow he would take Cindy Thompson's advice: he would drive down to the South Woods State Prison to meet the convicted killer face-to-face, to figure out whether Randall Thompson is exactly where he should be, or if the true killer is still prowling quiet suburban streets, watching school playgrounds from hidden vantage points, waiting, with weak-kneed anticipation, to sink his teeth into the next child.

Twelve

An early morning thunderstorm awoke Rory from the same nightmare he had awoken from a few nights ago—of the shore house getting torn apart by a vicious hurricane. Only this time, Nathaniel Foster, in his white First Communion suit, was there, standing quietly in the shadowy hallway to the back bedrooms. And every time Rory went to get him, to bring him to huddle in the safety of the living room with Marie and Kevin, he was inexplicably pushed back, as if they were magnets with the same pole, farther and farther into the dark house. When the roof began to lift from the house, blood spurted from the rafters and dribbled down the walls just as Nathaniel completely disappeared in the shadows and Marie and Kevin screamed from the living room.

For an hour or so, Rory simply lay in bed watching the lightning flashes against his curtained window and listening to the rain lash against the pane. The thunder was the kind that felt like it rumbled up from deep within the earth, the kind you could feel in the pit of your stomach.

The power had gone in and out, leaving the clock radio at his bedside temporarily useless, so Rory picked up his phone to check the time. It was ten of eight. For no particular reason, he scrolled through some old text messages and, for a moment, considered sending one to Kevin—ask if he had any exciting plans for the weekend—before remembering it wouldn't even be five o'clock yet out in California.

He lay in bed for another half hour before getting up to make coffee. It was still raining when he left a note for Kathleen on the kitchen table and began the hour-long drive to the prison.

South Woods State Prison came up suddenly just off Route 54. After dozens of miles of desolate Pine Barrens, the prison's football field-sized parking lot, barbed wire fences, and formidable brick austerity felt incongruous and alien. Visiting hours had just begun, so the parking lot was practically empty. Rory took a deep breath, grabbed his pen and notepad, and walked briskly through the drizzle toward a gated door marked *Visitors*.

Is this really a good idea? What makes me think I can even tell how guilty this guy is just from talking to him?

He was quickly buzzed in to a security checkpoint. When Rory told the guard he was there to see Randall Thompson, the guard shook his head and grumbled through his graying beard, "Hope you're not a friend of that fucking pervert animal."

They directed Rory to a blue-chaired visiting booth that smelled of both potent cleaning supplies and an intractable staleness. As he waited for Randall to appear on the opposite side of the thick Plexiglas, Rory flipped through the shorthand notes he had taken while listening to Cindy Thompson the other day. How Randall had been set up to buy that bag of horrific child porn. How he genuinely sought help after his first stint in prison. How he had nurtured an abused cat back to health when he was a child. Rory was ruminating on those details when he looked up to see the balding, middle-age man standing before him.

Randall Thompson was thin but round-faced. The little hair he had left was dirty-blonde and short-cropped. He looked down at Rory from dark-rimmed reading glasses and actually smiled, shyly, just as he had in his graduation photo from his mother's flyer. He sat down slowly; his shoulders and neck were tense, as if he were bracing for a punch. His orange jumpsuit seemed intentionally, even absurdly, unfitting, like a Halloween costume.

Looks more like a college professor than a killer. But what was that Shakespeare quote Marie used to say? Look like the innocent flower but be the serpent under it. Both men picked the phones up off their respective cradles as they studied each other through the Plexiglas. *He's probably wondering who the hell I am. And why the hell I'm here. Fair questions, both.*

"Randy Thompson," the mild-looking, orange-jumpsuited man said quietly, his tone hesitant and defensive, his voice slightly grainy through the phone.

"My name is Rory Callahan."

"You're the writer, right?"

"Yes. Well, ex-writer to be exact."

"Ma told me you might come to see me." Randall lifted his chin slightly, narrowed his eyes, and looked down at Rory from a slight angle. "What can I do for you, Mr. Callahan?"

"I had a long conversation with your mother. She was compelling."

Randall rolled his eyes. "I keep asking her to stop with the public relations tour. It's only going to make people hate me more than they do already. And it's put her life in danger."

"She really believes you're innocent."

"I'm not," Randall said forcefully. "I've been guilty for decades. It's why she needs to stop. I'm not a good person."

"Who is?" Rory asked. *Seems like his self-loathing runs pretty deep, understandably. I've got to get past that if I want to actually learn anything from him.* "Maybe being a 'good person' is a context-sensitive concept. Some of us are forced to carry baggage we never asked for. Maybe being a 'good person' looks different for a person whose back is breaking under a crushing burden than it does for someone who's scot-free."

Randall dropped his chin and relaxed his posture as he waited for Rory to go on.

"I know it's not a popular opinion," Rory said, "but after talking to your mother and even to a Hollingford police officer, I believe the prosecution's case was bullshit. I don't know if you're the kind of guy who would hurt a child, but I don't think you did on April 13th, 1992. At least not the way they said you did, anyway."

Randall didn't say anything at first. He looked away from Rory while still holding the phone up to his ear. When he finally spoke, his voice lost some of its defensive edge. "Even if that were true, what role do you play in this? Is this just a hobby for you now that you're not writing anymore?"

"Maybe. Maybe it started that way. But I was sitting there last night staring at this picture of Nathaniel Foster and I started to feel, of all things, pissed off. What if the guy who killed that kid was free, free to kill again—maybe he has already—while you rotted away in here? It would be a gross injustice, Mr. Thompson."

"Of course," Randall said. "But I have to correct you: I am not rotting away in here. I actually feel freer in here than I ever did living at home. Do you know how much guilt and boredom can eat away at you?"

Yes, Rory thought.

"It's a toxic combination," Randall continued. "Look." Although the visiting room was still empty besides the two of them, he leaned in closer toward the Plexiglas. "I know what I am. I thought I could change—I tried to change—but I couldn't. But in here, that guilty voice that gnaws away at my brain is quieter. I have a chance to serve my penance here, and that is liberating. I deserve worse than this. I would gladly accept worse than this."

"But you've never touched a child, have you? You've never hurt anyone."

"I've hurt plenty of people," Randall said. He hunched his shoulders, dropped his head, and ran his free hand through the patch of hair at the back of his head several times. When he looked back up at Rory, his eyes were wide and supplicating. "But no, I've never touched a child."

"So that night, April 13th, 1992, you were out walking?"

"Yes. Back then, I'd get anxious at night. Would lie in bed for hours, praying that I'd fall asleep. But I struggled to get that gnawing, guilty voice to shut up no matter how much I tried. So I'd take these long walks around town, try to tire myself out before bed. Sometimes I'd bring books on tape with me and listen to them through my Walkman. But that night I left it at home: I remember getting annoyed by the constant noise from the TV and just wanting some quiet."

"Do you remember where you walked that night?"

"I do. I remember that night vividly, actually. I guess with the news breaking about the missing boys the next morning, it just sticks clearly in my mind. That night, I left right around sundown. Walked down Central, did a lap around Crystal Lake, and then took 8th Street south all the way to the Route 54 interchange before I turned around for home."

"You were at the complete opposite end of town from the middle school," Rory observed.

"Yes. But I also didn't run into anyone who could tell the jury that. Not that it matters."

Rory glanced down at the open notepad on the counter, scrambling for a follow-up question to ask; it had been some time since his last serious interview, and he was feeling rusty. But he almost immediately noticed the note *video tapes = setup* from talking with Cindy, which prompted his next question: "Your mother suggested, about the video tapes they found in your closet?"

"I remember them."

"She suggested they might have been part of some kind of set-up."

Randall sighed heavily into the transmitter and shook his head. "Yeah, she's told me that, too. I think she might be grasping at straws there. Regardless of the intentions of whoever sold them to me, I still bought them of my own free will."

"How did you end up with the tapes in the first place?"

Randall's eyes darted down to the notepad and pen as if he were noticing them for the first time. He cocked his head, gave an askew, semi-smile, and asked, "What do you plan to do with all of this information, Mr. Callahan? Assuming you leave here believing I am innocent and the killer is still at large. Just out of curiosity."

"Fair question. And you obviously have the right to know. Honestly, I haven't quite figured that out yet. I'm considering doing a freelance piece for one of the Philly papers, if they're interested."

Randall ran his fingers through his hair again and nodded. "You live in town, Mr. Callahan?"

"Just recently."

"If you write anything—even start asking questions—prepare to be ostracized by the entire community."

Good point. Would any of it come back on my mom? "You're probably right there. But on the bright side, you've got at least one cop who's sympathetic to your cause."

"Really?" His eyebrows leapt up in surprise, or perhaps skepticism.

"Yeah. She sees holes in the prosecution's story that have never been explained away."

"She might be the only one. Cop, that is."

"Maybe. But she's a good cop and might prove to be an important ally."

"Good to know," Randall said. "Anyway, you were asking how I came across those tapes?"

"Yes. I was wondering how and when you got them."

"It's a bit of a convoluted story. You sure you have time?"

"Plenty."

"All right," Randall began. "The summer of 1992 was brutal. People in town had always known about me, why I had been in jail—word somehow always spreads in small towns—but up until that summer, except for wary looks at the Acme or mothers ushering their children away from me at Walmart, they generally left me alone. But things changed when those boys disappeared. People would stare when me and ma went out for dinner. They'd shout things like 'Where are the kids?' and 'child fucker' at us from their cars when we went out for a walk. Even the police talked to me a couple times. Nothing serious, but they knew I was on the list—"

"The sex offender registry."

Randall nodded. "They knew I was on that, so I was right in their crosshairs from the beginning. As the summer dragged on, that insatiable, nagging voice inside my head got worse. I'd hated myself since before I even knew what I was, but now I was ruining my mother's life as well. She'd act normal, pretend not to hear the insults or notice the stares, but I could tell it was wearing her down. It was getting to the point where she was afraid to leave the house, even to run to Wawa for some milk.

"One afternoon, maybe mid-July, I was pacing back and forth in my bedroom trying to figure out what I could do to make the voice finally stop. I had already tried alcohol, downing shot after shot of vodka till I was dumb."

And a sweet numbness it is, Rory thought.

"It actually worked for a week or two. The vodka drowned out the voice, and my mind was free to contemplate other things. It was freedom. Oftentimes, as I lay on my bed on the verge of passing out, some of my happiest childhood memories would come drifting back to me. Snow days spent sledding and building igloos with ma, last days of school, hayrides in the fall, things like that. But soon I would wake up not just with a hangover, but with the voice louder than ever and full of pent-up rage.

"So there I was, pacing back and forth, trying to clear the cotton from my brain long enough to think. I remember digging my nails into my palms till there was blood. The one thing I kept coming back to, the one idea that kept haunting me the more I tried to push it away, was that if I—" He hesitated, fumbling for the right phrase. "—could indulge in self-abuse, I thought maybe I could escape from my own head for a little bit, feel some kind of release, you know?"

"Sure."

"I'd been pacing for an hour, maybe two, going back and forth, making up my mind, then changing it. I suddenly found myself headed toward the front door, checking the clock on the microwave to make sure ma was still at work, and the voice quieted a bit. I kept going till I was down the block and the voice quieted even more, barely to a whisper. By the time I got to the old video store—used to be where the KFC is now on the White Horse Pike—the voice was completely silent. I hid my face from the clerk as I walked past and went directly to the backroom, behind that curtain. I understand video stores are now a thing of the past, but you remember how they used to have those back rooms?"

"Of course."

"I knew they weren't going to have anything that fits my—" Randall picked out an appropriate euphemism. "—interests, of course. But I hoped maybe they'd have something remotely close, but legal. It would have been perfect. A movie where they were all of age, where no kids were getting hurt, but they somehow made it seem..." He gesticulated to see if Rory got what he was implying without making him actually speak the words.

"I understand," Rory said.

"But of course they didn't have anything like that. It was insane to think they would, and I knew it was. I was scanning the shelves, looking for a video I figured I could try anyway, when a man came up beside me, uncomfortably close. I kept my eyes straight ahead on the video cases, just for the sake of discretion, and kept moving around the room, but he stayed right beside me the entire time. He was clearly following me. I finally picked a video and headed toward the curtain when I heard him mumble something like, 'They never have 'em young enough in this place.' That's when he grabbed my shoulder and turned me toward him. He was wearing khakis and a button down shirt. His hair was silvery-gray, and he had a goatee of the same color. I remember how strong his aftershave was. He looked like a mini-van driving dad or church deacon or something.

"I asked him what he meant and tried to move away, but he just smiled and held onto my shoulder. He was surprisingly strong. Then he pointed at the video in my hands and said, 'If that doesn't do it for you, give this a try,' and slipped an index card into my shorts pocket without breaking his stare or his smile.

"Even though he looked harmless—paternal, in a way—this guy completely freaked me out. I finally got away from him and hurried to pay for my video. I only glanced back once, but he must have still been behind the curtain because there was no sign of him. I just wanted to get out of there, so I paid with a five and left the change. Then, out of sheer paranoia, I took a different route home, glancing back every few minutes just in case he was following me."

"Why would he have been following you?" Rory asked.

"Not a clue. I told myself later that night that I was being irrational, but there was just something about the way he grabbed me, the way he smiled at me, that left me rattled. When I got home, I even locked the door behind me and camped out at my bedroom window upstairs, watching the street. I think it took about an hour for my heart to finally slow down to normal. And that's when I remembered the index card he had shoved in my pocket."

"What did it say?"

"Not much. A phone number written in Sharpie. Out of state area code. But I knew what it was for." Randall removed his glasses and placed them gently on the stainless steel counter before him. He closed his eyes and rubbed the bridge of his nose. "I came close to throwing

SEAN THOMAS

out that number so many times. I'm sure my mother told you why I went to jail the first time—trying to buy videos like that. I should have known better." He opened his eyes but kept them fixed on the counter. "And it's not the jail time. That's never been it, then or now. It's how everyone knows. This secret I thought I could keep buried deep inside me till my deathbed is now printed in the papers. Shows up on a registry anyone can see. Strangers I'll never meet look at me, read about me, and they judge. They hate me. But like I said, I know I deserve worse."

Rory waited, assuming Randall would continue the story in a moment. *There's no rush. And I can't blame the man for not exactly being enthusiastic about reliving this moment in his life.* But as Randall continued to stare down at his glasses on the counter, and many long seconds of silence passed, Rory finally prodded: "So you held onto the phone number that summer?"

"Yes. As I'd suspected, the video I'd picked up that day did nothing to help me get that release I craved. That time—even a brief moment—to get outside my own, guilt-addled brain. As the summer dragged on, there were a few times I grabbed that index card from my dresser, usually after staring at it for a while, and going down to the kitchen phone. A couple of times I even got so far as to start dialing the number. Then I'd talk myself out of it, convince myself it was another sting operation like before, and throw the card away. But inevitably, I found myself digging it out of the trashcan later that night or the next morning."

Randall still gazed unflinchingly at his glasses on the counter, his eyes taking on a remote, trancelike appearance. "I honestly can't remember a particular incident, or even a specific day, that finally pushed me to make that call. It was an early September morning; I remember that. And I remember feeling genuinely surprised when I found myself dialing the last digit in the number. It felt like I was in daze when I heard the ringing and then the voice—a man's voice—asking where I wanted to meet for the exchange. No, 'Hello' or 'Who is this?' Just, 'Where can we meet?' I hadn't even considered that, of course. When I started stuttering and stammering, he shut me up by saying, "AC Expressway rest stop, end of the parking lot on the Burger

King side, nine o'clock tonight. Bring a hundred dollars cash.' And then he hung up."

"Did you recognize his voice at all?" Rory asked. "Did it sound like the same man who approached you in the video store?"

Randall finally broke his stare. He looked at Rory, pursed his lips, arched his eyebrows, and lightly drummed his fingers on the edge of the counter as he thought. "Didn't really seem like it. Then again, it's hard to remember now, and I didn't really consider it then. I guess I just assumed it was. But both conversations—if you want to call them that—were so brief. I'm just not sure."

"That's understandable."

"You know," Randall said, a spark in his voice now, "something I've always found strange? How he automatically knew I'd be close to the AC Expressway. I figured because of his area code, he wasn't local. Maybe travels around looking for customers."

"Not staying too long to avoid attracting suspicion," Rory added.

"Right. I can understand wanting to maintain anonymity for both of us, but he never even asked where I was so we could figure out a place to meet. It almost felt he was waiting for me to call."

"You're right. That is strange," Rory said as he jotted down some notes. "How did the meet-up go?"

Randall shrugged. "Mercifully uneventful. I told ma I was meeting a college friend in Atlantic City for drinks and gambling that night, so she let me borrow the car and the hundred dollars. She was so trusting. Hopeful, maybe, because I was having a normal night out. Just another lie. Another thing to feel guilty about.

"When I got to the rest stop, he was exactly where he said he'd be: the only car in the back row of parking spots. A little, gray Toyota. I parked a few spots over, swiveling my head the whole time, looking for anything that seemed off. My heart was in my throat when I shut off the engine. The thought had crossed my mind that the guy might have a gun and rob me of the hundred dollars. Or I pictured cop car lights flashing any second, and I'd be calling my mother from jail again.

"But neither of those things happened. I got out of the car and walked slowly toward the Toyota. Suddenly, I heard a man's voice from the darkness off to my side: 'Leave the hundred on the hood. The bag is on the passenger seat.' I started to turn around to see who was speaking, but the man said, 'Stop. Leave the money, take the bag, and go.' So I did. I tucked the bill under the windshield wiper, grabbed the paper bag off the passenger seat, and practically threw it into the trunk before taking off. I never did get a good look at the guy. Not sure I even wanted to. Only a vague, dark outline from my rearview mirror as I drove off."

"Did you recognize the voice from the phone call or the video store?"

Randall shrugged again. "I was so nervous, I wasn't really paying attention to what the voice sounded like. I was just glad to put the rest stop behind me and get the hell out of there.

"I decided to drive to the mall and walk around for a few hours so my mother wouldn't ask why I was home so early. But I kept imagining that everyone in the mall was looking at me, that they knew the horrible thing I had just done, the horrible thing I had in the trunk of the car. I imaged them glaring, shaking their heads, thinking, *monster* or *child molester.* I tried to calm down, to act normal as I browsed through books or racks of clothes, but I couldn't. I checked my watch every minute to see if it was late enough for me to go home. I finally just sat in the car for an hour, pretending to read a paperback my mom had in the backseat, but really just counting down the seconds till I could leave.

"When I got home, I silently thanked God that the lights were out and ma was asleep. I snuck upstairs, trying to keep that paper grocery bag from crinkling as much as I could, and shoved it to the back of my closet, behind a mountain of old clothes. At breakfast in the morning, I lied again to my mother about how my friend from Rutgers was doing. I apologized that I'd lost all of the money at blackjack, promised to pay her back. She said not to worry about it. She wasn't upset. In fact, she seemed happy. Tried hiding a smile behind her coffee mug as she took a sip." Randall looked back down. His voice had lost its spark, becoming sullen. "Gave her false hope. Cindy Thompson's freak son might actually be normal."

"What happened next, Randall?"

Randall shook his head, slowly. "A few weeks later," he said, sounding defeated, "I'm sitting in the Hollingford police department and they're telling me they found the most horrifying child porn they've ever seen in my bedroom closet."

"Had you watched any of the tapes before your arrest?"

Randall shook his head again. "Never. Those tapes called my name every night as I tried to sleep. But I never could bring myself to watch one of them. Never even opened the bag."

Rory sat back in his chair, feeling the blue plastic creak beneath him. *If this poor son-of-a-bitch isn't lying, the whole thing does sound like a set-up.*

"But that's not the worst part," Randall said, mumbling now. "The worst part is, I never go to tell anyone the truth."

"The truth?"

"My lawyer thought it would be a bad idea, but I want to tell you. If you end up writing this article, it'll help me get clean." There were a few other prisoners in the visiting room now; even though they were all caught up in their own conversations, Randall still leaned in close once again. He whispered, "Those three boys? Too old for me. Far too old."

All Rory could do was nod and continue to scribble in his notepad. "Right," he finally said.

"I don't know if that makes me better or worse. Worse, I'd imagine. But that's the truth."

Rory was taken aback by this disturbing bit of honesty, but he kept his composure and asked, "I have your permission to include that information in a published article?"

"I want you to."

A passing guard, a squat, bulldog of a man, casually strode up behind Rory, rapped his nightstick on the metal counter, and said, "Time to wrap it up, gentlemen."

Randall Thompson nodded and slid his glasses back on as he made to stand up. "Feel free to come back if you have any other questions," he said. "It was nice talking to someone who isn't my mother." Then, he pursed his lips. "And thank you for not judging me. You're one of the few people who doesn't look at me like I'm Hannibal Lecter or a caged wolverine."

"Well, I appreciate your time, Mr. Thompson. And I'm sorry for reminding you of some god-awful memories."

"Don't apologize. I think about them every day. I force myself to. Part of my penance."

As Rory was about to hang up the phone, Randall said one last thing: "Mr. Callahan? If you end up finding the person who killed those boys, that is an act of justice of course. But don't do it for me. I'm where I belong. And I thank God every day for that."

Thirteen

On the drive back from the prison, Rory couldn't help but churn over everything Randall had told him. Randall may very well be a lying sociopath, an expert of manipulation and misinformation, but Rory's gut—which he had come to rely on and trust through his years of reporting—told him he wasn't; Randall seemed to fit the description provided by his mother of a sensitive, insecure man who, as a boy, would take care of an abused cat, not add to its torment.

Then again, isn't that exactly what a sociopath would have everyone believe? But the logistics—like Daniels said. Even if he'd wanted to kill those kids, how could he have?

Back at the house an hour later, Rory sat on his bed and pored over the notes he'd taken from talking to both Cindy and Randall Thompson before popping open his laptop and delving back into the dozens, if not hundreds, of archived articles about the murders, Randall's arrest and trial, and Cindy's hostilely-received campaign to resurrect her son's assassinated character. Hours passed and night began to fall when Rory pulled Officer Daniels's card from his wallet and dialed her cell phone: there was still more to know about the murders and the investigation if he wanted to figure out who really killed the three boys—which he was gradually realizing, he did. Badly.

"Officer Daniels," she answered.

"Officer, this is Rory Callahan."

"How are you, Mr. Callahan?" she asked. "Any updates on the death threats?"

"No, thank God. I'm starting to think it might not even have been a real death threat after all. Maybe just some misdirected practical joke or something. But thanks for your help with that."

"Not a problem."

"I was actually calling about something else, though. I was wondering if I could pick your brain about the Blueberry Hill murders."

"Oh," she said, without sounding overly surprised. "I'd be happy to. Why don't we meet for coffee, let's say 10:30 tomorrow at the diner on Central?"

"I'll be there."

"You don't have to come with me. I know church isn't exactly your cup of tea."

"Maybe not. But I'd like to. At least this week."

Rory and Kathleen sat over a breakfast of scrapple and scrambled eggs. Kathleen was wearing a sea-green summer dress while Rory had on a collared shirt, sleeves rolled up to the elbows, and suit pants.

"I can't even remember the last time I've been to Mass with you," Kathleen said. "It might have been your confirmation in 8th grade."

"Does my wedding count?" Rory asked, squirting a blob of ketchup onto his plate.

"No."

"Then it was probably my confirmation in 8th grade."

Rory had started drifting from organized religion in high school. He never minded going to church and listening to the priests, but the contradictions and pettiness of Church teaching always bothered him: Would God really get as upset about 14 year-old-Rory jacking off to the stunning blonde in biology class as He would about a corrupt politician taking shady campaign contributions or the rich yuppies ignoring the homeless man on the corner? So when his parents made attending Mass optional once he hit high school, he decided to sleep in on Sundays. When he and Marie had Kevin, they ushered him, halfheartedly, through CCD classes so he could get confirmed, but by the time the Church sex scandal was making front page news, they were both eager to put the Church behind them for good.

So when Rory found himself dressing to accompany his mother to nine A.M. Sunday Mass, no one was more surprised than Rory.

"Why do you want to come again?" his mother asked.

"I could use some grace," he answered, biting into a crisp slice of scrapple. "And maybe it'll remind you to pray for me."

"I always pray for you," Kathleen said.

"Thanks. I need it."

"Can you stay for coffee and donuts afterwards?"

Rory shook his head, swallowing his bite of scrapple. "I'm getting coffee with Jessica Daniels, the police officer here in town."

"I know her," Kathleen said. "Lovely woman. What are you meeting about?"

Rory hesitated. He felt bad enough for asking his mother about Evelyn and Nathaniel the other night, making her weep. When she'd expressed her strong disapproval of his visit to see Randall Thompson yesterday, Rory realized how irresponsible it would be traipse cavalierly through the minefield of still-painful memories, still-fresh wounds associated with the murders, as he had been. "I just had some questions for her," he answered haltingly. "Wanted to see what she knows about the Blueberry Hill murders. For an article I'm thinking about writing."

Kathleen continued buttering a piece of toast and nodded, though her eyes remained skeptical. "Just be careful, son. You know how I feel about you visiting that man yesterday."

"I know."

"Just be careful. Sometimes the dead should be allowed to rest."

The storms from the previous day left a sunny, mild, and breezy morning behind, so Rory and Kathleen decided to make the short walk up to Central for church. Despite her mental weariness, Kathleen walked with an energy and purpose that delighted Rory. *She looks good. Really good. I can barely keep up with her.*

The church building itself was post-Vatican II, so it featured few statues—just Saint Rose of Lima, the parish's namesake, the Blessed Virgin, and the Sacred Heart of Jesus—and simple stained glass windows bereft of saints and Biblical tableaus. The floor was carpeted, and there was no choir loft, but rather a piano off to the side of the altar. The air smelled faintly of Febreze and incense.

Rory had barely known the order of the Mass back when he'd been going to church every week; now, forty years later and with the service featuring new translations of certain prayers and responses, he was completely lost. He tried to participate, but when he found himself stumbling over his words, his mother shot him a look of embarrassment and annoyance. Ultimately, he decided to stay respectfully quiet instead.

The presider of the Mass was the parish pastor, Father George Santos. He was young, tall, and had a heavy, resonant voice. He seemed genuinely cheerful as he waved and shook hands during the procession and flashed frequent grins at the congregation from the altar—a sharp contrast from the weathered, white-haired, aggressively uninterested Irish priests Rory remembered from his childhood.

When it came time for the Homily, Father George displayed a calm, unassuming confidence as he casually leaned on the lectern and looked out at the congregation as if he were about to speak to a coterie of good friends. "It's great seeing a full house on this beautiful summer morning," he began, "but I don't think coming to church to pray for the Phillies will make them any better. Sorry to break it to you, but they're already screwed. I don't think God could do anything to help them even if He wanted to. But all evidence indicates He's clearly a Yankees fan, so there's that." The quip got a genuine laugh from the audience.

"Thank you for laughing," he continued. "Priest humor, mine included, is across-the-board awful. But that charity laugh does help me make a point about today's Gospel—it's actually a manifestation of the reading, and really the Gospels as a whole. By laughing at my terrible jokes week in and week out, you are demonstrating your care for me. You tolerate them with patience and kindness and love rather than heckle me like the failed stand-up comedian I am. That way, I go to bed each night feeling ok about my life instead of crying myself to sleep." The self-deprecation elicited another chuckle from the audience. "In the end, you've got my back, just as—I hope you know—I've got yours."

Father George stood up straighter, and his voice now featured a trace of chilliness—not enough to mask its inherent warmth, but just enough to signal that a tonal shift was coming. "Having each other's backs," he said commandingly, his miked voice bouncing off the back wall of the church. "It's what Jesus tells us to do. It's how he showed us to live our lives by example of his own life. And it's what I ask you to do now.

"We all know that hard times have visited us here in Hollingford, and they don't look to be leaving any time soon. The Mondelez factory that shut down last year still shows no signs of reopening, despite what the corporate offices told us when they announced the layoffs. Thousands of people, many of them belonging to this parish, lost their jobs. Soon, the unemployment checks will stop coming and tough times will only get tougher.

"We also all heard the news last week that two more anchor stores out at the mall are closing, in addition to the Olive Garden in the winter and the Pathmark last fall. We know this will mean more pain, misery, and hardships for our friends and neighbors. Therefore, let's have each other's backs. Christ calls us to. Share meals with one another. If someone loses their home or apartment, open your door to them. And if asking for help directly from your neighbor makes you uncomfortable, which no one would fault you for, make use of the parish. The food pantry and welcome table are always open to you, with absolute love and sincerity. Make use of the general donation fund to help pay your rent or mortgage so you can keep your home. These resources are offered freely, with love and compassion, and with the knowledge that, if situations were reversed and times were good for you, that you would be reaching out to lift up your unemployed, or sick, or disabled, or lonely, neighbor.

"Many of us have also heard the news of the young woman out in The Oaks who passed away last week, the latest victim of the heroin epidemic gripping not only our community, but many communities across the state. She was our fifth overdose of the year. And I say 'our' because she belongs to us. She is a member of our family—our human family—as much as we may want to forget that. So I urge you to harden not your hearts. The people who find themselves addicted to drugs are no less human, deserve no less dignity, and are no less loved by God than you, or me, or the pope. Even the people in town—an

81

increasing number, sadly—who manufacture and sell these drugs, do it to make a living, to make more money in a day than they would in weeks toiling away at a minimum wage job, to create, in a position of existential crisis, some kind of meaning for themselves when an economic engine that decides the fate of so many people—hundreds of millions—has decided it no longer has a purpose for them. If we want to start to solve the problems of drug addiction and the drug trade, this is the basic understanding we must all agree upon first.

"Finally, as we all know, summertime and the blueberry harvest bring with them, like every year, an infusion of migrant workers into our community. It is our responsibility to treat them as we would any of our other brothers and sisters in Christ, even if—actually, especially since—they do not speak the same language we do. We must treat them with the dignity, warmth, and respect they do not receive from their twelve-hour days of grueling, back-breaking labor. We must acknowledge not only their hands, which planted and picked our food, whenever we go to the grocery store or farmer's market, but we must acknowledge their humanity—their individual hopes, aspirations, struggles—even though, or, again, especially since, they live on the margins of society. It is our duty and responsibility, as followers of Christ, to welcome them in from the margins with warmth and kindness."

Amen. Where was this guy when I was going to church? Rory thought.

"Remember: the Church is not this building. It's not the diocese or the archdiocese. It's not some council of cardinals in Rome. It's us. The people. If we forget that, we risk losing everything." A pregnant silence followed Father George's speech as he sat back down and dropped his head in meditation. He arose after a minute or so and resumed Mass with the creed. "As we take care of each other, strive to have one another's backs, let us profess our faith."

When the service was over, Kathleen introduced Rory to Father George at the bottom of the front steps of the church. "This is my son Rory—the newspaper reporter I've told you about. He'll be staying with me for a while."

"Pleasure to meet you, Rory," Santos said, crushing Rory's hand as he shook it. "You write for the *Inquirer*?"

"Used to," Rory replied. "Doing some freelance work now." He shook out his hand jokingly as soon as he had it back. "Quite a grip there, Father. I think I'll get sensation back sometime next week."

"Sorry about that. Don't take it personally."

"Not at all. I'm going to guess you played football in high school. Maybe basketball."

"Both, actually," he said, grinning. "Up at St. Peter's in Jersey City."

"Ah, a North Jersey kid. That explains the Yankees remark."

"It's just the truth. As a priest, I've got a direct line to God, so I kind of know."

Rory laughed.

"So will we see you Thursday for our summer concert? You'll get to see me humiliate myself onstage with my guitar, and all proceeds go to the Food Bank of South Jersey."

"It's a fun night," Kathleen added, gently nudging Rory with her elbow.

"Why not?" Rory said, shrugging. "I'll be there." He glanced down at his watch to make sure he wouldn't be late for his meeting with Daniels. "I've got to run, but it was nice meeting you, Father. Your sermon was fantastic, by the way."

"Appreciate that. Giving homilies every week, it gets hard to tell if I'm actually reaching anyone."

"I'll see you at home," Kathleen said.

"See you, mom," Rory said, kissing her cheek. "Call me if you need anything."

He said goodbye to the priest as well, promising to attend the fundraiser Thursday, before turning and walking briskly back to the house. Once there, he grabbed his notepad and laptop before taking off in the used Ford Focus for the Hollingford Family Diner.

Daniels was already there when Rory arrived, hunched over a steaming cup of coffee in a corner booth of the quiet restaurant. As soon as Rory spotted her from the host stand, he hurried down the narrow aisle between the backless barstools and the four-seater booths and sat down across from her.

"Hey," he said as he slid awkwardly along the squeaky, turquoise plastic of the booth seat to the center of the table.

"Morning," Daniels said.

Rory nodded toward her uniform. "Just get off a shift?"

Daniels shook her head as she sipped her coffee. "It starts in an hour."

The waitress, a surly-looking middle-aged woman with painted-on eyebrows and an unexpectedly gentle voice, took Rory's order—coffee and a donut—and was back with it in what felt like seconds.

"So," Daniels began, "seems like you're obsessing over this case as much as I have."

"I think I am."

"Any epiphanies?"

"On Friday night, I asked my mother what she remembers about the murders. Turns out, she had been close friends with Evelyn Chandler, Nathaniel Foster's grandmother."

"Huh." Daniels looked slightly disappointed in herself. "I didn't know that."

"Neither did I. I mean, I knew they were friendly through church, but I had no idea that they had been such good friends. And then she tells me—believe it or not—that she has boxes and boxes of Evelyn's and Nathaniel's things in the basement. Apparently Evelyn had no one else to will them to when she passed away."

Daniels's eyes got wide and her jaw actually dropped. "Really? We have to look through them," she stuttered. "There's so much we could learn!" Realizing her volume had gotten louder than she wanted for a discreet conversation, she stopped and looked around self-consciously.

"I browsed through them that night. Lots of books, clothes, picture frames. I'm not sure we'll find any game-changers in there."

"Still, that's a pretty big development."

"Yeah. All these years, I had no idea those boxes were sitting in the basement."

Daniels simply shook her head in amazement.

"So as I'm looking through the boxes, I come across this picture of Nathaniel from his First Communion, and I all I can do is stare at it. Like I'd fallen into a trance. Staring at this sweet little kid in his white suit, hands clasped in front of him…still hearing my mother's sobs as she talked about Evelyn's heart slowly breaking for an entire year. And I suddenly feel like I have to know. I have to know for sure who the fucker was who killed that kid and, for all intents and purposes, his grandmother."

"I know the feeling," Daniels said.

"Well, I drove down to South Woods and talked to Randall Thompson yesterday."

Daniels's jaw dropped for a second time. "Jesus, Mr. Callahan—"

"Rory," he corrected. "Call me Rory."

"Jesus, Rory! Even I've never dreamed of doing that."

"You couldn't. Word gets back to the department somehow that you're visiting the most despised man in Hollingford history, and suddenly you have some difficult questions to answer."

"So what was he like?" Daniels asked, leaning forward. After years of researching the case, reconstructing the events of that night through dozens of different scenarios, analyzing court documents, police statements, and interviews, she was undoubtedly eager to hear Rory's impressions of the case's central figure and sole suspect; it was like hearing about a friend's first-hand encounter with a celebrity.

"Human," he answered. "Fragile, in a way. I had no idea what to expect, but he seemed like the person Cindy said he is."

"Which all could be the facade of a brilliant sociopath," Daniels reminded him.

"True. We can't rule that out." Rory washed down a bite of his glazed donut with a mouthful of hot coffee. "But I don't think so."

"How come? I'm dying to hear this."

Just as Daniels had done that day outside the apartment complex, Rory quickly scanned the restaurant—only three or four other booths and a couple of barstools were occupied—and dropped his volume as he began. "Remember how you said, if he is guilty, he must have premeditated the attacks, or he had accomplices?"

"Of course. Been my theory for years."

"Well, I don't think either is true."

"Which would mean," Daniels said, gently sloshing the coffee in her mug as she gestured toward Rory, "he didn't do it."

"Exactly."

"So what makes you think he didn't premeditate the whole thing?"

Rory shrugged slightly. "He just doesn't seem like the type. I know: it could all be part of a brilliant performance. But he seemed tortured. He knows that if he ever acted on his desires, even consuming the porn—"

"He'd be destroying the lives of children."

"Yes. The first thing he told me was, in his own words, that he is guilty, that he's not a good person. He said being in prison is actually liberating because it's a way of serving penance for his guilt—he doesn't have to bear sole responsibility for punishing himself anymore. It wasn't until I questioned him, even pushed him a little, that he told me he didn't kill the three boys.

"If he were the kind of guy callous, or psychotic, enough to scope out those children, stalk them into the woods, individually restrain, molest, and murder them, then vehemently deny it for twenty-two years, I imagine he'd leap at the opportunity to claim his innocence. Get 'his side of the story' published in the paper. Maybe catch the eye of a lawyer who can fight for an appeal or retrial. Manipulate people for his own ends once more. But he told me several times that he belonged in prison and wouldn't want to be freed. He agreed that finding the real killer would be an act of justice, but proving his innocence wouldn't. He doesn't seem interested in being found innocent because in his eyes, he's not. And I don't think he was bullshitting me. And believe me, I've been served my fair share of bullshit sandwiches through the years."

Daniels quietly considered this as she finished her coffee and greeted a perfectly-timed refill from the waitress with a smile. "Did he say anything else?" she asked after the waitress had vanished back into the kitchen. "Neither of us being sociopaths—I hope not, at least—we don't know how deep the levels of manipulation and reverse-psychology can go. Maybe the whole 'I actually belong in jail bit' is a minor gambit in his overall strategy to get released." She took a sip from her fresh cup of coffee and smiled. "Not that I necessarily believe that. Just playing devil's advocate."

"He did tell me something." Rory started to explain, but stopped as soon as he had started. He wanted to divulge Randall's secret in a way that made him sound sympathetic rather than monstrous. But Rory decided it was possible to be both and that Daniels would understand that. "He told me that Nathaniel, Christopher, and Andrew were too old for him."

As Daniels processed the information, her face tensed in a show of disgust before quickly relaxing again. Then, she frowned as she mulled over the implications of, and motivation behind, revealing this secret. "Either a brazen lie or another piece in Randall Thompson's tragic life."

Rory glanced down at the last bit of his donut but ended up pushing it away. "My gut tells me the latter."

Daniels nodded, waiting for Rory to elaborate.

"Realistically, what are the chances Randall ever gets a new trial?" he asked.

"Unless the real killer turns himself in and signs a sworn statement, or some earth-shattering piece of irrefutable, physical evidence suddenly emerges, none."

"He told me I could publish that information about him being attracted to younger children if I end up writing an article. Said it would help him 'get clean,' as he put it. Why give me that permission unless he's being honest? It wouldn't exactly paint a flattering portrait of him."

"Maybe he wants people to ask themselves that question," Daniels said, still playing devil's advocate.

"Maybe. If so, it's a desperate move."

"He's in a desperate situation. What does he have to lose?"

"His mother's safety, for one. Which he genuinely seems to care about."

"True," Daniels conceded. "And you're right, of course. It does seem like an usual piece of information to share for someone who'd want to trick people into thinking he's completely harmless and perfectly innocent."

"It was almost like an Act of Confession," Rory added, "told by a guy who genuinely believes he belongs in prison."

"Which he does, of course. He's never denied purchasing that horrible child porn."

"That's true." Rory paused and looked out the window for the first time since sitting down; he had been so immersed in telling Daniels about his visit to South Woods, he had barely even noticed it was there. The day was spectacularly sunny, with a clear blue sky stretching out to the horizon, but the street was quiet. No pedestrians. A couple of cars sat at an intersection before disappearing from view when the light turned.

In his head, he replayed Randall's story about buying the porn and realized that even if it wasn't a set-up—as Randall himself had said, he still bought and kept the bag of videotapes without anyone holding a gun to his head—it was at least worth recounting for Daniels to get her reaction.

As Rory retold the story, he particularly emphasized the way Randall was approached in the video store by the man with the silver hair and goatee, how, when he called the number on the index card, the man on the other end of the phone seemed to know who, and where, Randall was without asking, and the strange, carefully anonymous purchase in the dark rest stop parking lot.

"Some of it sounds like it might just be good practice for dealing child porn," Daniels said. "But other things definitely seem strange. If he's telling the truth, of course."

"It all comes back to that," Rory admitted. "Although if he were going to lie, why not just go all the way? Claim someone planted the tapes in his closet."

"Good point. But what about the other option? Maybe he had accomplices or was coerced into helping, and covering up for, the real murderer?"

"Then why talk to me at all? It wouldn't have taken much effort to tell me to fuck off if he was scared of someone, or trying to protect someone."

"Makes sense. And I think we both agree, there's no way he could have snapped, attacked, and killed the boys like the prosecution claimed. He wouldn't have the strength or time to carry out the attack, get the bodies back to his car, and clean up the footprints before the cops showed up."

"The timeline doesn't work," Rory agreed.

"Unless he didn't kill them that night. Maybe he only abducted them that night and killed them sometime later. All we really know, in the end, is that they disappeared on April 13th and were found five months later."

"Jesus fucking Christ," Rory said, sighing. "I'd never thought of that."

"Me neither. Till just now. Admittedly, it still seems like a stretch. There was obviously a vicious attack on the trail through Sattler's Woods that night, murder or no. And there's still the question of a single man somehow subduing three strong, healthy, pre-teen boys."

"Right."

"But until we learn something new—find something tangible—it's still his word, however convincing, against the state's."

"That reminds me," Rory said, reaching into the bag leaning against his thigh on the booth, "before you have to go." He pulled out his laptop and opened it up to reveal a Word document. The night before, he had collected every piece of information he could find about each of the victims, and typed them up in a file called *blueberryhill*. He scrolled up to the first page where information about Nathaniel Foster, including a school photo, was featured and turned it around so Daniels could see. "Anyone in town I could talk to who might remember anything about him? About his family or friends?"

Daniels shook her head and frowned. "Not that I know of. I'm afraid when his grandmother passed away, she took everything we might have learned about this poor little guy with her."

Rory turned the computer back around and scrolled down to a school photo of Christopher Fitzgerald, a fellow 7th grader of Nathaniel's and, by all accounts, his close friend.

Daniels shook her head again. "Only child. His parents moved out of town in '93 or '94. Wanted to put this place and all memories of it far behind them. Embarrassingly, I've tried to find them online a few times, but haven't had any luck. My guess is they don't want to be found or bothered."

"Neither would I," Rory admitted, feeling a shot of guilt pierce his conscience. *Of course they don't want to be bothered. Who the fuck would? And that's exactly what I'm looking to do.* He thought about closing up the laptop and giving the investigation a rest, at least for the day, before Daniels stepped in, anticipating his next question.

"As for Andrew Skelly? Had a younger brother. Last I heard he was working as a mechanic out in Sicklerville. His parents still live in town, over in Laurel Acres, but they keep to themselves. I'm not proud to admit it, but occasionally the thought has crossed my mind to stop by to ask them about the case—if they were happy with the investigation and Randall Thompson's conviction. But I always talk myself out of it quickly. It would be a horrible, tactless thing to do."

"It's a fair question to ask," Rory countered.

"Fairness is relative. It wouldn't be fair for me to ask about their murdered child. They have their truth. Their peace. What right do I have to disturb it?"

She's right, of course, Rory thought. *Sometimes the dead should be allowed to rest.*

"That doesn't mean I think you should stop your one-man investigation," she said. "I can even—" She hesitated and glanced out the window, then drummed her fingers nervously on the edge of the table, as if she were about to reveal a secret she had never told anyone before.

"Listen," she continued after taking a small sip of coffee. "The principal of Blueberry Hill is friends with my parents: they have game night every week with a bunch of other neighbors. Her name's Angela DeMarco, and her first year at the school was the '91-'92 school year. So I'm not sure how much she'll know about the boys, but there's a chance she might remember something. I mean, that year has got to be etched in her memory, right?"

"I can only imagine."

"If you want, I could try to—and I don't know what she'd say—but I could try to arrange a meeting with her."

The suggestion immediately piqued Rory's interest. "Yeah? Only if you're comfortable asking, Jess."

Daniels took a deep breath and nodded. "I think I am. It just feels weird. After all these years of doing research on my own, piecing together theories in my head, to actually be talking to real people. Real people who were there when it happened, were actually affected by the murders."

"You've never asked the principal about it before?"

"No, not really. Only in kind of a peripheral way once or twice. I was always worried I'd be prying into memories she'd sooner forget about. But if you're serious about finding the truth—"

"I am," Rory reassured her. *Maybe not at first, but I'm all in now.*

"—and I believe you are, because you actually drove down to South Woods to talk to Randall Thompson, for God's sake. I think it's time for me to start doing more than just concoct theories in the shower."

After they had paid and were on their way out of the restaurant, Daniels asked, "Can I reach you on the number you called me from yesterday? I'll try to get in touch with Mrs. DeMarco today. I'll let you know what she says."

"Any time," Rory answered. "That's my cell."

Out in the parking lot, just as Rory was about to make his way over to the Ford Focus, he turned to Daniels and said, "I've got to correct something you said earlier, though."

She gave him a confused look.

"This is no 'one-man investigation.' I would have hit a dead end without you."

She smiled briefly, the freckled skin around her eyes crinkling, before furrowing her brow and pursing her lips. "We just have to be careful now. Both of us. I know I have to be careful because of my job, my bosses, but you need to be, too, Rory. Remember what they did to Cindy Thompson."

She's right again. Emotions about a murder case, especially one like this, are always going to be volatile, unpredictable. "Good advice. Thanks."

The sky Rory drove home under was bright and cloudless, but he couldn't help feel a sense of uneasiness, as if he were driving into the heart of a storm and was powerless to turn back.

Fourteen

Sometimes the dead should be allowed to rest.

Kathleen's admonition echoed through Rory's head as he sat with her in the living room that afternoon watching the Phillies game.

The dead and their families should be allowed to rest. If some asshole showed up at my doorstep asking me what it was like to hold my father's hand as he died—as he lay in bed, his breath barely a rattle, the cancer leaving him a skeleton, a stick-figure, gasping for air, his skin yellow and cold—what would I say? The man who patiently explained football to me as we watched Eagles games in the front room of our row home, who took me fishing out at Brigantine, canoeing down the Delaware, camping in Valley Forge. The man who gave me a beer and had a long talk about treating women right when I had my first serious girlfriend in high school. Who pulled me aside during my wedding reception and said, "Be patient and kind, and no matter how shitty things get, you'll both be ok"—the man whose advice I failed to take. The man I wanted to be because he could bear anything— working unconscionably long hours down at the port, then joblessness, then two years of pancreatic cancer that absolutely ravaged him—with quiet determination. Who never wanted to talk about himself, always asked about you, and genuinely cared about the answer.

If I had forgotten the pain of the night he died, of feeling that last vestige of strength leave his fleshless hand, of the quiet rattle of his breath going silent, of the utter disbelief as the realization set in—my father is gone, he ceases to exist—if I had forgotten those things and were suddenly reminded by some asshole I didn't even know to satisfy his own curiosity, I'd probably punch him in the fucking face. If someone were to show up every day wanting to know what it felt like that night, if I could never escape the horror of that memory, I would move away and do my best to purge my name and contact information from the internet so no one could ever bring back that memory again. I would do what Christopher Fitzgerald's parents did.

93

Suddenly, the thought of doing more research into the case, of reaching out to family and friends of the victims to glean some overlooked bit of information that, in all likelihood, didn't even exist, made Rory queasy. He decided to take a break from the investigation for the rest of the day and simply enjoy the company of his mother. Maybe pick up a new book to read or go for a run through town.

Instead, when his mother had fallen asleep in her bright green recliner, he felt a quick jolt of panic at the prospect of a purposeless afternoon. He thought an hour or so of research would help assuage the anxiety, so he got up to retrieve his laptop. His hand on the doorknob of his bedroom door, he stopped himself and went back to sit in the living room with his sleeping mother.

Give it a fucking break. Sometimes the dead should be allowed to rest.

During the next commercial break, he paced back and forth in the living room thinking, *Sometimes the dead should be allowed to rest,* before breaking for the kitchen and helping himself to a bottle of Cape May Brewery double-IPA from the fridge. He had only planned on having one, maybe two, but ninety minutes later, he guzzled down the last bit of his sixth bottle. His head was swimming, but that sudden burst of panic from earlier was gone.

He reached into his pocket for his cell phone and opened the text messaging app. *having a good weekend? hows work?* he texted his son. He'd been meaning to fly out to visit Kevin in San Francisco for months now, but was afraid of how he would be received: Kevin had been furious about the divorce and put the majority of the blame on Rory's shoulders. *As he should,* Rory thought. Ever since breaking the news to him, Kevin responded to Rory's texts with curt, typically single-word responses, and he never returned Rory's calls.

He then scrolled down to the text-thread with Marie. *hey,* he texted. *how are you? my mom is doing well, all things considered. remembers some things clearly, is confused by other things. wishes you the best. i think she always knew you were too good for me.* He pressed *Send* and rested his phone on the arm of the couch for a second before furiously picking it back up to cancel the message. But it was too late.

Shit.

The double-IPAs were gone, but Rory returned to the fridge for a Yuengling. He downed it, then checked his phone for replies. Nothing. He set the phone down and managed to watch the game for five minutes before checking his phone again. Still nothing. He went back to the fridge for another beer.

When Daniels called an hour later, Rory's eyes were closed and he was drifting into a drunken sleep. The dream of huddling in the living room of the beach house being battered and brutalized by a wicked storm was just beginning when his ringing phone dragged him back to consciousness.

"Marie?" he answered, his voice raspy.

"Rory? It's Jess Daniels."

"Officer—I'm sorry. I was just taking a nap."

"You do sound groggy," she said. "Sorry about that."

"No need to apologize. I need to get my lazy ass up anyway." He arose on wobbly legs and went into the kitchen so as not to disturb Kathleen.

"I just wanted to let you know I talked to Mrs. DeMarco." Even in his drunkenness, Rory could detect the mix of anxiety and excitement in her voice. "And she agreed to talk to us tomorrow."

"Good. That's really good." He wanted to say more, but the beer made it difficult, like trying to swim against the current.

"How does noon work? Said she has a busy morning but would be willing to talk during her lunch break."

"Noon is perfect."

"Meet you outside the school?" Daniels asked.

"See you there."

When Rory returned to the living room, the Phillies postgame show was playing on TV and Kathleen was awake and yawning in her chair. She asked Rory what he'd like to do for dinner. He mumbled something in response, lay down on the couch, and was asleep within a minute.

Fifteen

Blueberry Hill Middle School was smaller and far less ominous than it appeared in the stark black-and-white photographs from the newspaper and internet articles. The boxy, brick building was cozily perched atop the gently sloping hill from which it bore its name. A well-manicured garden featuring soft-yellow trellises crawling with flowering vines sprung from the island in the middle of the drop-off circle near the school entrance. The school itself, as well as the small faculty parking lot off to its side, was fringed with lavender rhododendrons bursting from fresh, dark mulch.

Rory was ten minutes early, so he parked and wandered back past a small playground behind the school, to where Sattler's Woods once loomed. He wondered if the youngest, most imaginative middle schoolers once saw themselves in a dark fairytale—*Hansel and Gretel* or *Little Red Riding Hood*—as they wandered through those woods, dense with intangible evil, on their way home from school. For a while, at least, they would have been right to.

The baseball field that was built after all the trees were cut down, their stumps and roots ripped out and the tangled underbrush cleared away, was lush and green. Off to the right, sprinklers clicked and fizzed on a soccer field as they shot out streams of water in low, sweeping arcs.

As he walked behind the baseball field, Rory nearly tripped over the stone memorial to the three young lives ripped away in brutal, gruesome fashion. It rose several feet from the earth behind the home dugout and was shaped like a headstone. The plaque it bore read:

A.S. C.F. N.F.
Taken from Us Too Early
Rest in Peace

Rory looked around. The grounds were deserted: school was out for the summer, but it was only June—too early for day camps and sports practices yet. The air was perfectly still, heavy in anticipation of afternoon thunderstorms.

Rory stood quietly, alone by the empty fields, and tried to picture three boys emerging from the school one evening twenty-two years ago: Andrew was a year older and supposedly not friendly with the other two boys, so he took off, briskly and businesslike, out of a side door of the school building, through the playground, across the grass, and down the Sattler's Woods path without even looking back. But why had he been at school so late? Baseball practice ended at 5:30. And why had he told his parents he was getting pizza with teammates that evening? Was it a lie or a mistake? Maybe he'd gotten the night wrong—maybe his teammates had talked about going out for pizza Tuesday, not Monday, and he'd gotten days mixed up—then he lost track of time after practice playing the Game Boy that was later discovered in his backpack, and hurried home for dinner when he saw the sky getting dark.

Just as Andrew disappeared into the woods, Nathaniel and Christopher emerged from the same side door. The empty playground echoed with their voices and their laughter. Maybe they lingered a minute or two at the playground—swung across the monkey bars, glided down the slide—before continuing on across the grass. Perhaps they were singing songs from *Grease*, the play they had been rehearsing for, when they followed Andrew down the path through the woods. But then what happened?

Rory judged the walk from the school to where he now stood behind the dugout to be no more than forty or fifty yards. Off to the west, down the hill, was the Laurel Acres neighborhood where the Sattler's Woods trail had once let out and where all three boys had been heading. The entire walk—from the side door of the school to the safe haven of streetlights and warm houses of Laurel Acres—couldn't have taken more than a few minutes. Was it enough time for someone watching from a dark car in the parking lot to catch up to, and intercept, the boys? Maybe the attacker was in the process of subduing Andrew—wrestling him to the ground, binding his hands and feet, gagging his mouth—when he heard the laughter from Nathaniel and Christopher. Maybe he froze, dragged the bound Andrew off into the brush, then lay in wait, breathing heavily, until the next two boys came into view. Maybe he salivated with anticipation when he saw them. Couldn't believe his good luck.

A sudden and powerful sense of dread struck Rory in the pit of his stomach the longer he stood there attempting to reconstruct the events of that night. He felt a strong urge to put some distance between himself and the memorial, the silent athletic fields—the presumed murder site—as quickly as possible, so he hastily walked back to his car to grab his notepad and laptop bag before waiting at the front entrance of the school building.

When Daniels pulled up in her police cruiser minutes later, Rory was sitting on a well-worn, wooden bench beside the front door, looking over the questions he hoped Angela DeMarco could answer. He mostly wanted to get a fuller portrait of the three victims, particularly Andrew and Christopher—what they were like as students, who their friends were. Even the smallest, most mundane detail could potentially lead to a breakthrough.

"How goes it?" Daniels asked as she walked over from the parking lot.

"Not too bad," Rory answered, getting up.

Daniels held open the front door for him. "In case anybody asks, I'm getting lunch with my stepfather," she said, laughing nervously, before following Rory into the lobby.

From behind her desk, the receptionist in the main office seemed mildly concerned upon initially seeing flashes of the blue police uniform, but when she recognized Daniels's face, the look of consternation transformed into a beaming smile.

"Hi, Jessica," she said. "At first I just saw the uniform and wondered what the heck was going on."

"Good to see you, Denise. How's your summer been so far?"

"Quiet," she laughed. "Although I miss having the kids around. But I can't complain about the four-day work week." She looked down to check her appointment book. "You're here to see Angela, right?"

"Yes. Whenever she's free."

"I'll let her know you're here." She got up from her desk, shot both Daniels and Rory a quick smile, and disappeared into a hallway that branched out from the corner of the office.

"Angela's got a great memory," Daniels said quietly as they waited. "Remembers every student who passes through these doors. She's probably not going to reveal anything earth-shattering, of course, but she might be helpful. Could help us figure out where to go, or who to talk to, from here."

Rory nodded just as Denise returned from the back hallway. "You can go in now," she said, before sitting back down at her desk and turning to her computer screen.

"Thanks, Denise," Daniels said as they passed by. "Give Bobby and Karen my best."

"Will do," Denise said. Her tone was cheerful, though she turned in her chair and watched them carefully as they went down the hallway.

Angela's office was small—her desk barely fit in the corner of the room—but lovingly decorated. The cinder block walls were covered with student artwork, motivational posters, and pirate-adorned pennants, t-shirts, and rally towels with *BLUEBERRY HILL BUCCANEERS* printed in big, block letters. A massive corkboard behind her desk was completely covered with student portraits.

"Hey, stranger!" Angela exclaimed as she sprang up from her desk and gave Daniels a massive hug.

"Hey there," Daniels said, chuckling and patting Angela's back.

"And you must be Rory?" Angela asked as she released Daniels from her grip.

Rory stuck out his hand and smiled, but Angela ignored it, instead wrapping him up in a tight embrace as well.

"Don't mind me," she said. "I hug everyone."

"Thanks," Rory said. He couldn't help but smile.

DeMarco elbowed Rory playfully in the ribs and pointed at Daniels. "Not to date myself, but I was principal when Jess was in school here. She was easily one of the smartest, most driven, and kindest students I've ever known."

"I'm officially embarrassed now," Daniels said, her cheeks turning just the slightest shade of pink.

"Don't be!" DeMarco laughed. "Now, she's the best police officer we've got here in Hollingford. By far. And I'm not just saying that because I'm good friends with her parents."

Daniels shook her head but still smiled at the compliment.

"Well now, have a seat, have a seat," DeMarco ordered congenially, returning to the chair behind her desk. "What can I do for you?" she asked, scratching her curly, brown hair with a single finger and looking out at them through thick-rimmed reading glasses with sharp, quizzical brown eyes.

Daniels made sure to close the office door before settling into a chair in front of the desk. "Rory," she said, gesturing toward him as he sat down in the chair beside hers, "is investigating a rather sensitive topic here in town. One you have a slight connection to."

DeMarco nodded gravely. "The murders. You're writing an article about them?"

"That's the idea," Rory said, "but the research has raised some questions for me."

"Rory happens to share my skepticism about the state's case," Daniels said. "Thinks Thompson might actually be innocent."

"Did Cindy get to you?" DeMarco asked, sounding slightly amused.

Rory cleared his throat. "She did. I ended up listening to her whole speech."

"You're one of the few to give her the time of day. Most people treat her like road kill, if they don't want to turn her into road kill."

"Which is a shame," Daniels said. "She's a shattered woman trying, every day, to put the pieces of her life back together into something respectable."

"Agreed," DeMarco said, "although I have no problem with Randall Thompson being in jail. Guilty or no, a man who'd own videos like—" She hesitated. "—that, is a ticking time-bomb, a clear danger to the children in town. My children." She motioned toward the corkboard plastered with smiling, adolescent faces.

Rory nodded. "No argument here. Based on the conversation I had with him, he'd agree with you."

A brief look of disbelief washed over DeMarco's face. "You—met him?"

"That's the same reaction I had," Daniels said.

"His mother suggested I should. I didn't think I could know for sure without meeting him, face-to-face."

"And?" DeMarco asked. "What was he like?" If she had grown hardened over the years from fielding questions about the murdered boys—asked either out of genuine concern or idle curiosity—or weary of the horrid memories of the year she lost, or failed to protect, three of her students, that hardness cracked momentarily as she awaited Rory's answer.

"I drove away decidedly less convinced he's guilty. Which would mean—"

"Whoever did kill the boys might still be out there," Daniels concluded.

DeMarco looked back and forth from Rory to Daniels several times. "You think whoever killed my boys might have gotten away with it?"

Daniels nodded. "Or, at the very least, that Thompson had an accomplice—or accomplices—who were never caught."

DeMarco tapped a pen on her desk pad and gazed up at the ceiling. Roughly half the ceiling tiles were painted, covered in glitter, and otherwise decorated by the eighth grade classes that had moved on from Blueberry Hill in recent years. The earliest, and least adorned—it featured only the year in bold, black, 3-D lettering—was from 1998.

"I always thought that case wrapped up too neatly," she said, as if to herself. "I always found it strange how quickly they zeroed in on Thompson. It always seemed a little too convenient. If he were guilty, why the hell would he stick around, waiting to be arrested? If he killed my boys in a moment of boundless madness, wouldn't he flee in absolute horror after disposing the bodies?"

"Fair questions," Daniels said.

"I guess I always figured he was stupid—or arrogant."

"Arrogant, perhaps," Rory said. "Although, after meeting him, I don't think so. But definitely not stupid."

"And what about the conviction?" DeMarco asked. "Is it common to convict someone with no physical evidence like that?"

"It happens," Daniels answered. "Although you usually need something powerful to persuade the jury. Like an eyeball witness."

"Or a collection of horrific child porn," Rory said.

"Which makes me sick, just thinking about it." DeMarco looked like she might actually vomit; she closed her eyes, struggling to purge the very thought of those videos from her mind.

"Although the story behind how he got those videos," Daniels said, darting her eyes toward Rory, "is peculiar."

"Cindy Thompson told me she thought the videos were some kind of set-up to ensnare Randall," Rory said, returning Daniels's look. "Without sounding too conspiratorial, if Randall is telling the truth—which is a big 'if,' I realize—it's at least worth looking into."

Demarco's eyebrows dropped beneath the upper-frame of her glasses in a barely concealed scowl. "Regardless of how he got them, whatever I can help you with, and I doubt it'll be much, I'm not doing it to help a man who would own something like—that," she reiterated, words failing her once again to provide an adequately horrific description of the tapes. "I'd be doing it to protect my kids just in case, as you two say, a child killer remains on the loose."

Both Rory and Daniels gave her understanding looks.

"So what would you like to know?"

"It would be helpful to hear more about the boys," Rory said, readying his notepad. "What they were like as students. Who their friends were. My mother was close with his grandmother, so I have a pretty good sense of Nathaniel's—"

He was barely able to get Nathaniel's name out before DeMarco was singing his praises. "Such a sweet, sweet boy. Very intelligent, very quiet. Would rarely speak up in class, his teachers told me. If Christopher were ever absent, he'd sit by himself at lunch and read in one of the doorway alcoves at recess."

"Christopher was his only friend?" Daniels asked.

"I'd occasionally see him talking to different students coming into school in the morning, but Christopher was his only real friend. Christopher was so outgoing, never afraid to be loud or silly in front of people. I think that was good for Nathaniel. It was Christopher who got him involved in the drama club. Granted, Nathaniel only ever wanted to be a background character in the plays, but he loved it. I know it meant so much to his grandmother, too. She'd get front row tickets to every single performance and cry after each one." DeMarco smiled briefly at the memory.

"So Christopher was a more outgoing kid than Nathaniel," Rory said. "Can you remember any of his other friends?"

DeMarco scratched her hair with three of her long fingernails as she thought. "He was so friendly with everybody, it's hard to pick out individual names or faces." She smiled apologetically.

"That's ok. How about Andrew Skelly? What can you remember about him?"

"It's funny, but I don't remember as much about Andrew as I do about the other two boys. He was a year older—too cool to say 'hi' to the principal in the cafeteria. Maybe that's why I don't remember him as well. But he certainly ran in different circles than Nathaniel and Christopher. He was an athlete: played football in the fall, baseball in the spring. Other than that—" She raised her hands in defeat. "—I'm sorry."

"No need to apologize," Daniels said. "Do you remember who any of his friends were?"

Without another word, DeMarco whirled around in her desk chair and reached up for a bookshelf displaying, exclusively and in chronological order, every Blueberry Hill Middle School yearbook from the start of her tenure. She grabbed the first book on the shelf and flipped through the pages as she turned back to face Daniels and Rory.

"Kyle McCoy," she said, tapping her fingernail on the picture of a grinning adolescent boy with fire-red hair. "He's the only one who comes to mind. They played baseball together—I remember that clearly. I also have vague memories of seeing them leave school together, clowning around like pre-teen boys do."

"Do you have any idea if he's still local?" Rory asked, scribbling in his notepad.

"I can't be sure of that. No."

"I recognize the name," Daniels said. "And even the face a little." She looked down at the young face smiling up at her from the open yearbook. "He lives in The Oaks, that trailer park right at the outskirts of town."

"Might be worth talking to him," Rory said, looking over at Daniels.

"I think so."

"You know, I realize this sounds outlandish," DeMarco broke in, "but has anyone ever looked into that church—the nondenominational one down near Crystal Lake?"

"The Church of Christ's Healing Touch. Not that I know of," Daniels said. "How come?"

"What I've heard about them always struck me as a complete urban legend, but I couldn't help thinking about it when the boys went missing that night."

"Growing up, I used to hear from other kids that they had a dungeon, or torture chamber or something, in their basement," Daniels said. "But, according to my parents, that was a rumor they themselves spread to keep kids from riding bikes across their lawn to get to the lake."

"Probably pretty effective," Rory commented.

"Oh, it was. They had easily the nicest, greenest lawn in town."

"I've never heard that one," DeMarco said.

"What have you heard?" Daniels asked.

"Nothing in years," she replied, frowning. "But the summer I first moved here from Deptford, I heard the same story from a few different people. Neighbors, parents. Acquaintances like that. They said the church performed these terrible, violent rituals. They'd torture animals considered 'unclean' in the Bible—pigs, rabbits, mice. Make animal sacrifices to appease God. They'd even perform horrible surgeries on young people to make sure they stay 'pure.' Whatever that means. I didn't really give the rumors much thought—figured every town has its own, bizarre urban legends—till the night the boys disappeared. Then, I suddenly remembered one of the places they'd told me the congregation gathered to perform its rituals: Sattler's Woods."

"And the boys stumbled across them in the midst of one of those rituals," Rory said. *No fucking way. Of course no fucking way. Seems a little early in the night for a human sacrifice. Or maybe they kept the boys in the dungeon beneath their church until a more fitting occasion arose. Then again...there's always the sliver of possibility. We're not really in a position to dismiss any theories, no matter how far-fetched.*

"I know it sounds crazy. I know it *is* crazy," DeMarco said. "Still. It's a thought I haven't been able to shake even all these years later."

"You're right: there's probably nothing there. But it's at least worth checking out," Daniels assured her.

"Let me know if you do."

Daniels started to get up from her chair. "I'd hate to run, but my lunch break is almost over."

DeMarco checked her watch and did an exaggerated double-take when she saw the time. "Yikes, me too!" She came around from her desk to give both of them parting hugs. "I know I didn't have a ton of info for you, but I hope some of it was helpful."

"It was," Daniels said. "Extremely so. Thanks for your time. I know even during the summer it's a precious commodity."

"Not a problem. Not a problem at all." She swatted the air dismissively. "It's always a pleasure, my dear."

Daniels lowered her voice and gestured back toward the reception area. "And if you could, maybe—"

But there was no need to complete the sentence. "Not to worry. I'll tell her I called you in about someone tagging the playground equipment. And I'll say Rory was the concerned parent who spotted it." She winked.

Daniels exhaled sharply. "Thank you." She sounded relieved. "No one really knows we're doing this."

"And you're trying to keep it that way, understandably. It may not seem like it, but I can be discreet when the time calls for it." She smiled before cocking a concerned eyebrow. "By the way, will I see you at game night next Friday? Your parents happen to be hosting."

"If I have nothing better to do," Daniels chuckled teasingly.

"Oh, it'd break their hearts to hear that!" She gave Daniels one more hug for good measure before saying her final good-byes and settling back in at her desk.

Denise smiled and wished Daniels and Rory a good afternoon as they left the main office, though once again her eyes followed them intently.

As soon as they were outside, Rory turned to Daniels. "So what are your thoughts on the crazy cult theory?"

"Not gonna lie, my inner-child still gets butterflies every time I drive by the church property," she admitted before quickly conceding, "but it's bullshit, of course. Finding out about Kyle McCoy, though—that could be something."

"True. Should we reach out to him?"

"Why not?" She gave a shrug. "I think if we can get a clearer picture of the three boys, it could start to reveal some overlooked details. He might even have specific memories about the night his close friend went missing."

"Good thinking."

They walked across the empty drop-off circle in front of the school to the faculty lot where their cars were parked side-by-side.

"So where are you off to now?" Daniels asked, squinting up at Rory.

"I know it's a bullshit theory, but I'm going to stop by the church—The Church of Jesus's Touch."

"The Church of Christ's Healing Touch," she corrected. "Really?" She raised a single, skeptical eyebrow.

"I know there's no fucking way any of those rumors are true, but I thought it couldn't hurt just to check in there, get a feel for the place. Cross it off the list. Not that we even have a list yet."

"All right." She put her hands on her hips. "I actually don't know much about them. They've got a nice, thirty-some acre lot right by the lake where they pretty much keep to themselves. They don't seem to have a huge congregation, either, but they've been there for as long as I can remember."

"I guess as long as they don't lead me down to their torture chamber, I'll be all right."

"Good luck," Daniels laughed as she opened the door of her police cruiser.

"Thanks." Rory turned to climb into his Focus.

"And Rory."

He looked back.

"Let me know what happens." The laughter was gone from her voice. "I know it's a ridiculous urban legend, but sometimes there's a kernel of truth to rumors like that."

Rory smiled. "Don't worry: I'll be vigilant."

As they drove out of the school parking lot and down the gentle slope of Blueberry Hill, heavy, ink-black storm clouds swiftly spilled across the summer sky, and distant thunder rumbled in the otherwise still afternoon air.

Sixteen

By the time Rory reached the simple, wooden sign marking the entrance to the church's driveway, the sky was dark as night, and fat drops of rain sporadically slapped against his windshield. He also couldn't help but notice the ominously stark red and white sign given equal standing as the one for the church:

Private Property
No Trespassing

The paved driveway, lined with perfectly spaced, identically sized oak trees, was about a quarter-mile long and wide enough to allow two cars to pass with ease.

Looks like a goddamn plantation—and it's lakefront to boot. If Daniels is right about them having a small congregation, how the hell can they afford this?

As it came to an end fifty yards from the lakeshore, the driveway was flanked by two buildings: to the right, immaculately white and topped with a cross-adorned steeple, was the church, while on the left stood a small, single-story, rectangular building that looked like a school. Rory parked in a small lot beside the church. There was only one other car, a tan Lexus, parked there.

He got out and walked past the church toward the rectangular building across the driveway. A brick walking path wound down the slightly declining, freshly-cut lawn to the lake, where a long dock jut out into the tea-dark water. Forest-green Adirondack chairs dotted the lawn as well. The lake itself rippled with falling rain.

A sign above the doorway confirmed that the building was, in fact, a school: *Christ's Healing Touch Elementary & Sunday School.* The smooth limestone construction appeared fresh. Rory peered through the glass doors, not entirely sure what he was hoping, or expecting, to see. In the darkness, all he could discern was a massive cross at the end of an otherwise empty hallway. He took a few steps back and noticed a plaque screwed into the sandstone off to the side of the doors:

2 Corinthians 9:7
John P. Holling & Family

The rain and wind were picking up now, so Rory jogged back across the driveway and up the church steps where a wooden awning kept him, and his notepad, dry. He tried the door, figuring the church might be kept open during the day, but it was locked. He knocked and waited.

Rain was pounding against the small awning, and an intricate web of lighting lit up the sky. The subsequent roar of thunder rattled the small landing beneath Rory's feet. He knocked again, this time louder.

There's got to be someone inside: that's obviously someone's car in the parking lot.

He was about to knock again when a scuffling on the other side of the door caused him to freeze. He heard a deadbolt creakily slide out of place and suddenly found himself staring into a sliver of warm, white light as the heavy church door opened a crack.

A tiny voice leaked out from inside the church: "May I help you?"

At first Rory wasn't even sure he'd heard anything: the voice was almost inaudibly soft amidst the pouring rain and rolling thunder. He squinted into the light of the cracked door where a shadowy figure now stood.

"Hi, yes. My name is Rory Callahan. I'm a writer doing some research into..." He scrambled to think of a benign-sounding topic that also wasn't a complete lie. "...local history. I thought you folks out here might be a wealth of information, seeing as how you've been in the community for so long."

The shadowy figure in the doorway didn't move or speak for several moments.

"Mind if I come in?" Rory asked, feeling less and less certain about his decision to stop by the church like this. *What am I even going to ask them? Did you happen to defile the corpses of three children in some bizarre religious ritual before dumping them in the Pine Barrens twenty-two years ago?*

After waiting another thirty seconds without a response, Rory was about to turn and leave when the door opened a little bit wider. A young woman stood in the doorway. She couldn't have been any more than thirty, though deep lines spanned the entirety of her wide forehead, radiated from the corners of her eyes, encircled her mouth. She wore a conservative black skirt, cotton stockings, and a long-sleeved denim blouse. Her platinum blonde hair was slung over her shoulder in a single braid. She stared at Rory, smiling vacantly.

"I'm sorry to disturb you, miss."

The woman stood, smiling and staring.

"Do you mind if I come in?"

Without breaking her smile, the woman said, "Pastor Mark says we need to make ourselves more visible in the community."

"Your pastor? Is he here today?"

"Even with the secular thugs coming to kick in our doors, we cannot be perpetually circling the wagons and hunkering down, he says. That will destroy us before the SPs ever do."

"SPs?" *We seem to be having two different conversations here.*

"'Blessed are ye, when men shall revile you, and persecute you, and shall say all manner of evil against you falsely, for my sake.'" The smile suddenly vanished from the woman's face, and her eyes closed as if she were meditating. She moved her lips ever so slightly, uttering soft, unintelligible sounds.

It's not too late to get the fuck out of here, Rory thought. "Miss? Are you ok?"

A smile gradually crept over the woman's face, and her eyes reopened slowly. "Come in, Mr. Callahan. I would be happy to help you. I believe it will be the Lord's work."

Rory glanced over his shoulder at the long driveway that vanished among the trees. *Well, at least Daniels knows where I am. At least she'll come looking for me if I disappear. Right?* He squeezed through the doorway and stood in the vestibule as the blonde woman closed and locked the door again.

"I am Dana Gladwell," she said.

"Pleasure to meet you."

The inner doors of the vestibule were propped open, so Rory looked around the interior of the church. Perhaps a dozen pews, painted white, formed a column terminating at a pair of steps and a large landing at the far end of the building. A small table covered with a crisp, white, linen cloth, stood in the center of the landing. The only ornate feature in the whole church was a massive chair, also white, positioned behind the table. Elaborate designs were carved into its back, arms, legs, and apron. A massive cross rose from the top rail. The chair stood nearly as high off the ground as the table.

"We can talk in my office," Gladwell said.

"Great." Rory followed her over to a staircase that led into the basement. *Oh, fuck me. If only Daniels knew. My inner-child might start pissing himself soon.*

"I am the business manager of the church," Gladwell explained as they descended into the basement. "Pastor Mark may be the Lord's representative on earth, but he says even the wisdom of the Lord can use a little extra help when it comes to accounting." She chuckled mindlessly at her own joke. "So I take care of the bills, tithes from our members, and any larger donations we receive."

"I saw the new school building across the way. Was that a gift from a church member?"

"Mr. Holling was most generous to donate the funds for the school building. He knows how easily the secular world corrupts the youngest and most innocent among us. By helping us build the school, he declared war on Satan and his army. He sent a message, loud and clear, to all evildoers: not *our* children."

"Is Mr. Holling a member here?"

Gladwell sighed sadly. "Mr. Holling comes when he can, though his wife, who is tragically bed-ridden, prevents him from participating as much as he would like. Please keep them in your prayers," she requested solemnly.

"Will do."

Gladwell's spacious, well-lit office was one of several off a narrow, tiled hallway, though the others were all closed and dark. Wooden crosses of various sizes hung on the cinderblock walls alongside posters featuring Biblical quotes and serene landscapes. Gladwell's desk was cluttered with paperwork, but the bookshelves and filing cabinets that lined the walls appeared neat and organized. A small conference area with a table and two comfortable-looking lounge chairs was set up in a corner of the room.

"My deepest apologies for keeping you waiting in the rain," she said, offering him a seat in one of the lounge chairs. "Sometimes it is rather difficult to hear people at the door when I am down here. And this rain—" She raised a hand toward the small window where the wall met the ceiling and shook her head. "My apologies." She sat in the chair beside Rory, still smiling widely and regarding him with large, seaweed-green eyes.

"Don't worry about it," Rory said.

"So what are you researching, Mr. Callahan?"

He decided to come right out with it: "The Blueberry Hill murders. What people remember about them, how they affected the community. Maybe uncover answers to some questions in the process." He wasn't sure how Gladwell would react upon hearing this; he'd been purposefully vague out on the church steps and feared she might get pissed off by the bait-and-switch. *It was tactless, but it was also what I wanted: to see how she'd react just to being asked about the murders.*

But Gladwell didn't even flinch—just kept staring and smiling. "I was just a girl when that happened," she said, softly. "My mother and father were upset about it, I remember. They would not allow me to leave the house that whole summer. But that is all I can really remember."

"Do your parents still live here in town?"

"No. They moved to Florida when they retired. And we do not speak anymore."

"I'm sorry to hear that."

"Do not be, Mr. Callahan." She placed her hand on top of his; it was cold and dry. "Being persecuted and shunned for living the Truth, especially by those closest to us, only brings us closer to God."

"I see." *Holy shit. Her whackjob obsession with this church was enough to drive a wedge between her and her parents. Maybe she's brainwashed.*

"Pastor Mark would remember. A brilliant mind like his does not forget things."

"Do you think Pastor Mark would mind if I talked to him for a bit?"

"He would not mind. As I said, he wants us to become more visible in the community. To become a shining example to the corrupt, material world rather than allow ourselves be victimized by it."

"Right," Rory said, struggling to sound sincere rather than sarcastic. "Is he available any time this week?"

"Unfortunately, he is not. Pastor Mark is teaching a summer class at Foundations of the Family out in Colorado. He will not be home until the July Fourth weekend."

"Foundations of the Family?"

Gladwell smiled patronizingly. "Are you a Christian, Mr. Callahan?"

Rory was thrown off by the question. His first instinct was to tell her to mind her own fucking business, but at the same time, he was now eager to learn more about the reclusive church despite—or perhaps because of—Dana Gladwell's unsettlingly mannerisms. So he lied.

"I am," he said, returning Gladwell's deep stare and nodding slightly. "Very much so. At least, I try to be." He laughed at himself as if admitting an embarrassing bit of personal information.

Gladwell reached over and patted his hand again. "We are all imperfect, Mr. Callahan. We are all sinners. You are wise to recognize this."

"Thank you," Rory said, trying to seem appreciative of the comforting pat on the hand rather than reviled by it.

"Regardless of where you are on your faith journey, I highly recommend utilizing Foundations of the Family as a resource. It truly is manna in the desert." She reached over to the table between their two chairs and picked up a pamphlet from a stack of them, offering it to Rory. "You can sign up for online classes that help strengthen your relationship with God. And I would know: I have taken five myself."

"This looks great." Rory only glanced down at the pamphlet as he leafed through it, but he caught a glimpse of a few of the tutorials offered by Foundations of the Family for a nominal fee: *Speaking in Tongues*, *Living Chastely*, and *Fostering a Christian Family*.

"They also happen to be one of our greatest weapons in the war that has been declared upon us." For the first time since closing her eyes in prayer out on the front steps of the church, Gladwell lost her vacant smile. Even her wide stare narrowed slightly. "Do you know there are people out there—politicians, Hollywood actors, and their ilk—who would like to do nothing more than throw us in jail for being Christian? This very conversation would be illegal if they had their way." She leaned over and tapped the pamphlet in Rory's hands. "But Foundations of the Family will fight to the death to make sure that does not happen." She sat back in her chair as the smile and the stare returned. "And that gives me some peace of mind. Knowing they are willing to fight for us."

"Me, too," Rory said as he continued to flip through the pamphlet, feigning interest in it.

"There is only one thing I do not understand," Gladwell said, cocking her head slightly and smiling wider than ever.

"What's that?" Rory tucked the pamphlet into the pages of his notepad to give her the impression he intended to study it later.

"You said you hope to find answers to some questions in your research."

Rory shrugged. "It's unlikely, but possible. It could shed some light on the investigation and Randall Thompson's conviction, which some people think was a bit of a witch hunt."

"But suppose there is a witch, stalking and preying upon the weakest members of our flock—is a witch hunt, then, such a horrible thing?"

"I guess not. As long we know, beyond a reasonable doubt, that's what's actually happening."

"But *we*," she said, pointing toward herself, then Rory, before raising and spreading her arms to indicate all of humanity, "can never really know anything. Only God can."

While getting entangled in a theological debate with a hardline fundamentalist was not, Rory was realizing, a good use of time, he couldn't help saying, "But maybe God has also given us certain faculties, like intelligence and reason, we can use to establish knowable facts. But I guess using those faculties is optional."

Gladwell recoiled at the insult as if Rory had taken a swing at her. Her smile remained plastered on her face, however, although it shrunk ever so slightly. The corners of her thin lips twitched almost imperceptibly.

"God is fate, Mr. Callahan." She seemed to look past Rory now as she spoke. "If those young men lost their lives, God willed it. If that man is in jail, God willed it. What right do we have to question the will of God?"

"So God is responsible, either directly or indirectly, for the brutal murders of three innocent children?"

"We cannot pretend to understand the Lord's plan for us." Seeming to regain some confidence, Gladwell rested her elbow on the arm of her chair and leaned toward Rory. "We cannot pretend to understand the mind of God any more than an ant could pretend to understand *our* deepest thoughts and desires. To believe otherwise is hubris and folly." Whenever she spoke, Rory noticed, there was an artificiality about her cadence, as if she were constantly quoting something she'd memorized.

"But we are supposedly made in the image and likeness of God, right? If that's true, I'm not sure there should be this insurmountable disparity like there is between us and ants."

"Hubris, Mr. Callahan," she said sententiously. "Remember your place as a Christian."

Rory felt the simmering anger from before instantly boil up into a seething rage; he exercised every bit of restraint to keep it from spilling out in a powerful cascade of expletives. "You're right," he managed to say, hanging his head in acknowledgement of his error. *Can't shut her down yet. I don't think I've gotten the full scope of how crazy this woman—and maybe the whole congregation—truly is yet.*

"I must also take issue with a word choice you made earlier."

Rory looked up, trying his best to seem contrite. "Oh. Which one?"

"I believe you described the young men as 'innocent.' But as you yourself noted earlier, Mr. Callahan, none of us is innocent."

"That's true. I think I was just trying to convey that those boys were so young. Still children."

"But we are born guilty. We will die guilty. It is simply our natural human condition. We are fallen."

Rory nodded. "Right."

"And may I bring up another matter to consider? Perhaps a bit more personal."

"Sure." *Oh, boy.*

"Do you remember yourself at that age—twelve, thirteen-years-old—the age those young men lost their lives?"

"Of course. Not as well as I used to, though."

"Well, I still remember that time quite well. The powerful desires, the impure thoughts." She lowered her already-soft voice and leaned in even closer toward Rory. "I remember thinking about the cute boys in my class. Or seeing the men in those pornographic advertisements in the Sunday paper. There were countless quiet afternoons when I would sneak away with them to my room, where I could gaze upon them in secret, sometimes for hours." She whispered now. "I would sometimes even touch myself as I stared. The temptation was too great for me fend off then, and I did not have the relationship with Christ that I do now. I was completely lost.

"And I was a girl!" she exclaimed, placing a hand on her chest and laughing. "For a boy, those urges are all the more powerful and uncontrollable."

I was right, Rory though. *There was still a lot more crazy to uncover.* "That's quite a generalization," he said. "And—I just want to make sure here—are you implying that the victims were especially guilty because of raging, pubescent hormones?"

"That time in life is a trial, as I can attest to, and we simply do not know how those young men fared during such a trial. The young men in our youth group have many strategies for seeking God's help in combatting impure thoughts, but they must have the strength, and humility, to seek out that help."

"Just out of curiosity, what are some of those strategies?" *This ought to be good, if not appalling.*

"Prayer, of course. Prayer is the answer during any kind of adversity. It is the most versatile, and often the most powerful, tool the Lord has given us. Prayer can redirect our thoughts from baseness, from vileness, to absolute purity in a matter of seconds. If you can picture prurient thoughts as a plane taking off—" She began simulating the metaphor with hand gestures. "—prayer can keep the wheels of the plane from ever lifting off the runway. If you can instantly begin praying upon inadvertently seeing a salacious advertisement or picture online, the temptation will dissipate almost instantly."

"I see."

"But it does take time. It takes practice, discipline. And sometimes, even after time and practice, it does not always work for everyone. There is no universal recipe for living a holy life. Sometimes, as Pastor Mark calls them, we have to deploy the 'big guns.'"

"And what are those?"

Wordlessly, Gladwell arose and crossed the small office, her shoes popping softly across the tile floor. She stopped at her desk, reached into a drawer, and returned with two perfectly white, cloth bands. She continued to smile and stare intently as she held them out for Rory.

"What do you use them for?" he asked, holding them open-palmed. They were an inch or two wide and perhaps a foot long.

"The devil will often assault us with his strongest temptations when night falls. It is when many of us feel most desolate, as if God has abandoned us. He never has, of course, and never will. But when the devil is whispering in your ear, it is not always easy to remember that."

"I don't think I understand."

"We are fooling ourselves if we think being Christian is easy. Christ suffered for us. We must suffer for him." She took the bands back from Rory and laced one around each of her wrists. As she lifted her arms at a slight angle and stretched them out as far as she could, she grinned wildly. "Pastor Mark says using the Purity Bands on your bedposts makes you look like the crucified Christ. Do you agree?"

Rory felt a sudden twinge of trepidation. He had arrived at the church expecting nothing: cross it off the list, tell Daniels her skepticism was well placed. Maybe crack a joke about the quality and variety of cookies set out for the child sacrifice ceremony he had accidently walked in on. He had found Gladwell peculiar of course, when not enraging, to the point of wanting to know more about her and The Church of Christ's Healing Touch—not because he suspected there was a thread of truth to the urban legends about the church, or even that he'd learn anything valuable about the murders. Mostly, he was hoping for a good story to tell Daniels. He thought Gladwell was eccentric, even unsettling, but clearly harmless. Up until now, at least.

The longer Gladwell sat there, extending her arms like the crucified Christ, staring ceaselessly, giggling now, the less friendly her smile became. It was now aggressive, like the bared teeth of a snarling wolf. His only thought was *Maybe DeMarco was right* as he imagined several solid-bodied, cloaked and hooded figures suddenly emerging from the basement hallway to beat him senseless, restrain him, and prepare him for a ritual sacrifice.

There were tears in Gladwell's eyes as she continued to outstretch her arms and giggle. "There is joy in suffering," she said. "There is freedom in suffering. Christ showed us that."

Rory struggled to hide his growing sense of dread. "So true," he said. "So true." Awkwardly, he checked his watch and jerked his head toward the office door. "I'd better be going. Thank you so much for your time."

Gladwell slowly lowered her arms while watching Rory stick his pen into his jeans pocket, tuck his notepad under his arm, and stand up. "I will see you out."

"That's not necessary."

"I insist," she said. Then, before getting up, added, "I hope I did not upset you in some way."

"Not at all," Rory said, smirking as if the very idea were absurd. "I'm just running late for another meeting. That's all."

"Very well." The Purity Bands still tied around her wrists, she led Rory up the basement steps and back into the church vestibule. "I hope you will visit us again," she said, unlocking the heavy, white door.

"Thanks for the invitation. And for your time."

"I will pray for you, Mr. Callahan."

"Thank you."

She watched him as he stepped out into the light rain and hurried down the church steps. She was still watching as he drove out of the parking lot, past the church, and turned down the long driveway.

He called Daniels as soon as he was out on the road. "Can you meet up tonight?"

Seventeen

Rory was on his third beer by the time he'd finished telling Daniels, in as much detail and with as much animation as possible, about his encounter with Dana Gladwell at The Church of Christ's Healing Touch. They sat side-by-side at the bar in The Oasis, which was practically dead: a few business-suited men were scattered along the bar while a group of woman sat in a corner booth, talking and laughing loudly. There was no Phillies game on, so the TV on the wall played a program analyzing the various dismal lowlights from the weekend's games while occasionally offering brief, optimistic previews of the Eagles upcoming season even though it was three months away.

"I'm not going to lie," Daniels commented, taking a swig of her Guinness, "that's completely fucked up. Do you think parents are forcing their teenage children to use those...what did she call them again?"

"Purity Bands," Rory answered, swallowing a mouthful of Yuengling.

Daniels frowned in disgust. "Yeah—Purity Bands. Do you think church members are forcing their children to use them?"

"She told me kids in the youth group actively seek help in remaining 'pure,'" he said, using air quotes. "But it wouldn't surprise me."

"Wow." Daniels shook her head. "Completely fucked up. And if kids are being forced to use them, child abuse."

"Most definitely," Rory agreed.

"Although, if police showed up asking members of the congregation about it, there's no doubt they'd close ranks and stay quiet."

"I think you're right—like some kind of cult. To be honest, when we reached that point in the conversation, I started to think there might be some merit to those urban legends after all."

Daniels laughed sardonically. "I don't blame you. But still, there's just a tiny gulf between that and what Angela was telling us earlier." She held up her pointer finger and thumb, creating barely an inch of space, to punctuate the sarcasm.

"I know, I know," Rory acknowledged.

"But this pastor she kept referring to—what did you say his name was?"

"Mark Forsythe. Not surprisingly, The Church of Christ's Healing Touch doesn't have much of a web presence, but I was able to find his last name, at least."

"Mark Forsythe," Daniels repeated to herself.

"Ever heard of him?" Rory asked.

She shook her head. "He must not live here in town."

"I got the sense he's been at the church for a while. Gladwell seemed to indicate he was around when the murders happened."

"Maybe he's even the founder?" Daniels suggested.

"Certainly could be."

"We could ask. Want to stop in now and see if Dana Gladwell's still around?"

Rory laughed. "It's tempting, but I'm going to have to pass."

Daniels smiled and took another drink of her beer.

Rory lifted his beer to his lips as well, but then stopped and set it back down. "Something I just remembered," he said.

"Yeah?"

"That new school building next to the church was donated by John Holling. I get the feeling his financial contributions don't end there, either. Is he connected to the family that owns that huge mansion—you know, the one you can see when you're coming off the expressway?"

Daniels looked partly surprised but mostly confused. "John Holling? Yeah, that mansion is his. As far as I know, he and his wife are the only Hollings left."

"And they own the car dealership out on the White Horse Pike, right?"

"Yup. A bunch of the fast food restaurants, too. Maybe some of the places here on Central for all I know. They also have bought and sold tons of real estate in town."

"They must be worth tens of millions of dollars."

"Hundreds of millions, at least," Daniels corrected. "The Holling family founded the town back in the late 1800s and have essentially run things ever since. Nothing's ever been proven—I mean, no one's cared enough to really look into it—but the general consensus is that no one gets elected to the mayor's office or town council without John Holling's ok. And then he gets them to do his bidding."

"Have you ever met him?"

She frowned and shook her head. "I vaguely remember seeing him at the Fourth of July and Christmas parades they used to have down Central back when I was in elementary school. My mom would point him out to me because he'd always be on the same float as the mayor. Although, weirdly, he always just kind of sat there, surveying the crowds. Not really smiling or waving or anything. But I haven't seen him in years."

"Gladwell mentioned something about his wife being bed-ridden. Maybe that's why?"

"Could be. Elizabeth. I think that's her name."

"I just don't get it. I don't get why the wealthy town patriarch would take such an interest in supporting that weird little church." Rory drummed his fingers on the edge of the counter as he worked it out in his head.

Daniels gave a shrug. "Maybe he donates money to a bunch of local churches? He runs a pretty big charitable organization, too."

"It's possible," Rory said, nodding in thanks at Al the bartender, who had just dropped off a fresh Yuengling.

"How's your schedule look tomorrow?" Daniels asked.

"Well, I have coffee with my mom tentatively set for eight in the morning. I also have a nap penciled in for two in the afternoon, but I can move that around. Other than that, I'm pretty flexible."

Daniels laughed. "That bad, huh?"

"It's pretty fucking bad."

"Want to stop by and talk to Kyle McCoy late morning? I called him after we left the school. He said he remembers Andrew Skelly well and would be happy to talk to us."

"Damn, you're good," Rory said. "It's too bad you were in preschool back in '92. The police really could have used you on the murders. Hell, even as a toddler you might have done a better job with that investigation than they did."

Daniels suppressed a smiled. "I guess I couldn't have done any worse."

"And yes: I would love to go and talk to Kyle McCoy tomorrow morning."

"11 o'clock, then. I'll text you the address."

"Thanks." Rory took a sip of his beer and looked up at a replay of an error from yesterday's game. "What are the chances this guy remembers anything useful?"

"Not particularly good. But who knows? He'll tell us what he remembers about Andrew, we'll listen and write it down. He might reveal something that doesn't seem useful now, but could become important down the line."

Rory nodded and, for a moment, was silent. Daniels drank her Guinness and absently watched the TV up on the wall.

"Do you mind if I ask you something?" Rory asked, breaking the silence. "Feel free to tell me to fuck off if it's too personal."

"Not at all," Daniels answered. "Go ahead and ask."

"Don't take this the wrong way, but did you always want to be a cop? I mean, here, in Hollingford. Just curious how you ended up in a small town like this."

"Completely fair question," Daniels said.

"Again, don't feel like you have to answer. You just seem too good for this place. Too good for your department, at least."

"Like I could have gone on to do bigger and better things?"

"Something like that."

"To answer your question, no: I didn't always want to be a cop. And I never pictured myself winding up back in Hollingford. It took three years of college and a long conversation with one of my professors to help me realize I did, actually, want both of those things. And I haven't second-guessed myself since."

"Where'd you go to school?"

"Columbia."

"Halfway decent school, I guess," Rory joked.

"Shitty basketball program, at least when I was there," she said, laughing. "But it was all right."

"Not everyone can experience the magic of Big Five basketball," Rory said, toasting the beer-soaked memories of dozens of games he'd attended with his college buddies at the Palestra.

A fleeting but vivid memory of a game he'd gone to with Marie, only a month or two into their relationship, flashed through his brain: a brutally cold Saturday in February, holding her chapped hand to keep it warm as they walked from the train station. Forgoing the traditional post-game bar crawl with his friends to share his famous turkey chili with her back at his place that night. His radiator never worked in that shithole apartment, so the space heater whirred inches away from them as they ate.

The smile vanished from Rory's face as the memory came and went; he did his best to force one as he turned back to Daniels.

"How about you? Where'd you go to school?" she asked.

"Temple. Local boy, through-and-through."

"I'd planned on staying local, too: either Rutgers or Rowan for the in-state tuition."

"Understandable. College prices are a scam these days. My son just graduated from Bucknell. We said we'd help him with his loans, but I fear we'll be great-grandparents by the time we come close to paying them off."

"When that bubble bursts, shit's going to hit the fan."

Rory nodded in agreement. "So how'd you'd end up at Columbia, then?" he asked.

"One of my favorite teachers—my Physics teacher from junior year—encouraged me to apply to Columbia and Princeton. She said my grades and SAT scores were more than good enough to get in, and that they give need-based scholarships. Turns out she was right: they both offered me full rides. Perhaps the one and only advantage of having a stepdad out on disability and a mom paying the mortgage with tips from her waitressing job."

"Nicely done. I knew you were smart, but shit. I don't think they would have let me anywhere near an Ivy League campus, even for a tour."

"Thanks. College is college, though. The rest is name-brand recognition. Not really all that different from a box of cereal when you think about it."

"So what made you choose Columbia over Princeton?"

"It was farther away from here," she answered instantly, but then caught herself and looked suddenly contrite, as if she'd spoken ill of an old, loyal friend. "I mean, it's not that I hated it here—I didn't," she clarified. "But after eighteen years, this town felt a little stale. Like an episode of your favorite TV show you've seen way too many times. I mean, I love my mom, I love my stepdad—I never wanted to be too far away from them. But I did want to see what else was out there. Experience life outside of Hollingford for once."

"Sounds like you made a wise choice, then. Although here versus New York? Only slightly different, culturally speaking."

"Only slightly," Daniels laughed. "Even so, I loved it. The city was a little overwhelming at first, but once I figured out the trains and started discovering my favorite bars in my favorite neighborhoods—"

"Very important."

"—I really started to love it. I loved my courses, too. Never missed a class: even the eight AMs."

"You've got me beat there," Rory said. "What'd you study?"

"I double-majored in Sociology and Psychology."

"You must have waded into some deep, dark shit in those courses."

"That I did. In some of the courses, at least. My class on cults was pretty fucked up."

"I can imagine."

"You know what the weird thing is, though? I'm not sure I could ever explain why I wanted to study sociology and psychology—or at least, why I ended up majoring in them. I originally thought maybe there was some quantifiable way of understanding people, to demystify that oh-so mysterious human nature. I mean, people are constantly doing inexplicably horrific things to each other, right? Blowing each other up, shooting each other. Torture, rape, abuse. And then just good, old-fashioned selfishness and greed. Scary shit. I thought figuring out the *why* behind our unending clusterfuck as a species might make the scary shit a little less scary. You know, if those horrific things were no longer entirely inexplicable. But every time I thought I'd figured something out, a new piece of evidence would always come along to complicate it. I may have left with less certainty about human nature than I had coming in." She took a long swig of her Guinness and shook her head. "I guess that's what college is supposed to do."

"Sure," Rory said quietly. The beer was causing a handful of distant memories to come loose and meander through his brain. The moment he knew he wanted to be a journalist and nothing else: sitting in rapt attention, listening to Dr. Norberg, his Introduction to Journalism professor freshman year, deliver an impassioned lesson about the moral responsibilities of journalists, their necessity for society to maintain a modicum of humanity and justice. The long conversations he'd have with Dr. Norberg in his office every couple of months over four years. His first newspaper meeting, late on a Sunday night in October. How that dingy, over-crowded office above the dining hall immediately felt like home. "Sure," he repeated reflectively. "Do you mind if I ask you one more thing?"

"Shoot," Daniels answered.

"You said you realized you wanted to be a cop after a long conversation with one of your professors. What did he say that inspired your epiphany?"

"She, actually."

"She—sorry."

"Are you sure you've got time to hear this?"

Rory smiled wryly. "You could recite *Ulysses* from start to finish and I'd have time for it."

Daniels ordered a second Guinness and began her story.

"My plan since sophomore year had been to go to graduate school for Social Psychology, and I was looking at some of the best, most competitive programs out there. Stanford. Indiana. Emory. So I took my GREs. Asked professors for recommendations. Picked out the writing sample I wanted to send in. Figured out deadlines and set aside work-study money for the application fees.

"But the summer before my senior year, every time I sat down to write my personal statement, I'd freeze. I'd start, then stop and delete my first few sentences, over and over again, countless times. I'd stare at a blank Word document for hours, waiting for a lightbulb to go off in my head and the words that I'd been grasping for to finally come. But they never did. That little cursor would just keep blinking. Incessantly. I started seeing it when I closed my eyes at night to go to sleep. Like I said, I loved my classes and never failed to be fascinated by the ideas and the books and the discussions, but I had no fucking idea why I actually wanted to go to grad school. The idea felt comfortable at the time. Safe. Looking back on it, I realize fear was driving my decision to apply to grad school. And fear was not a good foundation to plan the rest of my life on.

"That summer, I was working as a research assistant for my professor up at school, but I decided to take off the last couple weeks to come back home before classes started up again. I thought the quiet, or the change of scenery, might finally help me write that pain-in-the-ass personal statement. But still, nothing. Just the blank Word document and that fucking blinking cursor.

"Then one morning I was sitting at the kitchen table, eyes glazed over—like they had been that entire summer—staring at my laptop screen, when my mom came in. She set a cup of coffee and a slice of lemon cake down next to me and ran her fingers through my hair like she would when I was a little girl.

"'Not now, mom,' I said, swatting her hand away.

"She sat down across from me and said, 'Going that well, huh?'

"'I'm never going to get into any of these schools—I have no idea what to write.'

"'You're the smartest person I know,' she said to me, sipping her coffee. That's been her refrain to me for years, whenever I've felt overwhelmed or lost. 'If you want to get in, you will.'

"'Thanks, mom.' I'm sure I sounded more annoyed than grateful.

"She watched me as I wrote my opening sentence for the millionth time only to delete it seconds later, jabbing the backspace key in frustration. 'Your heart's not in it,' she said, matter-of-factly.

"I slammed the laptop screen down and rubbed my eyes. 'I have no idea why I even want to go to grad school.'

"'Why'd you go to college in the first place?' she asked. 'Why did you pick your majors?'

"I told her what I just told you, about wanting to understand the fucked up things people do to each other. About finding some kind of logic behind the irrationality.

"'You're frustrated you never found an answer.' I'd never told her that. I didn't even know it myself till that moment. She just knew.

"'Yeah. That's definitely part of it. But maybe knowing there is no simple answer, no one-size-fits-all equation is the point of it all.'

"I looked at my mom for the first time since she'd sat down at the table. Even though she's always telling me I'm the smartest person she knows, I realized then that I will never be as smart, or wise, as she is. She didn't go to college—she got pregnant with me when she was a senior in high school—but that didn't matter. Some of the dumbest people on earth have graduate degrees from prestigious universities. She knew I had more to say, so she sat quietly and waited.

"'And as much as I love debating and discussing the readings with my classmates, there's no actual substance to it.' My mom nodded as I went on. 'Of course, there's value to understanding why people are violent, or racist, or abusive. We need to understand why if we're ever going to stop those things. Then again—'

"I studied my mom's face from across the kitchen table. Her deep brown eyes were sharp and bright in the morning sunlight. Her dark hair was pulled back in a bun. Her cheeks were covered with freckles, just like mine. People would often mistake us for sisters, and on that morning in particular, it felt like I was looking into a mirror. And then I noticed the scars. I mean, I'd always known they were there, but for so long I guess I'd chosen to ignore them, to look past them somehow. One was just above her left temple, snaking along her hairline all the way down to her ear. The other was a large, clover-shaped pucker off the corner of her right eye.

"'—then again,' I continued, ' there still needs to be *somebody* out there—actually in the world, not just a classroom—protecting people, keeping bad things from happening. There needs to be someone getting their hands dirty; it can't all be theory.'

"But as I spoke, all I could do was stare at her scars. She'd gotten them when I was six. Actually, I hate the passive voice so much—she didn't just 'get' them. My biological father gave them to her. He was an alcoholic and a gaping asshole. For years he beat the shit out of her. Who knows how it started? My mom never talks about it. But I'd guess with a shove, or a push out of the way, when she confronted him about leaving her alone, again, with the baby for another night. Or maybe it was about spending all of their meager savings on Jack Daniels. Yeah, it probably started with a shove and escalated, just a little bit, each and every time he got fired from another job or wasn't happy with what was for dinner.

"It got to the point when she must have feared for her life because, one afternoon before he got home from work, she brought me into their bedroom. We sat down, side-by-side, on the bed, and she picked up the phone from the nightstand. It was light pink. Cheap plastic. She turned the phone over in her hand and showed me the buttons. They glowed with this faint, green light whenever you picked it up off the receiver. She took my finger and lightly touched it to the 9 button, then twice to the 1. She said if I ever heard mommy crying and screaming because daddy was yelling, to push those numbers and to tell the person who answers to come help. She had me repeat the directions, the phone number, and our address and apartment number back to her five or six times so I'd remember. I had no idea why she was showing me this—I was six—but I nodded and started to cry as my mom's eyes filled up with tears and she held me in her arms. I could feel her shaking.

"Maybe a week or two later, I used that pink phone for the first and last time. I remember everything about that night. My mom and I were sitting at the rickety table in our tiny kitchenette. She kept checking the clock on the oven and sighing, but then smiling every time she looked over at me. It was dark out and I could hear a dog barking furiously outside. I could feel my stomach rumbling as the smell of dinner wafted over from the oven, but I could see in my mom's eyes that it wasn't the kind of night to complain about it. I just sat there, holding a stuffed animal, as my mom asked me half-heartedly about school.

"It might have been after eight when she finally got up and served dinner for both of us. My favorite, up until that night at least: crispy Shake 'n Bake chicken and creamy macaroni and cheese. I used to love spearing a bunch of macaroni, then a small piece of chicken, before dipping them both in ketchup and stuffing it in my mouth. I gulped down my glass of cold milk so fast, I got a brain freeze, but the feeling of the milk making a cool, smooth path down to my stomach was too good to resist.

"My mom had just filled up my plate with seconds and was pouring me another glass of milk when we heard the apartment door open and slam shut. My mom froze with the jug of milk in her hand as I watched her face tense up, almost like a wince. I could smell the whiskey before he even pushed his way through the kitchen door.

"'You fucking bitch,' he said, as he staggered in wearing his faded blue jeans and green flannel. His navy blue Wal-Mart vest—he'd been stocking shelves there—was draped crookedly over the flannel. I can't remember him wearing anything else now.

"'Are you hungry, Victor?' my mom deflected.

"'No, I don't want any of the fucking shit you call food.' His eyes were bloodshot and puffy.

"My mom was still standing, stiffly, next to me with the jug of milk in her hand. 'Why don't you have a seat and relax, then? Tell us about your day.'

"'My day was a fucking disaster.'

"'Oh. I'm sorry to hear that.'

"'Yeah, you should be. They fired me, Allie.'

"I wasn't eating any more, only staring at his face. For a moment, it looked like he was about to cry, but then his lips curled up in a nasty grimace and his eyes became fiery.

"He shuffled toward my mom, pointing an accusing finger. The cloud of whiskey stung my nostrils. 'You,' he croaked. 'It was your fault.'

"My mom's chest began heaving as she prepared for the inevitable, or perhaps as she desperately tried to think of a way of talking him down. 'No. Victor. How could it be?'

"'They fired me because I was late coming back from my lunch break. But I never would've been late if you'd made my lunch like you were supposed to.'

"'I didn't know I was supposed to. I'm sorry, Victor, I'm really sorry. You usually buy something for lunch, and if I knew you needed a lunch I would—' My mom's voice pinched off in a small squeal of pain as the asshole lunged at her and grabbed her behind the neck with his thick, calloused hands.

"'You lying cunt,' he growled as he shoved her to the floor and began to remove his belt.

"Without being fully aware of what I was doing, I found myself darting out of the kitchen and into their bedroom. Hoping he hadn't noticed me, I collapsed on the floor next to the nightstand, replaying my mom's directions in my head. I could feel my heart pounding in my chest and my hands shaking as I picked up that pink, plastic phone and dialed the number my mom had taught me.

"'911, what's your emergency?' The calm, measured voice of the dispatcher seemed surreal in my ear, like a voice in a dream. I didn't respond at first. I wanted to, but I couldn't make myself talk. All I could do was listen to the sounds from the kitchen: the looped belt whistling through the air, the sickening slap as it struck my mother's cowering body, my mother's desperate, garbled cries.

"'911, what's your emergency?' the dispatcher repeated, more urgency in her voice this time.

"I stuck my finger in my ear so I wouldn't have to hear those horrible sounds from the kitchen and was finally able to speak. 'My daddy is hurting my mommy. She's crying a lot.'

"'What's your address, sweetie?'

"I told her.

"'A policeman will be there soon. Stay somewhere safe, away from your daddy, ok? A policeman will be there soon,' she said.

"Before I had a chance to say anything else, I heard him start bellowing, 'Why did she go in there, Allie? Why the fuck did she go in there? What did you tell her to do?'

"When I realized what was happening, I leapt to my feet and sprinted to the bedroom door to close and lock it. But it was too late. He barreled through the doorway, knocking me to the floor. His eyes immediately went to the pink phone resting on the carpet by the nightstand before he turned to me.

"'Who did you call, Jess?' His voice got really quiet and his blood-shot eyes brimmed with tears. Maybe the thought of getting arrested forced him to realize what a monster he was. 'Did you call the cops on daddy? Did you call the cops on me?'

"I was doing my best to crawl slowly away from him, toward the corner of the room. 'You were hurting mommy.'

"'I know I was. I know I was. I know I shouldn't have. I can't help it, honey. It's not my fault. I don't want to, Jess.' And he started to cry.

"Whatever pent up remorse or self-loathing or pity he was feeling at that moment vanished when the 911 dispatcher's grainy voice from the phone, inquiring loudly if everything was ok, broke through his gentle sobbing. He immediately wiped his tears away with the sleeve of his flannel and whirled toward the phone, ripping it from the wall. He held it over his head, shaking it violently, as he loomed over me.

"'What kind of daughter calls the cops on her father, huh? What kind of daughter does that? One that's been brainwashed by her cunt mother,' he said, loud enough for my mother to hear him from the kitchen. She was crying and begging, in vain, for him to stop, to leave me alone. 'Or maybe cunts only breed cunts.' Flecks of whiskey-infused spittle stung my face.

"He bent over and grabbed my wrist, but I managed to break free and crawl past him before he got a good grip on me. 'Come back, you little bitch.'

"But I was already out of the bedroom and running down the hallway. He staggered into the hallway and launched the phone at my head. It missed by a few inches, crashing into the front door and exploding into a dozen pieces.

"I stepped over the debris as I flung open the front door, expecting to feel his strong, brutal hands on my shoulders any second, and scrambled down the wooden steps leading to the first floor units of our apartment complex. My bare feet were turned into pincushions from all the splinters from those steps, but I didn't care.

"I ducked beneath the bottom landing of the staircase and collapsed in the cool dirt, which was littered with cigarette butts, digging my fingers into the soil as I tried to catch my breath. I was terrified he'd come charging down the steps at any second. I looked up and listened. Light from the apartments filtered through the steps and fell across my little hiding place in gray bars. I could still hear him, screaming and cursing from back inside the apartment, and breathed a sigh of relief. I also listened for my mom, expecting to hear her whimpering, or crying, or begging—but nothing. I didn't know yet whether that was a good or bad sign.

"A skeletal tabby stalked up to me and rubbed against my thigh, scaring the shit out of me. I'd seen the cat wandering around the apartment complex for as long as I could remember, but never knew her name or who she belonged to, if anyone. Occasionally I'd convince my mom to a leave a saucer of milk out for her on the landing outside our door, which she always seemed to instantly discover and lap up in a matter of seconds.

"I picked the cat up and held her against my chest. Her fur was rough and her bones felt brittle, even in my skinny arms, but I clutched her tightly anyway. My heart was still racing, but my breathing was finally returning to normal.

"Where was the policeman? The lady on the phone said he would be here soon. I looked out at the dark street through the spaces in the steps, expecting, any second now, for a police car to come screeching up in front of the complex. I actually smiled as I imagined a police officer with huge muscles and a crisp, blue uniform dragging my dad out of the apartment in handcuffs, taking him away where we'd never see him again so my mom and I could eat Shake n' Bake chicken and macaroni and cheese, or play Candy Land, or watch TV, without being nervous the whole time that we'd hear him at the front door, drunk off his ass and in a nasty mood.

"Ten minutes must have gone by. My heart leapt when a car came zooming up the street. 'They made it!' I thought to myself. 'Finally! The police were here!' I started to push myself up with one hand, cradling the tabby with the other, and looked for the red and blue flashing lights that would free my mom and me from fear, from misery, from constant heartache. But I slumped back into the giant ashtray as the car I'd heard flew past the apartments and disappeared up the street and into the night.

"When a loud clatter shook the wooden steps over my head, I nearly dropped the cat. It was my dad. He came thundering down the steps, muttering obscenities and unintelligible comments to himself. For a second, I considered running away before he made it to the bottom of the steps. He might not even notice me if I was quiet and stayed in the shadows. Or even if he did, there was no way he could catch me in open space—he was drunk, and I was fast.

"But I hesitated, and he was surprisingly quick, thumping down the steps. When I saw the backs of his dirty Nikes stomp down on the bottom step, I pinched my eyes shut and waited for the rough hands to grab me. But nothing happened. I opened my eyes, one at a time, and saw him lurching across the grass toward the street. He clumsily unlocked his car door and spilled into the driver's seat. I held my breath. The police had to come now. If they came now, I could run out from my hiding spot, waving my arms, and direct them to the drunken asshole in the car before he got away. But they had to hurry. They had to come now.

"And they didn't. The squeal from the tires as my dad took off in his car reverberated through the entire apartment complex. I waited a minute or two, just in case he decided to come back, set the tabby down, and climbed carefully up the steps.

"The fragments of the shattered pink phone were still scattered near the doorway. The apartment was quiet. I glanced into the

134

bedroom as I crept down the hallway. A bunch of clothes were strewn across the floor and the bed.

"'Mom?' I whispered, barely able to hear my own voice. There was no answer.

"I found her lying, face down, in a pool of blood by the kitchen counter. I rushed over when I saw her and carefully turned her over on her back. Blood was trickling, slowly but steadily, from just above her left temple. Her eyes were blank.

"'Mom!' I shouted, shaking her, crying now. I thought she was dead.

"When the police finally showed up twenty minutes later, I was curled up on the kitchen floor, weak and exhausted from crying. There were two of them, identical-looking. Pudgy, disheveled, marshmallow-faced. The kind of cops biding their time till they can retire and move to Florida. I know that getting dozens and dozens of domestic abuse calls can desensitize you after a while, but these were some callous fucks; they looked annoyed to be called away from dinner. One of them crouched down and gave me a perfunctory pat on the back while the other called in an ambulance before feeling my mom's pulse.

"'She's alive,' the one cop said.

"'Hear that, kid? Your mom's ok. You can stop crying now.'

"She was alive, but only barely. Not only had the asshole broken three of her ribs, but when he punched her in the right eye, nearly blinding her, he knocked her unconscious, and she ended up catching a corner of the counter on her way to the floor. He'd fractured her skull. She was alive, but if those cops came five minutes later, she wouldn't have been.

"And the worst part? They never caught the asshole. They put a warrant out for his arrest, but nothing ever came of it. Five years later, my mom got a phone call from a detective in Indianapolis: they'd found his corpse in a back alley of the city. As far as the detective could tell, he'd collapsed back there after a night of drinking and died of exposure.

"We were honestly relieved to get that news—there were so many anxious nights when we were sure a branch scratching at a window, or the wind rattling the front door, was him coming back to terrorize us once again. But it wasn't justice. The fact that he even got away that night he almost killed my mom was an injustice. The fact that my mom lay unconscious and near death for a half hour, waiting for help to show up, was an injustice.

"There was a reason this memory came back to me, so vividly and powerfully, while I was sitting at the kitchen table with my mom the summer before my senior year of college. There was a reason I couldn't, and wouldn't ever, write my personal statement for grad school. Once I figured out why, it felt like something I'd known for years, even though I'd never come close to articulating it. It's because I didn't want to be a grad student or an academic. I wanted to be the person out there *doing* something, not just talking about doing something. I wanted to catch wife-beaters and rapists. I wanted to comfort crying children, tell them everything would be ok, and mean it. I wanted to be police. I wanted to be good police.

"On the first day of classes, I stopped into my professor's office— the one who was really pushing me toward grad school—and told her everything I told you. She listened sympathetically, nodded along as I spoke, and then sat for a minute, her hands tented on her desk, after I'd finished.

"'If you do this,' she said finally, 'you will work with people who are, in some cases, violent, short-tempered, racist, misogynistic. Or, sometimes, uninterested and lazy—like the men who kept you and your mother waiting over a half hour that night. You will work with some excellent human beings, too. Don't let the bad ones get to you, but don't just ignore them either and surround yourselves with the good ones. Challenge them, directly or by example. Make them better by your presence.'

"'I will,' I said.

"'You will be putting your life in danger. You will be often frustrated, work to the point of exhaustion. You'll be underpaid. Your pension will most likely get slashed even though you pay into it every paycheck. Your hours will be irregular. You'll miss holidays, birthdays, celebrations, vacations. You will sometimes even be hated and feared, no matter how good you are. You understand all this, right?'

"'I do,' I said. 'And maybe someday down the line I'll care more about self-preservation. But right now, I know this is what I am meant for. If I do anything else, it'll be a lie.'

"She nodded understandingly and smiled. 'Then you have to do it, of course.' She shook my hand as I got up to leave. 'Don't let the institution change you,' she said. 'You'll butt heads and make people mad, but they need you like you are.'

"And I walked out of her office for the last time. Later that night, I enrolled in the academy online and had my best night of sleep in years.

The Oasis was even emptier now: the group of chatty women in the corner booth was gone, as were a few of the lonely men at the bar. The fluorescent beer signs on the wall hummed softly. The TV above the bar, now muted, was replaying the earlier recap of the Phillies and the Eagles.

Rory sat quietly, sipping his beer and letting Daniels's story sink in. "So how's the job been treating you?" he asked after a moment.

"Like I told you outside Mrs. Thompson's apartment, I love it." As Al passed by, she ordered a water and took a long drink of it before continuing. "It doesn't mean everything my professor warned me about hasn't been true, though. As you experienced firsthand."

"Ackermann?" Rory asked, thinking back to the boney, dark-eyed jerkoff who brushed off Rory's concern about the threatening note the previous week.

Daniels nodded as she took another drink of water.

"He was only following orders," Rory said with mock sympathy.

"A popular excuse for the peddlers of banal evil."

"Well said."

"I do wonder if the job will one day burn me out. It hasn't yet, but obviously I'm only a few years in. I sometimes try to imagine what kind of police I'll be in ten, fifteen, twenty years. If I'll become complacent and apathetic too, as I wait for my pension to kick in."

"For some reason, I doubt that'll happen."

"Thanks," Daniels said. "I try not to get too caught up in those thoughts. Because right now, things are really good. My personal life hasn't been completely destroyed by work, which I've heard can happen pretty fucking often. I still have time to go to the gym every day. I've even had time to reread the *Harry Potter* series. And perhaps most impressively, I'm currently enjoying the most stable relationship of my life."

Of course you are, Rory thought. Besides an occasional, fleeting thought while drifting off to sleep, he'd never really harbored any hope of transforming his partnership with Daniels into something romantic or even sexual, so, if anything, the news was more of a relief than a letdown. *Not that it would have mattered—or should have mattered. Not only are you old enough to be her father, but she is far too good for a washed up, alcoholic, ex-newspaperman. Just picturing her reaction if I were to broach the subject with her is enough to make me sick.*

"That's great," Rory said genuinely. "How long have you been together?"

"Two years now," she answered. She looked up at the ceiling as she double-checked the math in her head. "A little over two years, actually." She sounded surprised. "I can't believe it's been that long. I met him, his name's Derek, randomly at a beef and beer fundraiser for the police and fire departments. He was gorgeous—reminded me of Idris Elba—but not exactly my type personality-wise. His opening line was asking my opinion about the Sixers acquiring Andrew Brynum. Little did he know that I couldn't care less about sports, which I told him, and that seemed to throw him for a loop. He mumbled something about getting me a beer, accidentally spilled his all down his shirt, and then looked at me like he was about to cry. I burst out laughing—I couldn't help it—and then he did, too. We started talking. I found out he was a new firefighter, not a cop, which was good—there's no way I could date another cop. We went out to dinner later that week, and that was it. Now we're looking to move in with each other later this summer."

Rory raised his glass. "Congrats."

"Thanks." Daniels raised her glass of water. "Cheers."

"Sláinte."

They both drank.

"How about you?" Daniels asked. "You mentioned having a son?"

Rory nodded, mindlessly watching the rerun of sports highlights on the TV. "A great kid. Way smarter than me. Must've gotten his brains from his mother." He paused and looked over at her. "My ex, as of recently."

"Sorry to hear."

Rory shrugged. "Completely my fault. I hated myself for losing my job, didn't want to take it out on her, so I shut her out instead. It was infantile."

"Any chance of reconciliation?"

"I guess it's possible, but not likely. I'd have to get my shit figured out. And even if I did and wanted to rekindle things with her, I'm not sure she'd want to. I wouldn't if I were her. I was a dick." He swallowed the last of his Yuengling and wiped his lips with the back of his hand. "So I'm staying out here with my mom for the time-being. Having some space has been good."

"How is your mother?"

"She's doing all right. Some days are better than others, but in general she's hanging tough." He sighed. "It was actually a bit of a blessing that she didn't really understand that note, kept mixing it up with memories from decades ago. I'd hate to imagine how paranoid and upset it would have made her."

"I still plan on getting to the bottom of that note," Daniels said. There was disappointment in her voice.

"I really doubt it was anything serious. It just caught me off-guard, finding it slid under the door like that."

"Of course."

It was a few minutes from midnight, and they were now the lone patrons in the bar. When Al came by to slide their tabs across the counter, Rory picked up Daniels's.

"Are you sure?" she asked.

"You got two drinks," he answered. "And thanks for meeting me."

"I'll see you at Kyle McCoy's tomorrow morning?"

"Let's learn something about Andrew Skelly."

Daniels offered him a ride as they walked out into the humid summer night.

"I appreciate it," he replied, "but the fresh air will do me good."

On the walk back, he dug his hand into his pocket to check his phone in the unlikely event that either Kevin or Marie responded to his text from the previous day. But there was nothing there: just the time—it was 12:03 AM—and an otherwise blank screen.

Eighteen

Kyle McCoy's tiny mobile home was tucked away in the farthest corner of The Oaks trailer park. It sat at the end of a small cul-de-sac and was surrounded by gray, sandy soil and gangly scrub pine trees. A colorful flower garden was boxed in at the corner of a small staircase and the front of the home, beneath a wide, curtained window that looked out onto the cul-de-sac.

As Rory parked behind Daniels's police cruiser, he tried to imagine what McCoy could possibly remember about his middle school friend from twenty-two years ago. *He must have been close friends with Andrew for DeMarco to be as confident as she was. The shock and disbelief of the murder might have preserved some surprisingly vivid details, too. Everyone remembers what they had for breakfast on 9/11, right?*

The man who answered the door looked remarkably little like the smiling boy from the Blueberry Hill Middle School yearbook. His once-vibrant face was pallid and deeply creased. His cheeks were sunken and covered with bristles of strawberry-blond scruff. His hair was still red, though the strands that poked out from beneath a sweat-stained Flyers hat were thin and flecked with gray.

Despite his haggard appearance, McCoy's voice was warm when he answered the door. "You the writer?" he asked.

Rory shook his hand. "Yes, Rory Callahan. Thanks for talking with us."

"Come on in. Your counterpart's already here."

He led Rory through a narrow kitchenette to a cramped living room lined with a collection of mismatched, dilapidated furniture. The floor was practically covered with toys—everything from dolls and stuffed animals to Legos and superhero action figures.

"Have a seat anywhere," McCoy said to Rory. Daniels was already sitting in a red love seat in the corner. "Get either of you something to drink?"

"I'm fine, thanks," Rory said as he sat down on a bright yellow couch against the wall.

Daniels held up her hand and shook her head.

"Just let me know if you change your minds," McCoy said. Kicking toys out of his way, he dragged a black, ladder-back from beside the TV closer to where Rory and Daniels were sitting. "Sorry about the mess. I sent my daughters out to play with their friend around the corner right before you got here."

"How old are they?" Daniels asked.

"Six and four."

"They must be adorable."

"Definitely the best part of my life. Give me a reason to get out of bed every morning," McCoy said wistfully. He clasped his hands together and he bowed his head, his back and shoulders wilting. "Ever since the plant closed last year, things have been real tough around here."

"You were at the Mondelez Plant?"

He nodded. "Eight years. Eight years and they gave us one month's notice they were closing."

"Jesus," Rory said.

"Yeah. Loaded trucks out of a warehouse up near Glassboro for a while after that, till I hurt my back. I think it's a slipped disk, but haven't had the money to get it checked out yet." He raised his eyes to see both Rory and Daniels looking back at him sympathetically. "But enough of my sob story. My girlfriend's got a good job managing the CVS downtown. I have my daughters and my health—at least, most of it. Things could be worse."

"Thank you then, again, for agreeing to talk to us," Daniels said. "Especially under these circumstances."

McCoy waved his hand dismissively. "It's no bother. Now what can I help you with? You two want to know about Andy?"

"Yes," Rory said, glancing over at Daniels. "Andrew Skelly. We're researching the Blue Berry Hill murders, trying to get a better sense of what happened that night."

"You mentioned on the phone that Principal Fanelli—guess it's DeMarco now—remembered me?" McCoy asked, looking at Daniels.

"She did. Almost as soon as we brought up Andy, she mentioned you. Pointed your picture out in the yearbook and everything."

"Sharp woman. Although the yearbook photo part is regrettable."

"Not at all," Daniels laughed. "You were cute."

McCoy smiled for a moment before wilting over again and grimacing as if in physical pain. The crow's feet at the corners of his eyes were pronounced. "I still think about Andy, you know. I still think about the good memories. Kidding around during baseball games on Saturday mornings, playing Nintendo in his basement, bitching about teachers and fantasizing about girls." He smiled, though once again, it was fleeting. "But even more so, I think about the nightmares."

"Nightmares?" Rory asked. He had his pen and notepad out.

"Yeah. Had them almost every night for a couple of years after he disappeared. They got worse after they, uh—" He hesitated. "You know, that fall. In the Pine Barrens."

"Right," Daniels said, to keep McCoy from having to name the horrible discovery in the forest.

"Almost every single night I'd have them," McCoy went on, shaking his head. "At first, I'd go to my mother's room to wake her up so she could sit with me for a while, tell me everything was ok, until I fell back asleep. But after it went on for months, I got too embarrassed to do that anymore. I'd just lay there, under my covers, too afraid to move."

"What were the dreams about?" Rory asked. "If you want to tell us."

McCoy frowned and shrugged his shoulders. "I don't mind." He inhaled deeply before continuing. "There were two main ones. They changed a little bit each time, but the basics were always the same. The first was in Sattler's Woods. It was pitch black out, and Andy and I were walking down the path wearing our baseball uniforms. In real life, that path was pretty short—you could walk the length of it in three or four minutes. But in the dream it always felt like we'd been walking for hours. We could see the end of the path and the lights from the neighborhood, but we'd never get any closer to them. We stopped 'cause we were out of breath, and Andy would always be standing with his back to the woods. Then I'd see them: the two, long, slender white arms that would slide out from behind a huge tree. They'd grab ahold of Andy—one hand was always covering his mouth—and pull him into the woods. That's when I'd wake up.

"The second dream I didn't start having till after the funeral and all. I'd be in the church where the funeral was, surrounded by all the crying people in black. But my eyes would always be fixed on the coffin at the front of the church. Then, suddenly, all the people would be gone and the lights in the church would go out. I'd start to panic, feel like I couldn't breathe. And I'd never be able to take my eyes off the coffin as the lid would swing open and Andy would sit up in it. I would say that he'd look at me from the coffin, 'cept he never had eyes—just these little pockets of pinched-up skin. His hair would be mangled, torn off in places, and his face would always be covered in blood. He'd try to say something to me, something important, but every time he'd open his mouth to speak, blood would come dribbling out and roll down his chin, onto his wrinkled suit."

From somewhere outside, the screams of playing children, soft from filtering through the thick summer air, leaked into the mobile home. McCoy raised his head for a brief moment as he listened to hear if they were from his daughters, but the screams quickly faded and silence reigned. He lowered his head again. "So didn't get much sleep those couple of years. Eighth, ninth grade. Rough years."

"Sounds like you and Andy were pretty good friends," Daniels said.

"We were. He was probably my best friend on the baseball team."

"I know it was twenty-two years ago, but do you remember much about April 13th?" Rory asked. "Anything that seemed off?"

"I remember a lot about that day. I remember they served hoagies, the only cafeteria food that didn't make me want to vomit, for lunch. I remember watching a video about the North Pole in science class, which made me think of the day my grandparents took me to the

Natural History Museum in New York over Christmas break. I remember it being warm and sunny for baseball practice; felt practically summer-like. And I do remember talking to Andy during practice. It's hard to tell if what happened afterwards is throwing a shadow on my memories, and it was so long ago, but he did seem a little off that afternoon. He was usually loud and goofy, making fart noises or playing jokes on us, but that afternoon he was quiet. I'd almost say withdrawn, like you'd say something to him and he was off in space, wouldn't even notice at first.

"Practice ended at 5:30. Andy would always walk home through Sattler's Woods, and I'd get picked up at the front of the school. I don't remember seeing him start walking home that night. I don't even remember saying good-bye to him. He might have still been packing up and putting away equipment when I ran around to the front of the school where my mom was waiting for me. Or maybe he went into the locker room to clean up, use the bathroom. I can't—" He stuttered, then paused. "I wish I could—"

"It's ok," Daniels reassured him. "It was a long time ago. And as far as you knew at the time, a normal day."

"The following day has stayed with me pretty clearly, though," he went on. "I woke up with a start in the morning. It was already light out and my alarm clock said 8:07 AM, so I started cursing 'cause I thought I'd overslept. But then I noticed my mom standing at the end of my bed, watching me. I started to yell at her, ask her why she let me oversleep, but she just came around, sat down on the bed, and put her hand on my cheek. She told me school was closed. Then she told me why. Three boys were missing. She asked me about Andy, if he ever mentioned anything about running away. I shook my head. Why would he run away? It was ridiculous she was even asking me.

"Maybe because I'd just woken up or maybe because the news was so unbelievable, it didn't sink in that Andy was one of the missing boys till my mom hugged me and told me over and over again that they'd find him. The longer she hugged me, the more I wanted to cry. It was weird—at the moment I was more worried about crying in front of my mom, of seeming like a weak little boy, than I was about Andy. Where he was, what happened to him. I stared at the *Indiana Jones* poster hanging on the wall and tried to will away the tears.

"My mom made French toast for breakfast; she'd taken the day off to be with me. I managed to eat a slice and take a few sips of orange juice before I threw it all up. I normally loved her French toast, but that morning it seemed scaly, like burnt human skin. I tried to watch TV—*The Price Is Right* was on—but all I could do was think about places Andy might've gone. When I saw a search party go by out the front window, I convinced my mom that we should go out and look for him. We checked the small creek about a quarter mile from my house. We used to catch frogs there when we were younger. We checked the park off Sycamore where we'd have catches and try to smack baseballs as far as we could into the overgrown grass.

"We started back to the house when we crossed paths with a search party heading toward the park. Four men. Two women. I'd never seen them before in my life.

"'We already checked here,' my mother told them.

"'Ah, ok,' one of the men said. 'Nothing in that tall grass?'

"'Do you really think he'd be hiding in tall grass like that?'

"'Not hiding,' the man said. He said it like we were idiots. 'They found blood on the trail in Sattler's Woods.

"I looked up at my mom, but she kept her eyes on the man, unblinking.

"'We're looking for a corpse,' the man said finally, pissed he had to spell it out for us.

"I thought of the burnt skin on the French toast and immediately threw up again. The walk home was a blur. I cried uncontrollably. My mother basically had to prop me up till we got home and I could collapse. And I did. On the floor, right there in the front hallway. The rest of the afternoon—" His voice broke. His narrow, pale blue eyes swam with tears. "I'm sorry. Believe it or not, this is the first time I've ever really told anyone about that day."

"There's no need to apologize," Rory said. He turned his head toward Daniels and exchanged guilty looks with her. "And no need to go on," he told McCoy.

"Thank you." He wiped the tears from his eyes with the back of his hand.

"Changing the subject," Daniels said in a soft voice, "do you remember guys on the team making plans to get pizza one night that week?"

McCoy scratched his scraggly beard and sniffled. "Not that I can recall. That's actually something I've never quite understood: why Andy told his parents he was getting dinner with us that night. We'd hardly ever go out for pizza, or anything like that, as a team. Maybe, rarely, after a game, but that would always be at lunchtime on a Saturday, never on a school night."

"And the police talked to the employees at both pizza places in town: Tony's on Middleton and La Vita's on Central," Daniels noted. "Neither of them remembers middle school kids, or even *a* middle school kid, coming in that night."

"Right."

"So do you think either Andy or his parents were lying about that?" Rory asked.

"Unless one of them made a really bad mistake, which seems odd, I guess I'd have to say so."

"What were his parents like?" It was Daniels asking this time.

McCoy lifted his Flyers cap from his head and ran his fingers through his thinning, copper hair. "Nice people. Came to all our baseball games. Always threw a birthday party for Andy when we were younger. Very patient with us when we'd do dumbass things like shoot each other at pointblank range with paintball guns or take wood from the garage to build a treehouse. His dad would play touch football with us in the backyard in the fall." He smiled to himself, briefly, and placed the cap back on his head. "They still live in the same house, as far as I know. Out in Laurel Acres. But I haven't kept in touch with them."

The smile returned to McCoy's lips for a moment. "There was this one birthday party when Andy got a brand new Super Soaker..." But his voice trailed off and the smile disappeared. His eyes became distant and he shook his head, slowly and solemnly. "I wish I could remember that night better. I wish I could rewind my memory like a videotape so I could see where Andy ran off to. There's just a blank space in my mind when I try to picture the end of practice that night. I was probably so hungry and anxious to get home, like I was every night after practice, I must've run around the school to where my mom was waiting as soon as coach let us go."

"And Andy always went straight home after practice. As far as you knew, at least."

McCoy nodded and sighed. "When my mom first told me he'd gone missing, that's what I pictured: him going straight home at 5:30. That's what he always did. His parents would definitely be the kind to worry if he didn't show up soon after practice. I mean, they were trusting, but protective, like any good parents. So at first, I figured if someone attacked him, it would have happened then, with the sun still bright in the sky and fresh dirt from the baseball diamond stuck in his cleats.

"But the more I thought about it, the more I realized that didn't make any sense. For one, there were other practices going on that evening. The softball team was usually out there pretty late. The track kids would be running around the school, sometimes even up and down the trail through Sattler's Woods. And there would've been other kids walking home on that trail, too. If someone attacked Andy anytime close to 5:30, someone would've seen it, or at least heard it.

"Then when we found out those other two boys got out of play practice at 7:30—"

"By the way," Daniels interrupted, "did you know the other two victims? Nathaniel Foster and Christopher Fitzgerald?"

"I didn't. I recognized their faces from passing in the hallway and such on all the fliers and news reports, but that's about it."

"Did Andy know them at all?"

"He wasn't friends with them, that's for sure. But maybe he knew them from a class. Seventh and eighth grades had gym class together, so it's possible. But I can't imagine that he was walking with them in a group or anything when—you know—it happened."

"Right," Daniels said. "Sorry for interrupting. You can go on."

"So when the news got out that Nathaniel and Christopher had been in rehearsal till 7:30, it made even less sense to me. If someone attacked Andy at 5:30, would they really wait around two more hours to go after the other kids? Makes no sense. My only guess for all these years has been that Andy went somewhere after school, maybe somewhere he wasn't supposed to be, so he lied and told his parents he was getting pizza with the team. Then he headed home, through the woods, around 7:30, same time as the other boys. That's the only thing that makes sense to me."

"And would you say," Rory hesitated as he prepared his next question. "Not to disparage Andy—"

McCoy held up his open hands, tacitly granting permission for the question.

"—but he wasn't the kind of kid who frequently lied, right?"

"Not at all, which is the real head-scratcher. I mean, he'd make up dumb bullshit like kids do—like how he sunk a ball in the basketball hoop in his driveway while standing across the street with his back turned and his eyes closed. Bullshit like that. But he wasn't the kind of kid to lie about serious stuff. He never hid bad test grades or report cards from his folks. I'd do that all the time, hide bad grades from my mom till the teacher called home. A lot of kids would. But not Andy. So telling his parents he was getting pizza with us just adds to the weirdness of the whole thing."

"It certainly does," Daniels acknowledged.

McCoy looked at Daniels, then at Rory, then back to Daniels. "Mind if I ask my own question?"

"Not at all."

"Just curious—what are you hoping to find out about Andy? All these years later, what's it matter? The police never talked to me then, so I've got to admit I was a little shocked to get your call twenty years after the thing itself."

"No one ever talked to you?" Daniels asked. Her tone was a combination of befuddlement and irritation.

McCoy shook his head. "They talked to coach Bryant. He's the one who asked us—everyone on the team—about getting pizza, if any of us had talked to Andy about it. We all shook our heads and looked at each other, confused and scared. And that was it."

Daniels performed a mild face-palm. "To call that investigation half-assed might even be a stretch," she muttered.

"We're actually not here in any official capacity," Rory answered McCoy. "We both think the murder investigation might have been botched, so we're doing a little digging to see if there were any stones left unturned."

"Or stones that were completely ignored the first time round," Daniels added.

McCoy twisted his pale eyebrows up in confusion, maybe anxiety. "Botched? I mean, they caught the guy, right? Thompson?"

"They did," Daniels responded. "He's serving life in prison."

"But you don't think he did it?"

Daniels shrugged. "Maybe not. Or maybe he did but didn't do it alone. Or, on the other hand, maybe the state's story is one hundred percent accurate."

"We just want to know for sure," Rory said.

"Jesus H. Christ," McCoy said. He hunched over in his chair and started cracking his knuckles. "Guess I always thought a jury convicting you like that meant you were pretty damn guilty. I suppose that's naïve."

"Not naïve," Daniels said. "The state obviously made a strong case that Thompson was a creep capable of killing Andy and the other two boys. We might have voted to convict, too, if we were on that jury."

"I guess the thought that the fucker who'd done that to Andy was in jail—that thought's given me some peace of mind these years."

"And he still might be. But if he's not, wouldn't you want to know that so we can get the piece of shit who actually did do it?"

As he thought it over, McCoy began to nod, slowly at first, then vigorously. "Damn right." He was quiet for a moment before repeating, quietly, "Damn right."

Daniels looked over at Rory to see if he had any more questions. Rory shook his head. "We can get out of your hair now," she said.

"Thank you for your time, Mr. McCoy," Rory said, hooking his pen to the pages of his notepad. "If you think of anything else, give us a call."

"I'd be happy to," he said. "And if you two have any break-throughs, feel free to keep me in the loop."

"We can do that."

"By the way," he said, getting up from the ladder-back chair, "did Zeke have anything helpful to tell you guys?"

Rory immediately brandished his pen.

"Who?" Daniels asked, looking up at him.

"Zeke Holling. I think Zeke's short for Ezekiel, but I'm not sure. He was Andy's best friend in elementary school till his dad sent him away to some military school out in Pennsylvania."

Daniels and Rory exchanged glances.

"Holling—as in *the* Holling family?" Daniels asked. "The Holling Mansion, the car dealership, all that?"

"I think so," McCoy said. "I guess so. The rumor was he lived in that big mansion out in the woods, so probably."

"Do you know him well?"

McCoy frowned. "Not particularly. I remember him from grade school a little. Very quiet kid. Never really talked unless someone spoke to him first. But he was Andy's friend way more than mine. I think they stayed friends even after he got sent away for school."

"That's really helpful," Rory said.

"Really?" McCoy sounded pleased.

"We actually hadn't reached out to Zeke yet."

"Because we didn't know he existed," Daniels added.

"Until now."

"Did we just get a break in this case?" Rory asked as they crossed the tiny front yard to the cul-de-sac where their cars were parked. He sounded incredulous and slightly excited.

"I wouldn't exactly call it a break," Daniels said, smiling. "But it's new information." As she thought it over, she shook her head and suddenly lost her smile. "Christ, I didn't even know John Holling had a son. How could I not have known that? They're only the richest, most powerful family in the county."

"Don't beat yourself up about it. Maybe there's a reason they've kept him out of the public eye."

"True. I just can't imagine what it would be."

They came to a stop beside Daniels's police cruiser.

"But between this and the school donation at that *Jesus Camp* church," Rory said, "we need to talk to John Holling."

"You're going to drive over to that mansion now." It wasn't a question. Daniels looked down and kicked a pebble across the cracked asphalt. "Shit. I wish my shift wasn't about to start."

"Sorry about that. I guess being out of work does have a slight silver lining."

"No need to apologize. I'd do the same if I were you." She opened her car door and paused. "As always—"

She didn't need to finish the sentence. "I'll let you know what happens."

She smiled as she got into the cruiser. "Text me—or call me—if you talk to him. Hell, even if he refuses to answer the door and you just see his silhouette in one of the mansion windows, I want to know."

"Of course."

As Rory walked over to his car, the faint sound of children laughing and screaming drifted into the cul-de-sac just as it had done in McCoy's living room earlier. Rory paused to listen before climbing into the Ford Focus, but the joyful sounds of children playing had already fallen into silence.

Nineteen

Pulling out of the trailer park to head north on Elmwood Drive, Rory felt a sudden twinge of guilt. He hadn't exactly lied to Daniels: he *was* going to the Holling Mansion…he was just making a brief detour on the drive there. He practically had to pass right by the Laurel Acres housing development on the way to the Holling Mansion anyway.

But he thought if he'd mentioned his plan of dropping in on Mr. and Mrs. Skelly to Daniels, she would have tried to talk him out of it. After all, it was their oldest son—not a student, or even a friend—who mysteriously vanished that evening after school, leaving behind only a bewildering cluster of footprints and a few traces of blood and brain matter. It was their son's knock on the front door they waited to hear, hope against hope, second after agonizing second, even as those agonizing seconds drifted into minutes, and hours—and then hours became days, days bled into weeks, and weeks somehow vanished into months. The glimmer of hope that he might still be alive—somehow, somewhere—served as only a temporary tormentor to a colder, more enduring cruelty: a thunderous silence that would only intensify once the arrest was made, once the trial ended, once the news reporters packed up and left town for good, once the people of Hollingford moved on with their lives and began to forget the horrific crime that made their community briefly infamous.

But the front door never to be knocked on, the doorbell never to be rung—excitedly, goofily, the way an 8th grade boy might ring it— would remain with them through the long years. Through the many Christmases that would never feel quite so joyous as they once had. Through the many birthdays that would go uncelebrated. The silence would then settle over the empty bedroom, over the baseball cards never to be flipped through and studied again, over the *Jaws* and Mike Schmidt posters on the walls, over the still action figures and dusty comic books.

The last thing this couple needed was a random, uninvited asshole to show up at their door, asking questions about their son, sharpening the teeth of vicious memories in the process. Daniels said the Skelly family was off-limits—questioning them would be *"horrible"* and *"tactless"*, Rory remembered her saying. And she might have been right.

But what if, on the off chance, they were hiding something? After the boys had vanished, both the Fitzgeralds and Evelyn Chandler, Nathaniel's grandmother, gave constant interviews to the papers and local news stations, perhaps believing that spreading word of the missing children could only help, however tenuously, cast a wider net to find them. By comparison, the Skellys were not just media-shy, but practically reclusive. In fact, they were featured in only one newspaper article, published three days after the disappearance in the *The Inquirer*. In it, they talked about the sleeplessness, the dark thoughts impossible to keep at bay, but also the hope that Andrew would be found, safe and unharmed. There was a photograph of them standing on the lawn in front of their house, cradling a framed picture of Andrew between them. Mr. Skelly's lanky arm draped over his wife's shoulder, their faces tired but not yet the gaunt, sunken masks of fear and despair they would inevitably become.

So maybe, just maybe—un-fucking-likely as it may be—there's a reason they wanted to stay out of the papers and off TV after the boys disappeared, Rory thought to himself, trying to justify his surprise visit to the Skellys as he made a left onto Laurel Acres Avenue. *And what if Andrew didn't lie about getting pizza that night at all? The only people he supposedly told about that were his parents. What if they lied?...And what reason could they possibly have for doing so?*

Before driving deep into the housing development, he pulled over and dug his phone out from his pocket. He opened the old newspaper article about the Skellys on his web browser, enlarged the image of the couple standing in front of their house, and propped the phone up in a cup holder near the radio so he could see the screen. He continued down the street slowly, glancing from one side of the street to other, scanning for the same house that glowed dimly on his cellphone screen in a grainy, black and white newspaper photo.

Of course, I'll come across as a complete fucking asshole no matter what. Besides, why would they talk now if all they wanted was privacy back in '92? My only hope is that maybe, after twenty-two years, they've got something they want to get off their chests.

He could feel his intestines tighten and his palms get sweaty on the steering wheel as the house from the photograph suddenly appeared on his right.

The house was modest: a small, attached garage, pale blue siding, white trim around the windows and the front door. A yard sign bearing the image of a yellow ribbon and the message *Support Our Troops* stood front-and-center on the freshly cut front lawn. A twisted willow, its long, gnarled branches contorted in elaborate knots, lingered in the corner of the yard; the same tree was visible at the edge of the *Inquirer* photo, only smaller and less deformed.

Rory stopped his car in front of the house and looked from the house to the image on his phone, and back to the house again, just to confirm it was the Skellys'. Despite the low quality of the photograph, and the decades that had passed since it had been taken, the house in the picture was clearly the same one he was now parked in front of. He shoved his phone back in his pocket and turned the car off.

For a moment, he sat there and looked up at the blue house. The curtains were all drawn and there was no car in the driveway. Maybe they were at work? It was early afternoon on a weekday, after all. The thought of starting the car back up, driving away and forgetting he'd ever stopped here briefly flashed through Rory's mind.

But what if? he then thought. *What if they know something? What if they have answers no one's ever bothered to ask them for?*

"Ok," he said, taking a deep breath and grabbing his notepad. The car door felt heavy as he pushed it open.

Other than a dog barking somewhere in the distance and the aggressive hum of lawnmower in a nearby yard, the street was quiet. Rory could hear his heart pounding in his chest as he walked toward the driveway. Several blocks up the street, Blueberry Hill rose like a massive barrow beyond a row of houses; the trees that once covered it had been cut down in the wake of the murders. Only a corner of the brick school building managed to jut out from the top of the hill.

Before he knew it, Rory found himself standing at the front door of the Skellys' home. With a sweat-laced finger, he rang the bell once and waited. The distant dog's barks became more frequent now—strained, distressed. The lawnmower continued to buzz uninterrupted in the summer haze.

After a minute or so of waiting, Rory backed up several feet and looked up at the house to see if, maybe, someone was watching from an upstairs window. But there was nothing. The house was not simply still, but lifeless.

What the fuck was I thinking? Rory thought, shaking his head. *Probably for the best no one answered.* He began to turn back toward the driveway. But then—out of the corner of his eye—he noticed a slight curtain flutter from the window closest to the door. He froze. He wasn't sure he'd seen anything at first. But then it fluttered, however slightly, once again.

When the deadbolt in the door clanked as it slid out of place, it seemed to echo down the empty street. The door creaked open soon after, but only by about three inches because the chain lock remained latched in place. The woman who looked out from the dark doorway with pale green, startled eyes, was in her sixties, maybe even seventies. It was hard to tell. Her white hair was like straw and her skin was papery.

"Yes?" was all she said, in a voice that snapped, but softly, harmlessly. Like a breaking twig.

Rory squinted at her, trying to determine if the woman who looked at him from the narrow opening in the door was the same woman from the old newspaper photo, her husband's arm wrapped around her shoulders, a picture of her missing son in her hand. *It's her,* he determined. *The years have worn away at her, but the eyes are the same. Warier now, but the same.*

"Yes?" the woman repeated in the exact same tone. Her eyes were no less startled now.

"Hi—" Rory began. Mrs. Skelly continued staring, her look one of confusion and expectant terror. Her tiny body, wrapped in a long white sweater, looked like it would shatter if she were to fall over. It had been so easy to interrogate the Skellys in his imagination, where they existed hypothetically, fictionally. Now, staring into the fleshless face of motherly grief, the idea seemed callous at best, exploitive at worst. *This is a bad idea. You should have told Daniels what your dumb ass was planning to do so she could have talked you out of it.*

"I'm sorry," Rory stammered. "I was supposed to drop something off at a friend's, but I think I have the wrong house." He leaned back and pointed at the house number hanging from the blue siding. "Yup." He forced himself to chuckle. "Wrong house. She told me it was a blue house on Laurel Acres Avenue. I guess there's more than one of those. Should've checked the house number before I got out."

Mrs. Skelly continued staring at him, her expression unchanged.

"Anyway, sorry to bother you, m'am. Have a good afternoon." He turned and hurried down the driveway without glancing back.

Out of embarrassment, mostly, he didn't dare look back at the house until he was in the car with the engine running. The front door was closed now but the curtain in the window next to it was peeled back an inch or two, and he could feel Mrs. Skelly's eyes on him. *Fuck you for not knowing what the endless years of heartbreak would have done to her. Fuck you for thinking this was a good idea even if she didn't look so fragile, in every possible sense.* He drove off quickly, trying to erase from his memory the image of Mrs. Skelly's horrified, green eyes and skeletal face as she stared from the house the way a prisoner might stare through the bars of his cell.

"Fuck you," he said to himself. "Fuck you."

Twenty

After winding along a houseless, heavily-forested road—which became a single lane as it crossed a narrow, concrete bridge—Rory watched with amazement as the Holling Mansion arose from the woods like a monolith. Although the mansion was only three or four miles northwest of Laurel Acres and the middle school, its wild surroundings made it seem a world apart from the rest of town: the vine-covered trees assuming giant, monstrous forms, the deep creek bed running parallel to the road, the piercing birdsong and relentless drone of cicadas practically drowning out the Guns N' Roses leaking from the Ford's stereo all served in making the remoteness tangible, enveloping, even though the expressway hummed with summer traffic only half a dozen miles to the west.

It was a short drive for Rory, yet it provided him ample time to dwell on the encounter with Mrs. Skelly. It had rattled him—made him wonder if his pseudo-investigation into a decades-old murder case, one that ended with a generally unprotested conviction, was anything more than an exercise in harassing the deeply traumatized, reopening old wounds.

She looked broken. Completely broken. If I'd opened my dumb mouth about Andrew, it would have broken her all over again. And for what? Because an investigation was done shittily? How many murder cases aren't done shittily? Or because a pedophile and his mother may or may not be delusional, if not flat-out lying? Maybe I need to find a new hobby before I do some actual fucking damage.

But for the time being, Rory was able to ignore this creeping doubt, primarily because of his growing curiosity about the Holling family. The two odd discoveries about John Holling—the money he'd given to the church rumored, however absurdly, to have conducted bizarre rituals in the woods behind the school, and then the mysterious son, Zeke, who'd been childhood friends with Andrew Skelly—may not have meant much taken separately, but together they were enough to spur unending thoughts and scenarios in Rory's head, from the simplest explanations to the wildest speculation.

A black, wrought-iron fence surrounded the Holling property, creating a border between the foreboding woods and the acres of meticulously maintained, golf course-quality grass encircling the mansion. The mansion itself was sprawling, almost ungainly: sharp gables of various sizes jutted up from different sections of the house while several turrets, each offering a panoramic view from wide, ceiling-to-floor windows, towered over the building and its grounds. Attached to the side of the mansion was a large, domed greenhouse that glinted in the afternoon sun.

When Rory turned up the driveway, he was immediately met by a gate—an extension of the fence, but taller and with an intricate, arabesque design rising, in a gentle curve, from the top rail. Ahead of him was a long, paved driveway that ended at a massive, multi-level fountain just before the front entrance of the mansion. The fountain, from the end of the driveway, at least, appeared moss-covered and unused.

Rory pulled his car over to the side of the driveway where a small panel featuring an intercom, a camera, and a keypad was perched on the end of a post—black and wrought iron, just like the fence. He rolled down his window and tapped the button on the intercom, regarding the camera from the corner of his eye, wondering who might be watching him on it.

"Who is this?" A woman's voice crackled through the intercom speaker. "Weren't expecting anyone today."

Rory cleared his throat. "My name is Rory Callahan. I'm doing some research for an article I'm writing and was hoping to talk to Mr. Holling."

There was a brief pause before the woman's voice crackled through the little speaker again. "Mr. Holling's not in. He's at the office today."

"Office?"

"At the dealership."

"Oh, right." Given John Holling's wealth, power, and age, it had never occurred to Rory that he would still have an active role in the day-to-day operations of his many businesses. It gave Rory an immediate, an unexpected, sense of respect for the town patriarch.

"You can stop over there if you want," the woman added. "He might be busy, but you can try."

"Thanks for your help."

Rory drove back into town on the same winding road he had taken out to the mansion, watching in the rearview mirror as the black fence disappeared from view and the array of sharp gables sticking up above the tree line slowly sunk into the dense forest and impenetrable vines, then, finally, vanished as well.

A plethora of gigantic, patriotic banners hung lazily in the still, summer air from dozens of light poles scattered across the expansive car lots of Holling Chevrolet. Most featured red, white and blue backgrounds, a few, firework displays, but they all made the same proclamation in bold, 3-D lettering: *Fourth of July Blowout Sale!* The sale appeared, at first glance, to be mildly successful: several bands of customers navigated the seemingly endless rows of new and used vehicles, some led by eager salespeople, others browsing unaccompanied.

The shadow from one of the sale banners fell over Rory's car as he parked in the small customer lot beside a row of used Chevy Cruzes. Notepad and pen in hand, he glided through the sliding glass doors of the showroom and into the frosty, sterile, air-conditioning. Expecting to be instantly solicited by a salesperson, Rory was surprised to be greeted only by the clank of the doors shutting behind him and a Counting Crows song piping softly from some overhead speakers.

As he was scanning the showroom floor, looking among the shiny, new cars adorned with red, white, and blue balloons for a salesperson or customer service rep he could ask about seeing John Holling, a quiet but monotone voice came from his right: "Welcome to Holling Chevrolet."

Rory turned to see a man hunched over a cheap office desk. He was in his thirties or forties—his face looked young, though his dark, curly hair was thinning. He had a bulbous nose, red with pores, and a long scar running from the inside corner of his eye down his right cheek where it disappeared into a thick, unkempt beard. His wide hands were positioned on the keyboard of a black Dell desktop stationed at the corner of his desk.

"My name's Mike," the man continued, pointing absently to the silver name tag pinned to his polo shirt. "All our sales associates are busy at this time, but may I offer you a soft drink, water, or coffee as you explore our showroom floor?"

"I'm ok," Rory said. "I was actually hoping to talk to John Holling. Is he available at all this afternoon?"

Mike looked up at him with dull, uninterested, brown eyes. "Do you have an appointment with Mr. Holling?"

"I don't. I'm a writer, doing a little research into Hollingford history for a piece I'm working on," he explained, using the same line he'd used on Dana Gladwell the day before. "I'd love to interview him for it."

Mike turned his eyes to his computer monitor and began scrolling through Holling's appointment calendar. "Looks like he's free this afternoon. I can go back and see if he wants to talk to you. What's your name, sir?"

"Rory Callahan."

Mike looked back up at Rory, only this time his eyes were wide with confusion, perhaps even fear. "Callahan?" Although he looked startled, his voice remained monotone. "Any relation to Kathleen Callahan, here in town?"

"Yes. I'm her son." Rory paused, expecting Mike to explain how he knew Kathleen—perhaps through Saint Rose, or maybe because Mike's mother was in the same card group. But Mike remained silent, looking up at Rory with that same, wide-eyed stare. "How do you know her?" Rory finally prompted.

Mike furrowed his brow and rubbed his protruding forehead, as if deep in thought. Rory found this sudden concentration strange, as it was Mike himself who asked about Kathleen—he shouldn't have been stumped by the question. "Kathleen. Kathleen Callahan," he said quietly, mostly to himself. "Did she buy a used Malibu from us a few years back?" He raised his bushy eyebrows, doing his best to replace his look of startled confusion with one of easy confidence.

"I believe she did."

"I thought so. I've got a memory like you wouldn't believe." He smiled uneasily and tapped the side of his head with a stubby finger. "I can tell you pretty much every car we've sold, and who bought it, for the past four years. From the Impala we sold to the Andersons in April 2010, to the Cruze we sold to the Rivases this morning, I pretty much remember them all."

Rory nodded, not sure what to say. "Impressive," he finally managed.

"How's your mother liking the Malibu?"

"No complaints, as far as I know."

"Well, here at Holling, we go above and beyond to provide quality vehicles at affordable prices. In fact, we treat our customers like family. You can let me know, personally, if she has any trouble with it and we'll take care of her ASAP," he added, handing Rory a glossy business card.

Rory briefly examined the card before sticking it in his back pocket. "Thanks," he said, though he was growing slightly impatient. The two burning questions he had about Holling—his connection to The Church of Christ's Healing Touch, and how good of a friend his son Zeke had been to Andrew Skelly—remained frustratingly unanswered the longer he stood here listening to Mike rattle off company slogans. *Christ, is he going to re-enact an entire cheesy TV spot, complete with awkward appearance by a member of the Phillies, or he is going to ask Holling about talking to me?*

The uneasy smile on Mike's face slowly faded the longer he stared up at Rory. Finally, he shook his head and pushed himself up from the desk.

"Let me go see if Mr. Holling's free."

"Much appreciated," Rory said.

Mike nodded before walking stiffly, and with heavy footsteps, across the showroom floor and disappearing into a corridor behind a gleaming Chevy Suburban. He returned only a minute or two later, the expression on his round, bearded face blank now. "He's happy to talk to you," he said as he returned to his post behind the desk. "You can head on back. First office on the left."

For belonging to one of the wealthiest people in South Jersey, if not the entire state, John Holling's office was surprisingly nondescript. The windowless room featured cinderblock walls, weak fluorescent lighting, and badly-scuffed vinyl tile. Two wooden chairs with worn blue padding stood in front of a generic executive desk. A speaker embedded in the ceiling just above the doorway emitted the same 90s soft rock that played out in the showroom. The plainness, even austerity, of the office was no doubt intentional: anything remotely luxurious would not only be out of place in a car dealership, but might drive a wedge between Holling and his employees. Already Holling was demonstrating his shrewdness as a businessman.

Seated in a large leather chair behind the desk was a small, wiry man with full, neatly parted silver hair. He was dressed well in a crisp, white, button-down shirt and blue suit pants, though he wore no tie, and his sleeves were rolled up to the elbow. Although he must have been well into his seventies, his fair complexion was smooth and practically wrinkleless. He appeared absorbed in his computer monitor, so Rory rapped gently on the open door to get his attention. The man looked up, grinned widely with a set of perfect, sparkling teeth, and rose to shake Rory's hand.

"Mr. Callahan?" he asked warmly. His handshake was cold and firm. "John Holling. Pleasure to meet you. Have a seat."

"Thanks for talking. I'm sure you're a busy man." The wooden chair creaked as Rory settled in it.

"Not at all. Not at all." Holling returned to his leather chair, which was comically large for his tiny stature; he looked like a child seated on a phonebook at the kitchen table. "If you don't mind, I just need a minute to get this email out, then I'd be more than happy to help you with your article."

"I don't mind at all. Take your time."

While Holling squinted at his computer screen, typing softly every few seconds, Rory glanced around the office. Besides the computer, a couple of picture frames turned toward Holling, and a black Bible with gold lettering on the cover, the desk was spartan. A file cabinet and small book shelf took up a corner of the room. Hung on the cinderblock walls were several photographs: a black and white aerial shot of Hollingford from the 1950s when most of the land was still undeveloped; a picture of a smiling Holling standing on a dock, a large red snapper dangling from the end of his upright fishing pole; and a faded photo of a much younger-looking Holling with another man, both sporting plaid 70s suits, both smiling widely, in front of the dealership showroom, a huge *Grand Opening!* banner hanging in the window behind them.

Rory paused on the last photograph. The man standing next to Holling looked somehow familiar. Rory racked his brain, trying to place where he'd seen him before. Even though the picture was easily forty years old, there was something about that man's face—the sharp jawline, the narrow, twinkling blue eyes, the full cheeks, the short, pointy nose, the impish smile—that reminded Rory of someone he'd seen recently. He was sure he recognized it. Another customer at the supermarket when he went shopping for dinner on Friday? One of the men sitting at the bar at The Oasis last night? He tried to think of everyone he'd met since arriving in town the previous week, but continued to draw a blank. *It was so much older than the one staring out from that photograph, but I definitely have seen that face before. Where? When?*

"All right," Holling said. "And with that—" He clicked the mouse with finality. "—I'm ready to chat." He pressed the button on his monitor to shut it off and looked over at Rory, grinning broadly. "Thanks for your patience."

"Of course. But before we begin, do you mind if I ask you about that photograph there?" he said, motioning toward the one of the dealership's grand opening.

"Not at all." Holling's face tightened, but he kept smiling as he turned his head toward the photo. "That was 1972, the year we opened this place. Feels like a lifetime ago."

"Who's the man in the picture with you?"

Holling sighed and pointed at the photograph. "That's my old business partner," he said. "He retired maybe twenty years ago. Haven't really seen or talked to him since."

"Does he still live here in town?"

"I couldn't even tell you. He'd always talked about moving to Florida, or maybe Texas, when he retired—he hated the cold—but I honestly don't know if he ever did." Holling pursed his thin lips and shook his head, his eyes still fixed on the photo. "Tragic, really—losing touch with him like that. Never could have opened the dealership without his help. It was his idea to start all of those fast food franchises out on the White Horse Pike, too. They've been nothing but a cash cow ever since, especially during the summer. People stop at them all the time for lunch on their way down the shore."

I know I've seen that face. But where? "Just out of curiosity, what's his name?"

"I'd rather not talk about him anymore, if you don't mind. Brings back some painful memories I'd prefer not to relive." Holling turned his face back toward Rory and flashed his sparkling white grin again. "But enough about me. Which paper did you say you write for, Mr. Callahan?"

"*The Inquirer.* Rather, I used to write for them. Now I just do freelance."

"And your article about Hollingford history—how's it going? Have you interviewed anyone else yet?"

"The article's going well so far. I talked to a woman at—" *Perfect chance to ask him about the church...just don't fuck up the name.* "—The Church of Christ's Healing Touch yesterday. Seems like an important local institution."

Holling nodded vigorously. "It certainly is. Good people over there, good people. Who'd you talk to?"

"Dana Gladwell."

"Isn't she the best?" he asked, still smiling widely.

"She's something else," Rory answered. Hoping to gauge Holling's relationship with the church, he added, "I noticed your name on the new school building over there. Congratulations on that."

"Thank you. That church has got such an important mission in today's world, it's the least I could do, really. And they appreciate knowing I've got their backs."

Oh, shit. Is Holling a full-fledged whack-job, too? "Important mission?" Rory asked innocently.

"Well, of course." He leaned toward Rory, resting his elbows on the desk. "The black tide of sin lapping at our shores has never been higher. Between the secular, homofascist Jews sitting on our courts, to the pornography being force fed to us on TV and the internet, we've got a real spiritual battle for the soul of our country going on, don't we? Pastor Forsythe and Ms. Gladwell and all of those good people at Christ's Healing Touch aren't going to let us go down without a fight, at least." Holling's leather chair squeaked as he leaned back in it. "Good people over there," he repeated.

Whack-job status: confirmed…with a generous dose of anti-Semitism and homophobia stirred in, just for good measure. "Are you a member of the church, too, then?"

Holling's eyes drifted down to one of the picture frames on his desk. "I am. Not as regular an attendee as I'd like, but yes." He looked away from the picture frame, up at Rory again, his blue eyes misty. "My wife Elizabeth is very ill, which sometimes makes getting out of the house difficult. We have a fulltime nurse, but I still feel guilty leaving, knowing she's lying in bed, suffering and afraid."

"I'm very sorry to hear that," Rory said quietly, dropping his chin.

"Please keep her in your prayers."

"I will."

"But yes," Holling went on, dabbing the corners of his eyes with a handkerchief, "the folks at Christ's Healing Touch have been nothing but supportive. They keep her in their intentions every week."

"That's good of them," Rory said. *This might be it—your chance to ask about Zeke.* "Is it just you and Elizabeth then at home?"

Holling put his handkerchief away and sighed again, deeply. "Unfortunately, yes. I wish I could say otherwise, but our only son is deployed overseas with the Army. He joined after 9/11—dropped out of college senior year, much to the chagrin of his mother and myself—and has been gone practically ever since. His latest deployment began in January, so we're holding out hope he'll be home for Christmas this year." He paused, picked up a different picture frame from his desk, and looked down at it reflectively. "We feel so torn about it sometimes. On the one hand, we're so proud of him for defending our freedom and liberating the world from terrorism and oppression. On the other hand, we miss him terribly. We worry about his safety every day. All these years he's been gone, I still get sick thinking about it sometimes." He flipped the picture frame around so Rory could see a handsome, clean-shaven, blue-eyed young man wearing a green military uniform and beret.

"Good-looking kid," Rory commented. "And brave as hell."

"Thank you," Holling said, replacing the picture frame. "We are very proud."

"Is he career military?"

"He didn't intend on it, but yes." Holling paused, raised a silver eyebrow, and squinted as his cool, blue eyes turned icy. "But again, enough about me." His formerly warm tone was now, suddenly, prickly: a mix of stern and suspicious. "Strange your questions should all be about my personal life thus far."

"I apologize," Rory said, trying to sound sincere. "I didn't mean to pry."

"What, exactly, is your article about, Mr. Callahan, and how can I help you with it?" His tone was no longer just prickly, but angry, accusatory.

Rory had a feeling his answer might not go over well—Holling had plenty of reason to want to protect the reputation of Hollingford, after all, so contributing to an article about the most horrific event in town history would not exactly be in his best interest—so he momentarily considered lying. Both unable to come up with a convincing lie and aware how foolish and unprofessional lying would be, Rory gritted his teeth before saying, "I'm doing a piece about the Blueberry Hill murders."

Holling closed his eyes and began breathing heavily through his nose. His nostrils flared with each breath, and his hands formed fists on the desktop. "I thought so." He sounded more disappointed than upset. "Why?" he whispered in a raspy voice. His eyes were still closed.

"I talked to Cindy Thompson, the mother of—"

"I know who she is," Holling snapped. "And I know what she's been doing." His voice was venom.

Holling's sudden, inexplicable transformation from kind and welcoming to bitter and cantankerous left Rory momentarily speechless.

"What did she tell you?" Holling spit out.

"Nothing new, I'm sure," Rory answered, sounding defensive. "But it was enough to pique my interest."

"Of course it was," Holling snorted, opening his blue eyes, now filled with hate as he glared at Rory. "What paper did you say you wrote for? *The Inquirer*?"

"Used to."

"Used to," Holling repeated, mockingly. "Once you've been contaminated by filth, you're always contaminated. There's no getting clean. I bet you lived in the city, too."

"My entire life, actually."

"Figures." He snorted. "That whole city became a festering canker of godlessness when the blacks invaded. Like vermin. Things only got worse when—God help us—they began running the city. Now I understand it's crawling with sodomites and perverts. What's next, a fag mayor and a city council as black as tar?"

Rory was momentarily stunned. He looked down at the notepad resting on his knee as if searching for some kind of guidance, some clue as to how to respond to Holling's unexpected temper and reprehensible bigotry. Unable to think clearly, he glanced back up to find Holling's hateful eyes locked on his.

"And now I understand why you went to Christ's Healing Touch yesterday: because you'd heard disgusting, nasty rumors about the church in connection to those murders and wanted to see if there was any truth to them. You wanted to drag those good people through the mud, write just enough about them that through suggestion, through hearsay, you could make your readers believe those horrible rumors might actually be true. And even worse—"

"Excuse me," Rory tried to interrupt, but his voice came out soft and feeble.

"And even worse," Holling continued, his voice rising and his ashen face turning crimson, "is what you plan to do to those poor boys. You want to exhume them from their graves, prop their skeletons up, and parade them this way and that for the entertainment of strangers. You want to turn the most tragic event in this good town's history into a mockery." Strings of spit were flying from his mouth now. "And what about their families? I imagine they are still haunted by nightmares these twenty-two years later. You will do nothing but dip your hand in the blood of their children and spatter it on their faces, smiling with derision all the while. Because your motivation is purely selfish—to sell an article. There must be less sadistic ways to earn a living, Mr. Callahan, than by torturing the families of those young men and defecating on the name of a good community. I suggest you figure out what one could be."

By the end of Holling's rant, Rory was no longer sitting in stunned silence, but instead trying to restrain the bitter rage forming at the back of his throat. "You finished?" he asked quietly.

"The question is, are you?" he shot back, wiping the corners of his mouth with the handkerchief. "If you had even an ounce of decency, you'd find something different to write about. Maybe a different tragedy to exploit."

"We're done here." The chair screeched against the vinyl floor as Rory slid it back and stood up. "Thanks for your time. I'll be sure to check the obituaries so I can celebrate when your name finally shows up in it."

Holling sat looking up at Rory, a smirk on his face.

"I think it'll be worth throwing back a few for," Rory continued. "One fewer old, angry, bigoted asshole sucking oxygen away from the rest of humanity."

"Something tells me you don't need much of a special occasion to throw back a few," Holling retorted, his voice cutting. "You Irish are all the same: pathetic, miserable drunks." He turned his computer monitor back on and flicked his eyes toward the screen. "Go back to your foul, homo-loving city, Mr. Callahan. You deserve nothing less."

Rory made a point to slam Holling's office door on his way out.

Mike, the man at the reception desk, attempted to exchange pleasantries with Rory, but "Have a good—" was all he managed to utter; Rory stormed past him without a glance, out the sliding glass doors, and into the blazing summer sun.

He waited several minutes for his hands to stop shaking before finally starting the car to drive back home.

Twenty-One

As soon as he pulled out of the parking lot of Holling Chevrolet, Rory called Daniels to get her perspective on everything he'd learned from talking to Holling—especially the dramatic turn in their conversation when Rory had revealed he was writing about the Blueberry Hill murders. He was still in utter disbelief over Holling's ugly diatribe and thought that talking to Daniels about it would somehow make it less surreal.

She didn't answer, so he left a voicemail: "Jess, it's Rory. I just had the most un-fucking-believable conversation with John Holling. Things seemed to be going well at first. We were making polite small talk when I found out that he's not only a big benefactor of Christ's Healing Touch, but apparently a proponent of their batshit crazy beliefs, too. I also found out his son is stationed in Afghanistan; he's been in the military for over a decade, so maybe that's why you'd never heard of him. And then, out of nowhere, he got suddenly suspicious and asked what my article was really about. When I told him, he started spouting off some putrid stuff—racist, homophobic shit—before I'd heard enough and stormed out of his office. I'm still in shock about it, to be honest. Would love to hear your thoughts on what the hell just happened back there. Give me a call back when you get a chance."

For the remainder of the short drive home, Rory drummed on the steering wheel anxiously. "Did that really just happen? Did that really just fucking happen?" he said to himself.

Back at the house, he had just walked through the front door when a commotion in the kitchen—pots and pans clattering, cabinet doors slamming—nearly made his heart stop. He rushed back to find his mother in tears, on her hands and knees, rifling through the drawers and cabinets. She was emptying them frantically, spilling their contents all over the floor. The air was also stifling: the windows were all closed and the air conditioning seemed to be shut off.

"Where is it? Where is it?" Kathleen wailed.

Rory walked carefully around the baking sheets, mixing bowls, whisks, and measuring cups littering the floor and placed his hand gently on Kathleen's shoulder. She jumped up in surprise, whirling around to face Rory. Her eyes were simultaneously wild and nebulous, as if she were peering intensely through a thick fog. Tufts of her gray hair branched off in different directions, and her flushed cheeks were streaked with tears.

"Oh, I can't find it, I can't find it," she cried, burying her face in Rory's shoulder. "He's going to be so disappointed." Rory could feel her entire, frail body shaking as he wrapped his arms around her.

"What can't you find, mom? What's wrong?"

"I can't find my springform pan! I must have lent it to someone, but I can't remember who."

"That's ok. We can always run out and get a new one."

"But it won't be ready for when he gets home. It'll take an hour to go to the store and get back." She pulled away from Rory and began walking back through the sea of scattered kitchenware, looking carefully down as she walked, like a beachcomber searching for a particular shell. "Maybe I missed it when I took it out," she said more to herself than to Rory.

"What do you need it for?" Rory asked, dreading the answer.

"For dad's cheesecake. I want it to be ready for when he gets home from work. I have the ingredients." She motioned to the kitchen table, where sticks of butter and cartons of cream cheese were stacked in a neat pile. "I just need to find that darn pan."

Fuck, Rory thought. *Just when I thought she was doing better.* "Dad's—" Rory began, but stopped when he realized the date: it was June 24th, his father's birthday. *And I completely forgot, like the asshole I am. Never said one word about it to her over breakfast this morning. God, I hope she doesn't think I'm as horrible as I feel.*

"Mom," Rory said, calmly, but firm enough that she stopped her desperate search for the springform pan and looked up at him. "Are you ok?"

She shook her head and walked toward him, accidently kicking a stray pot as she made her away across the kitchen.

"I'm sorry, mom, but dad's—he's not coming home tonight."

Kathleen stood in front of Rory, looking intently at him. She was still sniffling, but her eyes were clearer now, as if the fog had lifted. "What do you mean?" she asked.

"He's gone, mom."

"Gone." She hesitated. "He is?" Then, sadly, as the memory came slowly back to her: "He is."

"He's been gone over three years now," Rory said, softly. "I'm sorry, mom."

"That's right. He's gone," she repeated. "The cancer."

Rory nodded.

"The months and months in bed. Trying to get reception on that horrible little TV upstairs. Helping him use that shaky, plastic toilet by the bedside. The magazines in the hospital waiting room that never changed."

"Not the best memories, I know."

"I—I—" She stuttered as she formulated her thoughts. "I knew that. I knew all of that. I must have forgotten."

"It's ok, mom." He struggled to think of anything meaningful to say. "It's ok," he said again.

"It's not that I forgot, exactly. I mean, it's not that I completely forgot," Kathleen explained haltingly. "It's more like, sometimes, the memories of that time feel fuzzy—like remembering something in a movie, or a dream. And the older memories feel so much clearer. Not all the time, of course. But there are days—" She wiped her eyes with the back of her hands and even managed a slight smile. "—days when I'll actually listen for him at the door around seven. Wait for him to shuffle in, dump his boots by the stairs, hold me and kiss me for a long time. Wait for him to ask the same question he always used to ask as he got a beer out of the fridge: 'How was wrangling up the little snot-nosed ones today?'"

Rory reached out and took her tiny body in his arms.

"I miss him so much," she said, sobbing again.

"I miss him, too," Rory whispered. He could feel his eyes fill with tears. "Today would have been his seventy-sixth birthday."

"Can you imagine the jokes he would have made about the Sixers?" Kathleen said, making herself laugh through the sobs. "'I'm as old as their name and could still start for them.' Something like that."

Rory laughed, too. She was right, of course: between his wit and endless cynicism about the Philly sports scene, his father would have undoubtedly made countless jokes involving both his age and the hapless local basketball team.

"I think we should still make the cheesecake," Kathleen suggested.

"Agreed. A perfect tribute to dad." Rory released his mother from his grasp and looked down at the mess on the kitchen floor. "Why don't you get ready for the store so we can pick up another pan, and I'll put these things away."

Kathleen blew her nose and nodded. "It's a deal. Thank you." She kissed Rory on the cheek as she passed him.

Rory opened the kitchen windows and switched on the ceiling fan before bending over to begin sorting out the jumbled kitchenware and returning it to the cabinets. *Should I be leaving her alone as much I have been?* he wondered. *She's only going to get worse, right?*

With everything else organized and put away, Rory tried, unsuccessfully, to fit the baking sheets back into the narrow cabinet beside the dishwasher where Kathleen kept them. He gave a deep sigh and collapsed on the warm linoleum floor. *Crazy fucking day.* He thought about Kyle McCoy's heartbreaking memories, Mrs. Skelly's ghostly face at the door, the diminutive, silver-haired John Holling spitting out that disgusting rant. And then, coming home to this. *Crazy fucking day.*

Beads of sweat dripping down his forehead, he got back up on his haunches to try, one more time, to rearrange the baking sheets in the narrow cabinet so that the door would close completely and not remain a quarter-inch ajar. *How the hell did she have these in here?* he thought before giving up. He sat back on the kitchen floor and wiped his brow with his hand. *I just wish I knew what the fuck I was doing.*

Later that evening, with his mother watching reruns of *Law and Order* in the living room, Rory opened a beer and sat down at the kitchen table with his laptop. He checked his phone, expecting either a text or a missed called from Daniels, but there was nothing. He knew she'd left right from Kyle McCoy's to work a shift, which was most likely why she hadn't gotten back to him, but the thought flashed through his mind that maybe she was having second-thoughts about the investigation: maybe she'd realized the deeper she waded into this old case, the more she jeopardized her career, her future.

After all, unlike for him, there were actual repercussions for Daniels if the two of them happened to ruffle the wrong feathers— someone like John Holling's—or simply asked the wrong person the wrong question. As she had mentioned that day outside Cindy Thompson's apartment complex, her bosses at the police department would be pissed to learn she was actively working to undermine the outcome of the worst crime in town history. What would the consequences be if they found out? Demotion? Reassignment? An outright firing wouldn't be out of the question.

Rory kept his phone out on the table, just in case he heard from Daniels, but turned his attention to the laptop. He wanted to see what was out there about Holling's old business partner, perhaps even stumble upon an image to help him remember where he'd seen the man before. If he could find anything about Zeke—a social media profile he could contact would be ideal—even better.

Over dinner with Kathleen, the conversation with Holling had churned ceaselessly in his mind. The more he'd thought about it, the more he found Holling's sudden wrath less infuriating and more puzzling: it had gone well beyond mere annoyance at yet another reporter trying to exploit a local tragedy for personal gain. Rather, the vicious rant felt more like a defense mechanism, the way a cornered animal might lash out at an aggressor. Once Rory realized this, he kept coming back to the same two questions: Why had Holling felt so cornered? Was he hiding something?

But Rory also knew there was no way in hell he'd get any more information out of Holling himself. He could already picture that crimson face, hate dribbling from its lips, disappearing behind a slamming office door. He could already see the police car pulling up, the cantankerous-looking officers stepping out and approaching him, more than ready to lay hands on the man harassing the town's most distinguished and powerful resident.

No, going back to Holling was completely out of the question, of course; however, there were two people who still might know something, who might have some inkling of the secret John Holling was keeping if he, in fact, was. By reaching out to both Holling's son and old business partner, Rory hoped to discover even a hint of a missing piece to the puzzle.

His first few search attempts—*John Holling business partner, Hollingford John Holling business partner, Holling Chevrolet owner*—yielded nothing useful. He switched to Google Image Search, thinking he might be able to spot the somehow familiar face in an archived photograph and work backwards from there. But it was to no avail: all that came back were pictures of John Holling at various luncheons, community meetings, ground-breaking ceremonies, and charity functions. That vaguely familiar face in front of the Grand Opening sign at the dealership was nowhere to be found. He must have tried a dozen different search terms before slamming his beer down in frustration. "You've got to be fucking kidding me," he muttered to himself. "How can there be nothing?"

More surprising was how little he was able to find about Zeke. The old business partner was probably in his seventies, maybe even eighties, if he'd retired twenty-some years ago: it made sense he wouldn't have much of a web presence. But Zeke was young—midthirties, at the oldest. He was sure to have Twitter, Facebook, and LinkedIn accounts that, at most, a few minutes of searching would reveal.

But all Rory could find were two articles in the *Hollingford Herald*. One, from February 2002, announced Zeke's enlistment in the army. It featured several quotes from Zeke himself, explaining his desire to keep America safe and to personally slap the handcuffs on Osama Bin Laden, but little else. There was no picture. The second was from August 2008, before his third deployment to Iraq. There were quotes from his parents describing how proud they were of him and how they were going to pray for his safe return every single day. There were no quotes from Zeke this time and, once again, there was no picture. Rory tried Image Search and scanned carefully for the handsome young man in the green dress uniform Holling had shown him in the office. Not only did that image itself not appear, but Rory was unable to find any other pictures of the young man in the framed photo, or even photographs of anyone who looked remotely like him.

Rory drained his beer and sat back in the kitchen chair, arms folded, feeling defeated. *Weird. Really fucking weird,* he thought. He swatted irritably at a fruit fly buzzing around his head before grabbing another beer from the fridge. Formulating a new series of search terms to cast out into the vast, online ocean, he sat back down in front of the soft glow of his laptop screen.

Just then, the sound of his mother coughing from the living room caught his attention. He raised the beer to his lips and took a sip. *Dad's birthday. He'll be gone four years this November.* The empty Google search bar looked desolate, like an endless desert horizon, to his tired eyes. *Fuck it.* He closed the laptop. *This can wait till tomorrow.* He turned off the kitchen lights and went to go join his mother in the living room for an episode or two of *Law and Order.*

The nightmare came this time just around dawn. The familiar shore house being ripped apart by howling winds and bludgeoned by a relentless rain. Kevin and Marie huddling in the flickering lights. Nathaniel Foster watching from the shadowy back hallway in his First Communion suit. And Rory, standing in the midst of it all, paralyzed by fear as the windows shattered into millions of pieces, and a piercing scream—higher, louder, more desperate than even the sadistic wind—filled the small shore house.

Rory's heart was racing when he awoke and instinctively realized that the sounds from the nightmare—the shattering glass, the screaming—were actually coming from upstairs.

Twenty-Two

Rory's hands were shaking uncontrollably as he leaned over the kitchen table—where he'd placed the brick that had come crashing through Kathleen's bedroom window minutes before. Although he was wide awake and full of adrenaline—his heart was pounding in his chest—part of him felt oddly dazed, befuddled, as if the delineation between his nightmare and reality were still fuzzy. The seven or eight beers he'd downed watching *Law and Order* last night weren't helping.

Kathleen stood beside him in her bathrobe and slippers, a scowl on her face. "I'll get the light," she offered, and went over to flip the switch. Neither of them had thought to turn it on before. Instantly, the gray, shadowy kitchen became brightly—for a moment, blindingly—lit.

"Let's see what's inside," she said, returning to the table. She did her best to sound more irritated than afraid, but there was a slight tremble in her voice.

"You sure?" he croaked. His voice was still scratchy with sleep.

Kathleen nodded.

The brick itself was unremarkable. It was older, weather-beaten. The corners were chipped. It left an outline of powdery debris on the tablecloth. A thin layer of moss grew in its many small cracks and crevices. But around the center of it, a thin, white rope was tied. And wedged between the rope and the brick was a bulging envelope.

Rory slid the envelope out from behind the rope. The flap was bubbled up in places; it popped open on its own as soon as Rory removed the envelope from behind the rope. Unlike the letter that had been slid under the door last week, waiting on the hallway floor to be picked up, this envelope had nothing written on the outside of it. Rory carefully emptied it onto the table.

They both gasped when six copper bullets rolled out across the tabletop. "Holy shit," Rory stuttered.

Kathleen covered her mouth with both hands.

The bullets came to a gradual stop, pointing in various directions. Some had rolled all the way to the edge of the table, while others had barely moved from where Rory had dropped the envelope. They looked like corpses in an aerial shot of a battlefield.

With a tremulous hand, Rory reached out for the single piece of folded paper that had dropped out of the envelope along with the bullets. He opened it. As he'd feared, the note was written in the same neat print as the previous one.

> *Three for the old blood. Three for her son. The brain, the heart, the intestines. They must both keep the secret or else blood will soak through their mattresses and I will taste it on my tongue and rejoice. I'm watching. Day and night.*
>
> *-The Guardian*

Kathleen leaned on Rory for support. "This wasn't Billy," she said, her voice shaking. "Billy would never do this."

"Yeah," Rory whispered. He was still trying to make sense of the neatly written note laid out on the table before him, of the six bullets—one of which pointed directly at him—surrounding it.

"Who would do this? Who would do this to us?"

Rory wanted to say something comforting, something reassuring: *It doesn't matter, mom. The police will get him. No one's going to hurt us.* But as much as he wanted to, at first he was unable to say anything at all. More than fear, or dread, or paranoia, Rory felt a creeping sense of paralysis: it was not unlike the sensation from his nightmare, as the shore house groaned mournfully just before being dismembered and tossed into the endless black sky by the merciless winds.

Kathleen looked up at Rory, her eyes wide with confusion and fear. "Rory?"

Rory looked away from the kitchen table and down into his mother's eyes. He gave her shoulder a squeeze and cleared his throat. "I don't know, mom," was all he could manage. "I don't know."

Twenty-Three

Early morning light pierced through the stand of pine trees across the street from the house. The air was already thick and hazy. Rory could feel a film of sweat forming over his legs and arms as he sat on the front porch drinking a cup of coffee and waiting for the police car to show up. He'd thought about texting Daniels but, since he hadn't heard from her since calling yesterday, decided against it; she was probably enjoying a rare day off, and it would be nothing short of a dick move to interrupt that. Instead, he called the police station. The tired-sounding officer he'd spoken to promised to send someone over immediately.

Rory tried futilely to steady his shaking hands as he raised the coffee cup to his lips. He managed to take a sip before the coffee sloshed around too badly and he had to lower the cup back into his lap.

Who the fuck? he thought to himself. *And why?* His first idea had been John Holling, given the tenor of their conversation yesterday. But then, would the town patriarch really risk his reputation and status over thrown bricks and anonymous death threats? It didn't make any sense. Besides, what about the other note? It featured the same handwriting, the same disturbing language, the same signature—*The Guardian*—as this one and had been slid under the front door at least a week ago, long before Rory had even met John Holling.

Various faces floated to the surface of his mind. Dana Gladwell's seaweed-green eyes and wide, relentless grin. Kyle McCoy's sunken cheeks and strawberry blonde scruff. Cindy Thompson's stringy white hair and gray skin, both sickly-looking from years of absorbing cigarette smoke.

But just as quickly as the faces surfaced, they would vanish. Nobody he'd met since arriving a week ago had any reason to threaten Kathleen or himself, now or ever. None. The one possibility he kept coming back to—the one that caused his insides to tighten with dread—was that a deranged man, with no rhyme or reason, randomly picked a home to watch, and terrorize, solely for the pleasure of it. If that theory were true, and it was presently the only one that made any sense to Rory, there was no telling what this man might do next.

Rory put his coffee down on a plastic, patio end table and walked out across the dewy lawn toward the driveway. He turned around and looked up at the head-sized hole punched through the center of Kathleen's bedroom window. Spidery cracks radiated through the jagged glass that hung like fangs around the edge of the frame; a gentle breeze could have brought it crashing down on the sill to shatter into miniscule fragments. Luckily, the muggy air showed no signs of stirring that morning.

He was still looking at the shattered window when the police car pulled up to the curb behind him. When the car door slammed, he turned to see Officer Ackerman, the same cop who'd brushed off the note Rory had taken down to the police station, walking hesitantly toward him.

"Mr. Callahan?" he said sheepishly.

This fucking guy, Rory thought, but he offered his hand cordially. "Thanks for coming out."

They shook hands—even in the summer heat, Ackerman's handshake was cool and clammy. He looked ready to say something but then stopped, removed his cap, and ran his fingers through his short, black hair. "Look, I'm—" he began. He was staring down at his feet. "I have to apologize about last week. I really had no idea—"

"You did what you thought you had to," Rory said. "Self-preservation. I get it."

"I'm sorry." He looked at Rory with his coal-black eyes. He seemed genuinely contrite.

"Don't worry about it."

Ackermann replaced his cap and squinted up at the broken window. "How's your mother doing?"

"Scared, of course, but holding up ok. She's upstairs cleaning up the broken glass."

"Not hurt, is she?"

"No, thank Christ."

"Good," Ackerman said, sounding relieved.

Yeah, helps cover your ass, Rory thought.

They went inside so Rory could show him the brick, the letter and the bullets on the kitchen table—untouched since they'd spilled out of the crinkled envelope half an hour ago. The sight of them on the table was still jarring to Rory: he'd specifically gone outside to avoid looking at them, contemplating their violent intrusion into his mother's home.

"Jesus," Ackerman whispered, eyeing the bullets.

"And just in case the message wasn't clear enough," Rory said, tapping the note.

Ackerman leaned over to read it. "They're referencing you now," he observed.

Rory nodded. "Whoever did this must actually be watching the house."

Ackerman removed his cap and ran his fingers through his crew cut again. It must have been a nervous habit. "I'm going to take these down to the station. Might be able to pull some fingerprints from them. Let me run out to the car to get some gloves and evidence bags." He replaced his cap and turned to leave the kitchen, but paused instead. He dropped his head and sighed. "I'm incredibly sorry, again, for last week. If I knew this would happen…" His voice trailed off.

Rory was still mildly pissed about it, but he was starting to appreciate Ackerman's apologetic attitude. He also knew what it was like to be young, worried about your career, and eager to please your bosses at every turn. In his first year at the paper, his editor ordered him to abandon the article he'd been working on for weeks, one about the city's criminally underfunded rehab centers, to instead write a piece about some low-level employees in the mayor's office who'd been caught sending each other porn through interdepartmental mail. The story was complete nonsense, of course, but it would sell papers. Instead of arguing, Rory forced a smile and wrote the new article. He never got a chance to finish the one about the rehab centers.

"Like I said, don't worry about it," Rory said.

Ackerman nodded wordlessly before heading out to grab his supplies from the car. Within a minute or two, he was back.

"If we can get prints off them, who knows what we'll find?" he explained, pulling on a pair of rubber gloves and shaking open the plastic evidence bag. "Or if we make an arrest, prints could be hugely important."

Rory leaned back against the kitchen counter and watched as Ackerman methodically picked up each bullet with a pair of tweezers and dropped them into the bag.

"What kind of bullets are those?" Rory asked quietly.

"Hollow point. Particularly brutal," Ackerman said, carefully placing the letter, along with the envelope, into a second bag. He opened a third one for the brick. "State of New Jersey has a few regulations about buying them, but they're still pretty easy to come by."

Just as Ackerman was sealing the three evidence bags, a voice broke over the radio clipped to his belt. "Officer Ackerman, Chief McGarry has requested you call his office as soon as possible."

Ackerman removed the gloves and grabbed his radio. "Copy. I'll give him a call in a second." He nodded at Rory. "Just gonna drop these off in the car," he said, lifting the three transparent bags. "See what the chief wants. Be back in a minute or two."

"Take your time," Rory said. After listening to Ackerman walk down the hallway and leave through the front door, he slumped down into a kitchen chair and stared at the dusty outline of the brick that remained on the tablecloth. His earlier adrenaline had dissipated; now he just felt exhausted. He could practically feel the bags forming under his eyes.

The cup of coffee he'd left out on the porch was suddenly beckoning him. He was just about to get up to retrieve it when he felt a gentle hand rest on his shoulder.

"You doing ok?" Kathleen asked.

Without looking up at her, Rory patted her thin, bony hand. "Yeah. How about you?"

"All right. Got the glass cleaned up. I'll call the window guy when he opens in a bit."

Rory nodded absently.

"What did the police say?"

"Not much yet. He did take everything for possible fingerprints."

"Good. That's good." She squeezed his hand. "I'm glad you're here," she said.

"I am too, mom." Maybe it was the exhaustion, or the guilt, or the feeling of helplessness—having no idea who was terrorizing them and therefore no solution, no course of action to stop them—but Rory's eyes brimmed with tears.

At that moment, Ackerman came back into the house. He stopped at the entryway to the kitchen and quietly rapped on the doorframe. "Sorry to interrupt," he said.

He came over and introduced himself to Kathleen which, much to Rory's begrudging pleasure, seemed to comfort her.

"Thank you so much for coming out here," she said effusively.

"My pleasure, m'am. I'm sorry you've had to go through all this. Rest assured we will find the person, or people, doing this. I just received word we'll have an officer stationed on your block 24 hours a day for the next few weeks, at least."

"Oh, thank God," Kathleen said, placing her hand on her heart. "That'll help me sleep at night."

"Which is important," Ackerman said. "I know you're both understandably worried, but please make sure you take care of yourselves."

"That's good advice. We most certainly will."

"Now if it's ok with you two, Chief McGarry would like to stop by to talk to you, personally, later this morning."

Kathleen and Rory exchanged glances.

Glad to know they're taking this thing seriously now, Rory thought.

"Of course!" Kathleen said. "That's very kind of him to make time for us like that."

"Have you met him before?" Ackerman asked.

Both Kathleen and Rory shook their heads.

"Well, he's a great man. You're in good hands under his watch."

As Ackerman headed out, he promised to send an officer out as soon as possible to watch the house and the street. "Mid-afternoon, at the latest. And please call me if I can help with anything else."

They watched him from the front doorway as he walked across the lawn to his police cruiser. After a minute, he pulled away from the curb, and the house became suddenly, disturbingly quiet.

Twenty-Four

Neither Kathleen nor Rory was particularly interested in breakfast, so they put another pot of coffee on and sat in the living room to flip through the channels, finally settling on *The Price Is Right*. It was just mindless enough to keep them, to an extent, from dwelling on the swift and violent theft of their most fundamental sense of security—the security of being inside your own home. The plan seemed to work for Kathleen: within a half hour, she was snoring from her recliner. Rory, too, felt his eyes getting heavy, though he fought to keep them open. He found his gaze drifting from the pathologically excited contestants jumping up and down on the TV over to the bay window every time he heard, or even thought he heard, a car go by. He decided to lay his head down on the arm of the couch so his view would be directly out the window. But it was a quiet morning on a quiet street—maybe one car would pass every fifteen minutes—and soon he was nodding off.

Whenever he drifted into sleep, he was back in the storm-battered shore house. Only it wasn't the wind and sand that smashed the windows, splintering them into countless pieces, but bricks—dozens of them—each one carrying a bulging envelope, affixed by a thin, white rope. And each time he heard the awful sound of the shattering glass and the ear-piercing screams, he jolted wide awake to find himself in the sunny living room, his mother gently snoring and the sounds from the TV soft and indistinct.

Eventually, he sat up, downed the cup of now-lukewarm coffee to help shake off his drowsiness, and went to retrieve his laptop from the bedroom. Even though the bedroom was only one room over, he felt a sudden, swelling desire not to be alone, so he brought the laptop back out to the couch in the living room.

With a heavy sigh, he popped the screen up and, for a solid minute, stared blankly at it. He wanted to continue digging for information about Zeke Holling—more as a distraction than anything, to keep the horrible, soft, metallic patter of the bullets dropping onto the tablecloth from playing over and over in his head—but seemed to lack the mental energy to get started. After procrastinating by checking the weather, the headlines on *Philly.com*, and baseball scores from last night, he went to Google where, several times, he started to type in a search term only to delete it seconds later. Finally, he came up with a combination of words he hadn't tried last night: *Ezekial Holling Hollingford New Jersey United States Army 2002 Afghanistan Iraq*. And once again, nothing came back.

Am I really this stupid? he thought. *I give up.*

Before closing his laptop and looking for the TV remote, he decided, fully expecting to discover nothing, to Google *the guardian NJ death threat*. He thought there might be a chance, even just a tiny sliver of one, that someone, at some point, had received similarly signed threats and that, just maybe, the incident was recorded in a newspaper article, police report, a post on someone's blog—anything, really. But, as he'd expected, nothing relevant came up, even after he sifted through dozens of pages of search results.

Lacking the motivation for any further internet searches, he shut the laptop down and reached for the remote resting on the arm of Kathleen's recliner, careful not to wake her. After flipping through a seemingly endless array of infomercials and cable news talk shows featuring hosts who were all blonde, well-tanned, and exceedingly angry, he finally settled on *SportsCenter*. It was innocuous and at least mildly diverting—easily the best option for the circumstances.

And yet, he was only able to watch it for maybe five minutes before feeling restless. He got up, walked over to the window, and peered outside. The street was empty. *Do you really think this asshole would be back again already?* He shook his head and tried laughing at himself, but it come out as more of a pained grunt. *Maybe. He might not be completely rational, right? But still: you can't let him get inside your head like this.*

He decided to go upstairs and check Kathleen's bedroom to see if there were any pieces of broken glass she'd missed: he thought that doing something useful might be the best cure for his own, troubling thoughts. Her queen bed wasn't made—a rare sight—and the broken window made the entire room seem not only compromised, but irreparably damaged. It was the most vulnerable he'd felt standing in that room since the last days of his father's life, as he stood over that same bed and held his father's fleshless hand, wincing every time a labored gasp for air escaped from the bundle of bones resting beneath the blankets.

Rory knelt beneath the window to inspect the carpet. From the look of it, Kathleen had done a thorough job of cleaning up the glass: he only managed to pick out a few tiny shards from the carpet, visible only because the morning sun was beating down through the window, causing them to glint if he looked from just the right angle. He dropped the shards into his open palm, walked them over to the bathroom, and gently brushed them into the trashcan.

Just then, a knock came from downstairs. Although it was a quiet knock, it still sent a shot of adrenaline racing through Rory's system. *Who is that?* he thought, before instantly remembering the chief was supposed to stop by that morning. He tried chuckling at himself again, feeling embarrassed to be so on edge. *Get it together. Get it together*, he repeated internally as he hurried downstairs to invite Chief McGarry inside.

Rory opened the door to find a husky, pale-faced man in uniform raising a fist to knock again. He looked to be Rory's age—mid-fifties— and his slicked-back hair had the streaks of gray to prove it. Pock marks cratered his round cheeks, and a thick, brownish mustache crawled across his upper lip like the bristles of a poison ivy vine. He slowly lowered his hand and looked intently at Rory through thinly-framed glasses.

"I apologize," he said. "I didn't want to startle you with the door-bell." His voice was soft and high-pitched, practically falsetto.

"Appreciate that. And thanks for coming out." Rory shook the chief's warm, sweaty hand.

"It's my pleasure, Mr. Callahan."

"Come inside," Rory offered, holding the door open so McGarry could squeeze through. "My mother's sleeping in the living room, but we can use the kitchen."

"Your mother's home is lovely," McGarry remarked as Rory led him back to the kitchen.

"Thanks. I'll tell her you said so."

As soon as they arrived in the kitchen, McGarry plopped into a chair, which groaned under the sudden shock of weight, and dropped a manila folder he'd been carrying under his arm onto the table. "I understand she's been experiencing some poor health recently?" McGarry asked, looking up at Rory while caressing the tips of his mustache with his thumb and pointer finger.

"Unfortunately, yes. I'm just glad I can be here for her."

"That's wonderful of you. Really wonderful." His voice was melodic, almost soothing. "I'll keep her—and you—in my prayers."

"Thank you. I'll tell her you said that as well," Rory said, trying his best to smile. "Can I get you anything to drink? Coffee?"

"Yes, please. I take mine with three sugars and cream."

Rory turned and dumped the remnants of the earlier coffee into the sink so he could make a fresh pot.

"I don't want to take up too much of your time," McGarry said, "but, on behalf of the entire department, I really wanted to come out here and apologize in person."

"That means a lot." Rory's back was turned as he shook the ground beans into the filter and turned the Coffeemaker on, but he was listening carefully.

"I understand Officer Ackerman was made aware of an earlier threat slipped under your mother's door and chose to take a 'wait and see' approach."

With the water percolating, Rory turned to face McGarry. "More or less." *If you want to be euphemistic about it.* He thought about mentioning Daniels, her willingness to call in favors and pull strings to get a set of eyes on the house after Ackerman had turned him down, but immediately decided against it: it might have been an act of breaking chain of command, or at least insubordination. If Daniels had kept McGarry in the dark about it, it was certainly with good reason.

"There's something you must understand about our department—our entire town, really," McGarry explained in his smooth falsetto. His meaty hands were folded across his bulbous stomach. "We may project an image of suburban bliss, but I'm not going to sugar coat it for you: times are tough. We took a hit during the housing crisis we never really recovered from. Have you ever been out near Evergreen Terrace?"

"Can't say I have."

"Block after block of foreclosed homes. Been sitting empty for five years now. So whenever I hear politicians and people on the news talk about economic growth and being out of the recession, I look around and, frankly, I don't see it.

"And with that, sadly, we've also seen an influx of crime." He dropped his head in solemnity, causing a double-chin to bubble out from his neck. "Burglaries are up. Armed robberies, too. And now some unsavory outsiders are poisoning our community with drugs. Feeding off the despair and misery of people going through some hard times." He raised his head, his lips curled in disgust. "Using the vacant homes to sell from. Cook from even. Good, family homes now being used for such awful purposes. It makes me sad, Mr. Callahan," he said, shaking his head.

The kitchen was now filled with the warm, rich aroma of freshly brewed coffee, so Rory turned to prepare a cup for himself and McGarry. "Understood," he said, pouring in the sugar and grabbing the cream out of the fridge.

"So it's with no cynicism, but rather hope—hope that we can turn this community around, help it survive these dark days—that I tell you Officer Ackerman's actions—"

Inaction, Rory thought.

"—were for a reason. A necessary evil, so to speak. As seriously as we take each and every complaint, each and every call from our community members, we simply don't have the manpower to give equal time and attention to all of the incidents that get called in during a typical day. Dozens and dozens of them."

"I understand that," Rory said, carrying over the coffees. *And I understand you didn't even hear the self-contradiction you just blurted out.* "I wrote about city politics back in Philly for twenty-some years. The unending mantra for all government agencies was 'do more with less.'"

"Exactly. And thank you," McGarry said, graciously holding up the steaming cup of coffee as Rory joined him at the table. He blew on it before taking a sip. "The other consideration we've had to take into account concerns our most prized possession: our reputation. There's no doubt it's been tarnished of late—there's simply no denying that. So we decided that perhaps we could, even in a small way, help in restoring our once sterling image. Make Hollingford once again a shining beacon for families looking for a good, safe community to settle. So if we must be a little pickier in deciding how to classify, or if to report certain minor crimes, well…" He flicked his small, gray eyes up at Rory in a knowing manner and sipped his coffee again.

"The end justifies the means." *A philosophy that always blows up in your face.*

"Exactly," McGarry repeated, smiling weakly. "But rest assured, finding the person—the criminal—terrorizing you *is* a priority. And please trust me when I say, we will keep you and your mother safe."

Why does this guy seem more like a sleazy lawyer than a cop? Rory drank his coffee and nodded wordlessly.

"Now, a question I have to ask you—" He paused, licked his pasty, thin lips, and started over. "Actually, it was a question Officer Ackerman should have asked you, but I think he was feeling a little reticent, given your previous encounter." He smiled, revealing a row of tiny, yellow teeth, like kernels of corn. "I'm sure you've already run through a mental checklist, but can you think of anyone who might have a reason to be angry with your or your mother? Someone bearing a grudge?"

Rory shook his head. "My mother is the sweetest lady in town, and I've only been here a week."

McGarry watched Rory with his beady grey eyes and nodded. "So no arguments with anyone? Heated conversations? Even the smallest things can set some people off."

The image of Holling's red face, strings of spittle bursting from a mouth lined with perfectly white, perfectly straight teeth, automatically popped into Rory's head. He was able to quickly dismiss it, though, as he remembered his earlier conclusion: that it made no sense whatsoever—on any number of levels—for Holling to be behind the threats.

"None," Rory answered.

McGarry set his coffee mug down on the table and tapped the side of it with his wedding band. "Baffling," he said.

"So no one else in town has had this happen to them?"

McGarry shook his head. "Nothing that's been reported. My only guess—and this is pure conjecture, mind you—is that, perhaps, it might be related to our drug problem. Some of these drugs out there now, especially the synthetic stuff, can cause strange, often horrible, behavior."

Rory peered skeptically at McGarry over the edge of his coffee mug as he raised it to his lips. *In other words, he has no idea who's doing this, so he's making shit up.* He swallowed his coffee and asked, trying to disguise the derision in his voice, "Do you really think drugs would make someone do this—something so drawn-out and methodical? Watching the house, waiting until the middle of the night to deliver the threats. That takes forethought. Planning. Time."

McGarry held up his hand defensively. "Like I said: pure conjecture." He smiled and even chuckled to himself. "You leave the police work to us, Mr. Callahan. Whoever's doing this will be in custody long before he can do any harm to you or your mother." He lay his hand over his heart, adding, " That's a promise."

Rory tried to take comfort in McGarry's words, but there was something about the chief—the verbose, overly-polished language, the calculating grey eyes, the soft, sugary voice—that inspired more doubt than confidence.

"Speaking of police work," McGarry said, smiling again, "I hear you've been working on an investigation of your own. The Blueberry Hill murders?"

Rory felt his shoulders suddenly tighten and the black coffee sitting in his stomach churn, but he managed to appear unfazed. "Yeah, if you want to call it that. For an article I'm working on."

"I see," McGarry said, steepling his hands in his lap.

"How'd you hear about that?" Rory asked, nonchalantly sipping his coffee.

"When you've been chief as long as I have—twenty-five years last March—you tend to know everything going on in town, whether you want to or not."

Holling, Rory thought. *Who else would tell the cops about it? And who else would even have the ear of the cops, not to mention the chief, about something so insignificant?*

McGarry must have detected a hint of trepidation on Rory's face because he laid a hand on Rory's shoulder and shook it playfully. "I'm not here to discourage you—or even lecture you. In fact, quite the opposite." He turned, with some effort, toward the table and picked up the manila folder he'd placed there when he sat down. "This is something that's been weighing on me for quite a while now, and I thought you might be able to help me with it."

He opened the folder, producing a hefty case file. "I sunk hours, too many to count, putting all this together." He handed it over to Rory. "His name was Jacob Neville. An accountant with a wife and three daughters down in Anne Arundel County."

"Maryland?" Rory asked. He flipped through the case file as he listened, but didn't know where to start. There were dozens, maybe hundreds, of pages of police reports, court records, and transcripts of police interviews.

"That's right. Arrested and charged with the murders of eight boys, all between the ages of ten and thirteen. All of them sexually assaulted, killed with a blunt object, and buried in a shallow grave outside of town. He was found guilty on all counts."

"I remember this," Rory said. "Vaguely. The story went national, I think."

"Evil incarnate, that man," McGarry said, nodding toward the case file.

"And you think—?"

McGarry cut him off. "I have no proof of anything." He leaned in toward Rory, darted his eyes around the kitchen even though, besides Kathleen asleep on her recliner in the living room, the house was empty, and lowered his voice. "But there are some pieces from his case that align in interesting—very interesting—ways, with regard to the Blueberry Hill murders." He licked his lips before continuing. "Neville's *m.o.,* if you remember, was to tell his family he was going on a business trip, only to drive hours away, sometimes up into Pennsylvania, other times down to Virginia, but never more than three or four hours from Baltimore, to a small, suburban town he'd picked out in advance. He'd find a cheap motel to stay in and always check in under the same alias: Charles Rankin. A reference to some old movie.

"Then, he'd spend days watching the local elementary or middle school. Watch the children arrive in the morning. Watch them at recess. Watch them as they'd walk home at the end of the day. He'd get a sense of timing and patterns: which children walked with friends and which walked alone. He'd methodically pick out his victim and plan his attack. Figure out some lie to get them into his car, or else follow them down a lonely path through the woods, or along a quiet field, on their way home from school. Sound familiar?"

Shit, Rory thought. Questions were multiplying in his brain, but he wanted to hear McGarry out before saying anything, so he simply listened.

"Anyway," McGarry went on, "The towns he chose were so arbitrary, so unrelated, and the murders were spaced out over the course of a decade—not to mention the fact he was meticulous in cleaning up after himself—it took years for him to be caught. But he eventually slipped up in a small town near Harrisburg. Caught disposing the body of a twelve-year-old he'd offered a ride home to by pretending to be the high school football coach. Some deer hunters who'd lost track of time and stayed out past dark came across him digging a shallow grave for the body in the woods outside town.

"When he was caught, he told the county police he'd killed other children—many of them. Bragged about it really. Claimed he was ridding the world of 'monsters that had not yet transmogrified,' whatever that means. But he wanted the FBI to figure out exactly how many, and when, and where. And they did, eventually. Jacob's wife, once she got past denial, was incredibly cooperative: she showed the agents all her old calendars, all the weeks she had blocked off for Jacob's 'business trips.' They cross-referenced those dates with unsolved murders of pre-teen boys in the Mid-Atlantic, and maybe a dozen came up. They then pulled guest logs from every hotel and motel in and around the town of each murder, and sure enough, 'Charles Rankin' was checked in at seven different hotels, in seven different towns across Maryland, Pennsylvania, and Virginia at just the same time a boy disappeared only to be found in the woods, beaten to death, sometime later. Including the young man he was caught burying, that was eight total.

"Now here's where things get interesting," McGarry said, shifting his weight on the kitchen chair and leaning in even closer to Rory. "A few months after Neville's arrest in '95, after the story had gone national, I got a call from the manager of the Mermaid Inn, down route 54, that a Charles Rankin, who, according to her, looked remarkably like the Jacob Neville all over the newscasts, had checked into her hotel for about four days in February of 1992. She had the records still to prove it.

"At the time, I brushed it off. Did the manager down there at the Mermaid, an older woman named Joanne, really expect me to believe she remembered what this guy's face looked like from three years ago? She also had a reputation for jumpiness, and for stretching the truth. One time, she called 911 because she swore she overheard two guests loudly debating how they were going to rob and kill her as soon as they had the chance. It turns out, they were college buddies who'd had too much to drink and started arguing about sports—maybe where the 'murder the manager' idea came from. The responding officer asked her how she'd heard the conversation in the first place. Apparently, she had pressed her ear to their door because she thought they looked, somehow, up to no good when they checked in.

"So, I hope you understand why I didn't jump in my car and bolt down 54 to talk to this lady when she called. I assumed maybe she was trying to insert herself into this big, sensational narrative that was making headlines. The crime story *du jour*. Besides, we didn't have any unsolved murders in the area, so what difference did it make?

"Well, after a while, that phone call gnawed at me. Or, more accurately, while it didn't keep me up at night exactly, it stayed in the back of my mind to pester me, like a mosquito bite that never goes away. Just so I could be rid of it, I finally drove down there to take a look at her guest log." He stopped and pointed to the massive case file in Rory's hands. "If you don't mind, turn to the second-to-last page."

Rory flipped to it and looked down at a photocopy of a page from the Mermaid Inn guest log. It was hand-written in tiny, cursive script. And sure enough, from Tuesday, February 18th to Friday, February 21st, 1992, a Charles Rankin had stayed in a room with cable and a queen bed at a rate of fifty-nine dollars a night. He'd paid in cash.

"Jesus," Rory whispered, running his fingertips over the paper as if testing to see that it was real.

"My reaction exactly."

"But the timeframe doesn't work," Rory pointed out. "By almost two months. The boys disappeared on April 13th."

McGarry sighed. "You're right, of course. And there are plenty of other conclusions you could draw from that piece of paper that don't involve Jacob Neville killing our three boys. For one, we can't rule out the possibility that someone actually named, unfortunately for him, Charles Rankin did stay at the motel for those few days in February 1992."

"It's possible," Rory acknowledged. "Just weirdly coincidental that it fits the pattern of Neville's behavior. Hollingford is, what, maybe a three hour drive from Baltimore?"

"Two-and-a-half to three. Yes."

"And do you know if Jacob's wife had those days marked out in her calendar for a business trip?"

McGarry nodded gravely. "I was able to confirm with an investigator who worked on the case that, yes, he claimed he was away on business that week. And, to complicate matters, none of the murders linked to Neville—the confirmed ones, that is—were committed in February of '92. Which means he was free, so to speak, to pay a visit to Hollingford."

Rory scratched his stubble and looked down at his feet as he thought out-loud. "It's a random suburban town a few hours from Baltimore, a small, cheap motel, and, whoever this Charles Rankin is, happened to stay there while Neville was supposedly away on business. At least, according to his wife's calendar."

McGarry chuckled softly. "If it was an innocent guy who happened to be named Charles Rankin just looking for an inexpensive place to stay while visiting family for a few days, it's just bad luck."

"But you're right: it's possible," Rory said. "It's not a particularly uncommon name."

"The other possible explanation is that Joanne made the whole thing up and forged the page in the guest log." McGarry slanted his eyebrows and stroked the corners of his mustache. "There's that strange human desire to feel connected to tragedy, even tenuously. She might have been trying to create that for herself."

"But if she just made it up," Rory said, as he worked it out in his head, "then why not just make the date he stayed there April 13th? It would give the story some credibility, right?"

"You're right," McGarry answered. "And I've thought about that. Plus, there's no way Joanne could have known that Mrs. Neville had those days in February blocked out in her calendar."

"Good point," Rory said.

"But maybe she just got lucky." McGarry shrugged.

For a moment, the two men sat in silence, Rory scratching his chin as he considered the overwhelming number of angles this new scenario presented, and McGarry watching Rory with a slight smile at the corner of his lips.

McGarry cleared his throat, glanced down into his empty coffee mug, and wet his lips again. "It may take a slight stretch of the imagination," he said, "but I ask you to consider this scenario, Mr. Callahan."

Rory looked up, eager to hear what McGarry had to say.

"Let's consider for a moment," McGarry continued, "that it was Jacob Neville who checked into the Mermaid Inn on February 18th, 1992. Let's also consider that he parked in a remote corner of the Blueberry Hill Middle School parking lot each morning that week to watch the children arrive and was still there at the end of the school day when the children left for home. Perhaps he stayed even later. Perhaps he stayed until the end of practice for the school musical, which would have been in full swing at the time, and took note of the children who left for home after dark had fallen. Two children in particular—Nathaniel Foster and Christopher Fitzgerald—walked home through a dense stretch of woods behind the school, a place where they were alone, and isolated, and vulnerable.

"Maybe he had them marked and was ready to follow them into Sattler's Woods with rope to restrain them and bandanas to gag their mouths, when something—who knows what—spooked him. Maybe a custodian or teacher noticed him in the parking lot, knocked on his window, and asked what he was doing there. Maybe something back home in Maryland took him away from the task at hand. Or maybe he waited for the two boys to emerge from the school one night, watching from the dark playground, and they never did because play practice had been cancelled, unbeknownst to him.

"Whatever the case, he didn't get a chance to satisfy his bloodlust, so he returned home, depressed and disappointed. Weeks passed, and as much as he wanted to forget about the two boys from the small town in New Jersey, he couldn't. He obsessed over them, fantasized about assaulting them, then crushing their skulls in with a baseball bat. He needed to feel the ecstasy of killing them; he couldn't stand it anymore.

"So one night in April, after work, he tells his wife he has to stay late at the office, and drives straight up to Hollingford, right to the school he had watched so carefully that week months earlier. The timing is perfect: play practice is just letting out. And there they are, setting off through the woods on their way home. Only this time, there's a third boy with them. Neville knows that it's reckless, but he doesn't hesitate. With rope and bandanas in hand, he follows them into the woods.

"It's after midnight when he returns home. His wife and daughters are asleep. He takes an extra-long shower, making sure to rid himself of any blood spatter and dirt from struggling with the boys or from digging their grave. He crawls into bed and falls asleep instantly, not only because he's exhausted, but because he finally feels satisfied after weeks of frustration and disappointment. He wakes up in the morning, smiles as he makes breakfast. Kisses his daughters on the way out the door and goes to enjoy a normal day at work."

McGarry stopped to let the story sink in. The kitchen was intensely quiet. The gentle ticking of the clock on the wall seemed to thunder through the house like sonic booms.

"And unfortunately," McGarry said, almost in a whisper, "there's no way to question Neville himself about it. Used a razor on his wrists in January '96."

Rory let silence settle over the kitchen again as he thought. "Why are you telling me this?" he finally asked.

McGarry didn't hesitate. "Because the more I think about this scenario, the more possible it seems. Not only possible, but plausible. What makes more sense: a kid with no history of violence, no history of even touching a child, killing those boys? Or a serial killer who reveled in stalking and killing children? Our three boys were found buried in a shallow grave in the woods outside town, just like Neville's victims. That's a fairly significant detail, in my mind at least."

For the first time in their conversation, McGarry seem to lose his calm, unwavering confidence. His voice shook, and his gray eyes swam with tears. "And yet, I'm responsible for putting that first man in jail. A kid, really. He was still in his 20s. I'm responsible for ruining his life. For ruining the life of his mother. He's in jail on some weak—very weak evidence—for something I'm not sure he did anymore. I thought so at the time. When we found those videos in his closet, I was convinced. But now…now, I don't know anymore."

McGarry's sudden show of emotion, the boiling over of guilt and self-doubt that had simmered perhaps for years, caught Rory off guard. *Maybe he's not the soulless, career-obsessed robot I thought he was.* But at the same time, he was curious why, if McGarry had been consumed by doubt and guilt because of his theory about Neville, he hadn't done anything about it—why he let it eat away at him rather than talk to a judge or D.A. or even the FBI agents who'd investigated Neville. Why not go to Randall Thompson himself? Perhaps the information about "Charles Rankin" checking in to the Mermaid Inn would be enough to test DNA samples from the boys, from the apparent murder weapons, against Jacob Neville.

Rory retrieved a box of tissues from the counter and offered them to McGarry. "Thank you," McGarry said, removing his glasses so he could dab his eyes. "I'm sorry for getting emotional." He replaced his glasses and smiled in an embarrassed way.

"It's all right," Rory said before adding, gently, "You must have had this theory for a long time."

"I'm ashamed to say how long," McGarry mumbled, turning his eyes to the linoleum. "I've tried ignoring it, tried convincing myself it's so far-fetched, there's no way it could be true. And sometimes, I can ignore it, even for days at a time. And then it'll come raging back—I'll see Cindy Thompson wandering the streets with her fliers or get a complaint about her disturbing customers in a store—and I'll think of Randall's young, petrified face as he sat in court. I'll think of how his face must look now, how the years in jail must have hollowed it out, toughened it. Made it blank and senseless."

McGarry suddenly looked back up at Rory, his gray eyes burning with self-loathing. "Once they showed the jury those videos, there was no way he'd ever see the outside of a prison. And I knew that. And I thought that was justice." He motioned toward the massive file in Rory's hands. "I can't do anything with that, Mr. Callahan. I can't undermine my own department, my own D.A. I'd lose the respect of everyone who works for me, from my deputy all the way down to the rookie patrolman."

"Maybe not everyone," Rory said, thinking of Daniels.

"Enough of them to risk my job, or at least the ability to do my job well."

But by sitting on this information, you're not doing your job well, Rory thought.

"But if the information came from an outside source," McGarry went on, "if it showed up in an article…" He let Rory complete the thought.

"You could clear your conscience while protecting your career," Rory said.

"And free a man who never should have been convicted with such paltry evidence." McGarry licked his lips again. "It's a *quid pro quo* situation. You get an explosive article, I get peace of mind."

Rory nodded, trying to come up with an ulterior motive McGarry might have in turning the case file over to him, but was unable to do so.

"Conduct as much of your own research as you want. Use any of the details from that case file. The only thing I ask is to leave my name out of it," McGarry said.

"Of course," Rory replied, thumbing through the pages of the file. He felt dazed by all the new information McGarry had given him; he was simultaneously excited that his doubts about the state's case against Thompson were well-founded, but also strangely disappointed that his suspicions about John Holling and The Church of Christ's Healing Touch might not mean anything.

"You have a chance here to rectify my mistakes, Mr. Callahan. To save a life." McGarry's broad, bloated face was solemn. He removed his glasses, exhaled on the lenses, then wiped the fog off with a cloth he'd extracted from his breast pocket. When he looked back up, there were tears in his eyes again. "Not just Mr. Thompson's—" His silky, falsetto voice was breaking. "—but my own."

Twenty-Five

While dusk fell over the quiet street, Rory stood on the front lawn and sipped a tumbler of Jameson. From the corner of his eye, he glanced at the tan Camry parked across the street, perhaps thirty yards away. It belonged to the police officer Ackerman had promised would watch over the house for the time-being. Rory felt a momentary wave of guilt break over him—watching this sleepy neighborhood had to be the worst, most soul-crushing assignment imaginable—followed by an even stronger wave of comfort, knowing that he, and especially Kathleen, could sleep soundly and safely tonight. He sipped some more whiskey and listened to the tinny music from an unseen ice cream truck float through the yard from a nearby street.

Sometime in the late afternoon while Rory was poring over the case file about Jacob Neville, Daniels had called. She apologized for not getting back to him sooner: she and her boyfriend Derek had had a rare day when they were both off from work, so they decided to drive into Philly to eat dinner at a fancy restaurant and spend the night at a nice hotel. She purposefully avoided checking her work phone while she was away, but had heard about the latest death threat from "The Guardian," including the details about the brick and bullets, as soon as she stopped at the station that afternoon to check her schedule. Now she wanted to meet up not only to discuss the bizarre meeting with John Holling, but just to see how Rory and Kathleen were holding up.

"I could stop by around 8:00, 8:30, before my shift starts tonight," she'd offered.

"Yes—for the love of God, yes," Rory had said. "There's a lot we need to catch up on."

It was nearly dark when Daniels pulled up in her police cruiser a few minutes past 8:30. Rory was sitting on the porch with his tumbler of Jameson, which he raised to her as she walked up the driveway to the house. "Welcome back," he said. "You leave for a day and the whole town goes to shit."

Daniels laughed as she leaned on the railing of the porch steps. "How are you doing?"

Rory swallowed a sip of the whiskey and looked away from Daniels's caring brown eyes. "All right. My hands finally stopped shaking."

"Which window was it?" She tilted her head back to look up at the house.

Rory got up and walked out onto the lawn to stand next to her at the edge of the planter. He pointed up at Kathleen's bedroom window. "That one. On the left. Window guy fixed it this afternoon."

Daniels sighed and shook her head. "I'm sorry, Rory."

"Don't be. You did everything you could to help us after the first note."

"How's your mom doing?"

"Not too bad either. Calmed down a lot, but she was really shaken up this morning."

"Shit. I would be, too."

"They actually sent Ackermann out when I called. Officer Dickface, as you affectionately referred to him. If I remember correctly."

Daniels smiled at that. "You remember correctly. I stand by the moniker, actually."

"Fair enough," Rory said, laughing. "He was actually halfway decent today, though."

"Really?" She sounded genuinely surprised.

"Yeah. He seemed remorseful about ignoring the first note. Even got the wheels in motion pretty quickly to get someone out here to watch the house." He gestured toward the Camry across the street.

Daniel turned her head to look at the unmarked police car and nodded approvingly. "For a man born with a dick for a face, not bad at all."

Rory burst out laughing. It felt good to laugh. "Do you want to sit?" he managed to ask, walking across the cool grass back to the porch.

"Thanks." Daniels followed him up the steps and settled in the plastic patio chair adjacent to his. "So what the hell happened with John Holling?"

"Oh, what a shit show that was." Rory detailed his entire visit to Holling's office in the car dealership: how it started with innocuous pleasantries only to turn into snarling attacks as soon as Rory revealed he was writing about the Blueberry Hill murders. He also explained his maddeningly empty Google searches for any information about Holling's mysterious ex-business partner or his son Zeke.

"Sounds like he was trying to scare you away," Daniels said.

"Scare me away?"

"Yes. What were you discussing before he suddenly got suspicious and asked what your article was about?"

"I'm pretty sure we were talking about his son. He told me he's deployed with the army and showed me his picture."

"The son you can't find any information about online? Absolutely zilch? That's weird, Rory."

"It is," Rory agreed. "I thought at the very least I'd find a Face-book page, a Twitter. Anything."

"So maybe he's hiding something—maybe about his son, maybe something else—and figures if he spits a bunch of nasty racism and homophobia in your face, you'll want to leave and never talk to him again. I mean, who really wants to get into a prolonged conversation with a bitter, racist, homophobe?"

"True. If that's what he was trying to do, mission accomplished. I have no desire to speak to that insufferable prick again."

"Which is maybe what he wants."

"Could be," Rory acknowledged, taking another sip of his whiskey. "He also talked about protecting the families of the victims from media snooping and keeping the town's reputation intact. Maybe that's why he was trying to scare me away. Not so much that he's hiding something."

"Hmm," Daniels said as she thought it over. "He does have a lot at stake in ensuring the good fortune of the town—his own name, for one. So that makes sense, too."

"And then there's the business partner," Rory said, sounding exasperated.

"Seems like he didn't give you much about that guy."

"Not really. Just that photo of the dealership's grand opening." Rory slid an ice cube from the tumbler into his mouth and slowly crunched it between his teeth. "As strange as it sounds, I swear I've seen him somewhere, though."

Daniels sat up in her chair. "Here? In town?"

"I think so. It was recently, I know. But fuck if I can remember when or where exactly." He shook his head and sighed. "Don't get old, Jess." *And don't drink yourself to sleep every night either.*

"I wonder where he lives," Daniels said. "Assuming he lives in town."

"And assuming I actually did see him," Rory noted.

"It would have to be Northwest Estates, back in that little neighborhood of McMansions in the far corner of the development. Those are the biggest houses in town, besides the Holling Mansion, obviously." She balled her hand into a fist and gently bounced it off her knee as she spoke. "But I know all the families who live back there. As far as I know, none of them have any connection to Holling or the car dealership."

Just then, the screen door creaked open and Kathleen stepped out onto the porch.

"Oh, hello!" she said when she saw Daniels. "I was wondering who my son was talking to out here."

"Great to see you, Mrs. Callahan. How are you this evening?"

"Hanging in there. I'm sure you know all about the—" She paused to rearrange her words. "—what happened last night."

"I do."

"Even Billy Dannucci wouldn't do that. Not even Billy."

"I want you to know that you and your son will be safe here. We've got your backs, so you've got nothing to worry about."

Kathleen smiled broadly at that. "Thank you. For all that you do."

"It's my pleasure, of course."

"Are you planning to stay a while?" Kathleen looked from Daniels to Rory. "I've got some peach cobbler and vanilla ice cream."

Daniels shrugged. "Can't say no to that."

"That would be great, mom," Rory said. "Thanks."

"All right. Just give me a couple minutes." She turned to go back inside, the screen door closing slowly behind her.

"So on a scale from one to ten, how spoiled were you as a child?" Daniels asked in a low voice.

"She wasn't always like that. She could be scary when she needed to be." He took a long sip of his whiskey, diluted now by the melting ice cubes. "And with me, she needed to be scary more often than not. And besides," he continued, setting his glass down beside a leg of his chair on the uneven planks of the porch floor, "I'm sure your mom is the same way."

"It's true," Daniels admitted. "She's honestly heart-broken I'm moving out this summer. Sure, she's happy for me, of course—and it's not like I'm going far—but I've been living with her and my stepdad since college. It's a big change. For both of us."

"From what you've told me, she sounds like an incredible human being."

"She is," Daniels said. Her eyes were on the cluster of dark pine trees across the street, fireflies drifting slowly through them like sparks falling from a firecracker across a night sky. Her voice sounded distant, too. "She's my best friend. My inspiration. I've never known anyone stronger."

The screen door creaked open again, and Kathleen reemerged out onto the dimly-lit porch with two bowls in her hands.

"It's still warm," Daniels said excitedly as Kathleen set one of the bowls in her hands.

Kathleen handed the other bowl to Rory. "There's plenty left, if either of you wants seconds."

They both thanked her profusely.

"If you need me, the Phillies will be putting me to sleep in the living room," Kathleen said as she pulled the screen door back open and stepped inside.

"Have a good night," Daniels managed to say in between spoonfuls of cobbler. "Oh my God." She turned toward Rory. "This is amazing."

"My dad could cook, too: he'd pick up fresh vegetables and these unbelievably tender steaks from the Italian Market on his way home from work," Rory said. "Irish parents who could both cook—maybe I was spoiled as a child."

"My parents still save me a plate of dinner every night. Even when I work overtime and don't get home till one in the morning, it'll be there in the fridge waiting for me."

"Think you'll miss that?"

"Yeah. Derek's going to have to step up his game, that's all."

Rory finished his last bite of dessert and set the bowl down on the floor beside the empty tumbler. "There's something else I need to talk to you about before you go." His voice was quieter now, more urgent. "You've got to keep this one completely between you and me, though."

Daniels put her spoon down and set the bowl in her lap. "Yes. Of course."

"Chief McGarry paid me a visit today."

"McGarry?" A deep crease appeared across her brow. "Why?"

"Believe it or not, he wanted to help with the investigation. At least, that's what he told me."

Daniels's face contorted in puzzlement. "That doesn't make any sense. Why would he want to help poke holes in his own department's case?"

"Guilt, mostly. He thinks that Thompson might be innocent."

Daniels actually gave a small, mirthless laugh at that. "I find that a bit hard to believe. He was chief back in 1992. He probably hand-picked the detectives who worked the case. Why would he suddenly have doubts about it now?"

"If you want to believe him, he's had doubts about it for years now, mostly because there's another, credible suspect he's discovered."

Daniels gripped the arms of her plastic chair, whether out of anticipation or anxiety, Rory couldn't tell. "Who?" she asked breathlessly.

Rory told her about Jacob Neville—the methodical, carefully planned murders of pre-teen boys all within a certain radius from his home. He told her about Charles Rankin, the alias Neville always used at the cheap motels he checked into when planning and committing the murders, and how McGarry got a call from the manager of the Mermaid Inn claiming that a Charles Rankin had stayed there for four days in February 1992. He told her about the photocopy of the guest log and about McGarry's theory that Neville scouted the location and picked out his victims in February, but actually killed them two months later. And finally, he told her that if Neville had really killed Nathaniel, Christopher, and Andrew, that secret died in 1996 when Neville picked up the razor blade to slit his wrists.

The endless loop of cicada rattle—the slow build before the crescendo, then the sudden drop-off into silence before starting all over again seconds later—filled the silence. From across the dark yard, the street, bathed in yellow light from the lampposts, seemed somehow distant and set apart, as if Rory and Daniels were looking at it through a thick piece of textured glass. The wind chime hanging from the corner of the porch dinged and clacked softly in a slight, warm breeze.

Daniels took a deep breath before exhaling slowly. "Wow. Just, wow," she said.

"That was my reaction, too."

"I don't know whether to feel vindicated of frustrated. This could mean everything or absolutely nothing." Daniels's brown eyes were dark in the weak porch light as she looked at Rory. "What do you think?"

"I haven't had a chance to look everything over—"

"Everything?" Daniels interrupted.

"McGarry gave me this massive file about Neville. Court documents, police interviews—you name it. He wants me to use it for my article, leaving his name out of it, of course. Hopes it'll cast a new light on the case and maybe exonerate Thompson."

Daniels slowly shook her head in disbelief. "He really thinks Thompson is innocent. Maybe I've been wrong about him all these years."

"Why? What'd you make of him?"

"Career-obsessed asshole. Doesn't even acknowledge you around the station. I doubt he even knows my name."

"He got pretty damn emotional talking about Thompson. About feeling complicit in maybe putting an innocent man away." Rory sighed. "Then again, there was something about him that rubbed me the wrong way. I just can't put my finger on what it was."

"He's an asshole, that's what rubbed you the wrong way," Daniels said. "Unless, of course, he really does have a heart and some sense of integrity. I've misjudged people before. I mean, why else would he be doing this?" Daniels pinched the bridge of her nose and groaned. "My head officially hurts now."

"Mine, too."

Daniels checked her watch, and then sprang up from her chair. "Shit, I'm late for my shift."

"I'll take that off your hands," Rory said, reaching for her dessert bowl as he stood up as well.

"Thanks." She looked over her shoulder at the screen door. "Will you thank your mom again for me, too? That cobbler is good enough to create world peace. We should really contact the U.N."

"I certainly will," Rory laughed.

Daniels started down the porch steps, then stopped and looked back at Rory. "This whole serial killer angle is a mindfuck, and maybe even the truth for all we know. But don't give up on Holling, either. You've got to listen to your gut, and my gut, at least, is telling me that outburst yesterday is shady. I really think he was trying to scare you away from—" She hesitated, then threw up her hands. "—from something. But God knows what."

"Once again, good advice," Rory said.

He watched her drive away then glanced over again at the tan Camry sitting in the ethereal yellow light of the lampposts. He tried to let the wave of comfort that had hit him earlier wash over him once again, but instead he felt a steady, rising sense of coldness, of emptiness, even as he turned to go inside where his mother was watching TV.

Twenty-Six

It was mid-morning, and Rory had been sitting wide awake in bed for hours. His night had been long and restless: every time the house creaked, he would jolt awake and imagine a masked figure, knife in hand, standing just on the other side of his door, waiting for the right moment to come bursting in. At one point in the early morning hours, the sound of squealing tires had sent him racing to the window. When he'd flung back the curtains, he was momentarily, and embarrassingly, frightened by his own reflection in the dark window before he could look past it onto an utterly still street.

And even when he hadn't been on edge about every little sound from inside and outside the house, he lay motionless in bed, staring up at the ceiling while hundreds of disturbing details about the Jacob Neville case swirled ceaselessly in his mind. What haunted him most were Neville's own words from the police interviews: they were so cold, arrogant, and callous. Neville somehow convinced himself that his killings were morally imperative, and he seemed to enjoy being persecuted for them.

Before trying to fall asleep, Rory had spent a long time lingering over the school photos of Neville's eight confirmed victims, which McGarry had included in the file. The gap-toothed smiles, shaggy haircuts, brightly striped polo shirts. He couldn't help but think of his own son Kevin at that age. The obsession with *Pokemon* and *Guitar Hero*, the awkwardness around girls.

As he'd turned slowly through the photographs, he kept waiting for the faces of Nathaniel Foster, Christopher Fitzgerald, and Andrew Skelly to appear next, smiling up at him. They didn't, of course—but he was starting to think that maybe they should be in there, included among Neville's victims. Maybe McGarry's theory made more sense than anything.

Just after sunrise, he'd had a thought. Neville had spread his murders out to deflect suspicion: among his confirmed cases, there was always, at least, an eight month gap between them, and sometimes as much as a year and a half. It was an integral part of his *m.o.* and one of the reasons it was so difficult to track him down. So if Neville had committed a murder shortly before or after April 1992, it would be a huge aberration from his pattern and a strong reason to doubt McGarry's theory.

After that thought dawned on him, Rory had scrambled for the case file, which was on the floor at his bedside, and flicked the lamp on. According to the charges brought against Neville, he'd killed an eleven-year-old boy in Fairfax County, Virginia in October 1991, before killing a thirteen-year-old boy outside York, Pennsylvania in January 1993. A six-month gap between the Fairfax murder and the Blueberry Hill murders. It was shorter than Neville's typical quiet period between murders, but not short enough to put any major dents in McGarry's theory.

Ever since then, Rory sat upright in bed with the back of his head resting against the wall, watching the room slowly brighten as he tried to put the pieces of the Jacob Neville puzzle together in his mind. *There'd be no doubt about it—or at least far less doubt about it—if he'd checked into that motel in April. Would he really stay for four days in February only to drive back two months later to murder the boys? He didn't do anything remotely like that in any of the other cases. Still. It's possible. Those details—the pre-teen boys accosted while walking home from school, the shallow graves in the woods outside town... just the fact that a Charles Rankin stayed at a cheap, local motel at all—are all too similar just to be coincidences. Right?*

The longer Rory sat in bed thinking through the information in the case file, the more he agreed with McGarry—it must have been Neville. There was one question in particular McGarry had asked that played like a refrain over and over again in his head: *Does it make more sense that a kid with no history of violence, no history of even touching a child, killed those boys? Or a serial killer who reveled in stalking and killing children?*

Rory still had a hard time letting go of his suspicions about John Holling and The Church of Christ's Healing Touch, but as the morning wound on and approached noon, he began to. *I guess you can extend that question,* he thought. *What makes more sense: A wealthy, well-regarded businessman killing those boys, or a serial killer who reveled in stalking and killing children?* He sighed. *That question just sounds goddamned absurd. Just because someone is a racist homophobe and belongs to a creepy, fucked-up church does not make them a killer.*

As he slowly concluded that Jacob Neville was worth exploring further, and perhaps even writing an article about, Rory felt unexpectedly disappointed and couldn't figure out why. *This is probably the guy,* he thought to himself. *Spend a few months doing research, conduct as many interviews as possible, maybe I can confirm it. Or at least make a strong enough case to clear Thompson's name. Maybe even catch the eye of the Innocence Project, and who knows? They could, potentially, retest the evidence for Neville's DNA and find a match.* He stretched—sitting upright in bed had made his back sore—rubbed his eyes, and checked the clock on the night stand. It was a few minutes past noon. *Remember this all started when Cindy Thompson poured her heart out to you about her son. And you believed her. And now you have a chance to prove her right, to help her reclaim her son's name. To reclaim his life.*

Rory stumbled from bed and checked out the window. The tan Camry was gone, but a different car—a gray Honda—was parked in the same place. He assumed it was another police car, but decided he would go out to make sure after he'd gotten something to eat.

He shuffled into the kitchen, where Kathleen was reading a book, and headed to the fridge for a beer.

"Good afternoon," Kathleen said. "I guess you slept as poorly as I did."

"I'm sorry to hear that." He opened a Yuengling and sat down at the table with her. "Did you get any sleep at all?"

"Drifted in and out." She closed her book and rubbed her forehead tenderly. "I know the policeman said they'll keep an eye on the house to make sure nothing happens, but it'll still take me a few days to feel back to normal."

"Me, too." Rory took a long sip of his beer. "We could switch rooms tonight," he suggested. "Change of scenery might help you sleep."

"I'll be fine. But thank you."

Rory casually flipped through the *Philadelphia Inquirer* as he drank his beer. He heard his stomach rumble and thought about getting up to reheat a piece of leftover pizza from last night, but instead, feeling completely sapped of energy, decided to sit for a little while longer.

Kathleen groaned as she picked up her book again. "I'm going to take a nap after lunch—don't want to be completely exhausted for the concert at Saint Rose tonight." She reached over and gently brushed Rory's arm with her fingertips. "You still interested in going with me?"

Rory bolted upright: he suddenly remembered where he had seen Holling's ex-business partner before.

Twenty-Seven

Father George Santos's office, located off the first floor hallway of the rectory, was tiny and modestly decorated. Several family photographs adorned the wood-paneled walls, and a portrait of the Sacred Heart of Jesus was displayed prominently behind the desk. A small, wooden crucifix hung over the doorway. Early afternoon sunlight poured through a large window, illuminating a thick stream of dust motes riding a gentle breeze from the air-conditioning. The office, and the whole rectory for that matter, had an earthy, warm smell, seemingly inherent to all old houses.

"I wasn't expecting you until this evening," Santos said. He loomed over his desk, and was nearly as wide as it; Rory had forgotten how much the priest was built like a linebacker. "How are you adjusting to suburbia? It's no Philly, but I know the pace of life around here can be pretty break-neck."

Rory laughed at that. "It's going all right," he answered. "And to be honest, the quiet's not so bad after all those years in the city. I'm beginning to understand why my folks moved out here in the first place."

The smile disappeared from the priest's face, replaced by a look of grave concern. "Speaking of your mother, how is she?"

"She's hanging in there. She's tough, as I'm sure you know." Rory didn't mean to sound brusque, but he was eager to reveal the nature of his visit, to see if the priest could help him.

"Glad to hear that." He smiled again. "I'm looking forward to seeing her tonight at the concert. I'm not sure she can say the same about me, though: she's heard me sing before." He pantomimed covering his ears while making a face of utter disgust.

"I'm sure you're not that bad," Rory said, laughing again at the self-deprecation. "She's excited about the concert. Been talking about it for weeks."

"I'm covering a handful of George Harrison songs. I just hope I can do the man some measure of justice." Still smiling and chuckling softly at himself, Santos folded his massive hands on the desk. "But anyway, what can I help you with, Rory?"

Rory didn't hesitate. "There's a man I've seen a few times since moving here. He's always wearing a fedora and a pinstripe suit, always walking here, to Saint Rose, down Central Avenue in the middle of the day. I even offered him a ride once because I thought he might pass out from the heat, but he declined. Couldn't have been nicer about it, though. Do you know him?"

If the question perturbed Santos in the least, he didn't show it. He smiled casually and said, "Of course. His name's Henry Shaw: he's one of my parishioners."

Rory felt his heart leap in his chest. "Henry Shaw," he repeated, savoring the name that had eluded him the past two days. "Do you have any idea if Mr. Shaw used to work with John Holling? If they were business partners?"

Santos continued smiling, but his broad shoulders seemed to tense up, and his fingers, which were laced together, tightened. "As much as I'd love to talk to you about Henry, I'm afraid much of what he's told me about his past has been in the confidence of Confession."

Of course, Rory thought, feeling his heart sink again. "I understand," he said.

Santos tilted his head slightly and crossed his large, muscular arms. "You said you're doing freelance writing, right?"

Rory nodded.

"Do you mind if I make an educated guess about your interest in Henry?"

"Sure," Rory said. He answered with easy confidence, but could feel his palms begin to sweat: he had no idea where Santos was going with this.

"My guess is that you were minding your own business out somewhere when Cindy Thompson came up to you—probably with fliers—

talking about her son being wrongly convicted. You were either just intrigued, or bored, enough to listen to what she had to say, and it stuck with you. Your reporter instincts kicked in, so you did some research on your own, started talking to people in town about it, and soon began to realize she might actually be right: her son might be wrongly convicted. So now you have an article idea that's not only begging to be read and debated, but one that might even have social impact if it helps exonerate an innocent man. And all of that has led you to this office to ask about Henry Shaw."

Stunned, Rory could only stare blankly at Santos for a moment before clearing his throat and asking, "How did you know all that?"

Santos uncrossed his arms and smiled. "The archdiocese has reprimanded me on more than one occasion for not always—how did they phrase it? 'Sticking closely enough to the orthodoxy of Church teachings.' Their words, not mine. They said it's not 'priest-like' of me. Maybe. But I do know how to read situations. And people. And I think that's more helpful in being pastoral than throwing rules from the Catechism or ancient quotes from the Bible in people's faces."

I knew I liked this guy. "Couldn't agree more," Rory said.

"Listen." Santos rested his elbows on the desk and leaned forward. "I can't tell you much about Henry."

Rory sighed and looked down at his lap. *Catholic rules—they'll fuck you over even when you're not Catholic.*

"However, there's no reason Henry can't tell you about himself."

Rory's eyes shot up. "Really?"

"Henry is the kind of man who appreciates solitude. He doesn't even leave his house unless he has to. But he does walk here every day—every single day in that suit and fedora—so that I can hear his Confession." Santos reached into his pocket and extracted his phone to check the time. "He hasn't shown up yet today, but it's almost one, so he'll probably be here soon." He placed the phone on the desk and slid it toward Rory. "Give me your number. I'll ask him today if he wants to meet with you, explain to him why. I'll let you know what he says, either way."

Rory picked up the phone and enthusiastically punched his number into it. "Thank you, Father. You have no idea how helpful this is."

"I don't know what he'll decide to do," Santos said as he took the phone back from Rory and returned it to his pocket, "but I have a feeling he'll say yes."

As Rory got up to leave, he thanked Santos again before pausing. "Are you sure you're comfortable doing all this?" he asked.

Santos's gaze drifted up to the crucifix above the doorway before returning to rest squarely on Rory. "I may not be orthodox enough for the archdiocese, but I am a spiritual person: I pray for an hour each night before I go to sleep and for an hour every morning when I wake up. And for the past few months, God has been telling me something—telling me to do something. It's been driving me a little bit crazy, frankly, because I haven't been able to figure out what it is He wants me to do." He leaned back in his chair, glanced up at the crucifix again, and shook his head as if dumfounded. "I wish I could explain how, but when you stopped in here today and asked about Henry, suddenly, I knew what God has been telling me to do. I think I know why, too—and I think you'll find out for yourself soon enough."

It was three hours later when a call from Santos woke Rory from a fitful nap.

"He told me he'd be willing to talk to you," Santos said. He spoke slowly and seriously, and his words felt heavy. "Wants you to stop by tonight, around seven."

"So soon?" Rory asked, trying to shake off his grogginess.

"That surprised me, too. It might be for the best, though: if he waited, he might be more tempted to change his mind."

"Right," Rory said, rubbing his eyes.

"He gave me his address. Do you have a pencil?"

"Sure." He rolled out of bed and grabbed his notepad and pen from off the dresser. "Go ahead."

"He's at 210 Euclid Avenue. Described it as a small, brown duplex. His side has the overgrown garden."

Rory sat on the edge of his bed and scribbled the information down. "Got it. Thanks, Father."

There was silence on the other end of the line.

"You still there, Father?" Rory asked.

"Yes," Santos said. "God bless you in your work, Rory." And then he hung up.

Twenty-Eight

"I'm sorry about the mess," Henry Shaw said as he removed stacks of yellowed newspapers from his kitchen table. "I never get rid of the paper till I finish the crossword puzzle." He dropped an armful of the papers into a large cardboard box in the corner of the room and returned to the table for another load. "And as you can see, I rarely finish the crossword puzzle."

It felt almost surreal for Rory to watch the man from the photograph in Holling's office—the man he'd futilely tried to track down on the internet for countless hours—shuffle around his tiny kitchen.

"I don't have many guests over," Shaw continued apologetically. "Don't go out much either for that matter." He exhaled sharply, almost in a whistle, after depositing another stack of papers, then turned to open the fridge. "Care for a soda, Mr. Callahan?"

"Sure," Rory answered.

"And please have a seat. Make yourself comfortable."

Rory sat down at the table and watched as the old man removed two cans of Coke from the refrigerator. He then reached up into a cabinet for a couple of glasses before pivoting to the freezer to grab a handful of ice cubes, which clicked softly as he poured equal amounts of soda into each glass. He moved slowly and deliberately and always shuffled his feet when he walked, as if he were afraid he might topple over if he picked his feet up. His gray trousers and short-sleeved, collared shirt were wrinkled; his suspenders were twisted in the back. Even for a man well into his eighties, he seemed frail, but his face somehow retained its fullness and vivacity. His narrow blue eyes twinkled even in the low light of the kitchen.

"Now," Shaw said, taking his time as he placed the glasses of Coke on the table and lowered himself into a chair. "You want to know about John, huh?"

"Whatever you feel comfortable sharing." Rory turned to a new page in his notepad and uncapped his pen.

Shaw waved his finger toward the notepad. "And this is for a newspaper article?"

"Yes," Rory said. "Is that something you're ok with?"

"It's why I'm doing this. I'd been waiting years for God to give me a sign to do the right thing. I just never thought it would come directly from a priest during Confession. I guess God doesn't always work in mysterious ways—sometimes He can be about as subtle as a kick in the butt." He smiled playfully.

"Were you and Mr. Holling business partners at one time?"

Shaw took a long drink of his Coke and nodded solemnly as he swallowed it. The soda fizzed softly when he set it back down on the table. "For thirty years," he answered.

"How did you meet?"

"We met at Wharton. I was in the MBA program. John was only an undergrad, but he was taking graduate-level classes just for the hell of it. We started talking after class one day—a course on the fundamentals of entrepreneurship—and ended up at a bar, where we drank and shot pool for hours. Talked about all the business ideas we had, how we both planned to strike it rich and retire young.

"We became friends after that. He was my only friend in Philadelphia, really: all my college pals were back home in Toledo, which was not exactly a short train ride away, you see. And he knew the city—all the best restaurants, clubs, theaters. Even though he was younger, he looked after me in a way.

"Eventually he convinced me to move out to Hollingford with him after we both graduated in '61—him with his BA, me with my MBA. Promised to get me a job through his family. Explained there was real money to be made in mini-malls and real estate out in the suburbs. And I believed him, so I followed him out here. Even convinced my wife Julia, still my fiancé at the time, to come out here with me, even though all our friends and family were back in Ohio.

"And for many years, times were good. His family gave us a generous loan to help us start a commercial real estate company, and we made a fortune building up the White Horse Pike with strip malls and shopping centers. A year before they finished the expressway, we opened a handful of fast food restaurants and gas stations right off the exit; you've probably seen for yourself how packed they are during the summer months. John moved into his family home—you've probably seen that, too, all the way from the expressway—when his mother passed away in the early seventies. And I bought a sizeable new house out in Northwest Estates for Julie and me. Had a second home, a beautiful old Victorian, down in Cape May, too—block off the beach."

Rory's fingers were cramping from all the notes he was taking. He paused and shook out his hand. "Did you stay pretty close with Mr. Holling throughout those years?"

Shaw stroked his beardless chin before running a hand through his tuft of wavy white hair. "We were good friends for a long, long time. But things started to change around 1979. Whenever I think back on it now, that year stands as the beginning of the end, in my mind. That's when the rumors started."

Rory gripped his pen tighter. *Here we go.* "Rumors?" he asked.

Shaw looked down at his hands resting in his lap and picked at the corner of one thick, yellowed thumbnail with the other. When he looked back up, his narrow eyes seemed somehow smaller, as if they'd shrunken into his skull. "John got married a couple of years after we'd graduated, to a woman named Elizabeth. Frail, waifish little thing. Like a moth. Very sweet and quiet, but not John's type at all. Back in Philadelphia, he preferred the loud, voluptuous girls who could keep up with him at the bar. Elizabeth, on the other hand, would barely speak above a whisper and would get nauseated at even the thought of liquor."

"How did they meet?"

"Through his family. Her father was a trustee at Penn and a good friend of John's family, so John and Elizabeth had known each other since they were children." Shaw sighed and took another drink of soda. "He called her up for a date one night maybe a year after we'd moved out here. They dated long distance for a month or two—she lived out on the Main Line—before he proposed. Six months later, they were married."

"That was fast."

Shaw laughed darkly. "No kidding: my head was practically spinning from the whole thing. I actually asked him once after he'd proposed—we were both drunk—why he was marrying Elizabeth. The few times I'd seen them together, they acted like strangers. There was no warmth there. No love. At least, it seemed to me. And I'll never forget his answer. He got all worked up and told me, practically screamed at me, that it was a moral obligation. He said the intermingling of the classes, and especially the races, would spell the end of America as we know it. Having children by Elizabeth, he told me, would ensure the survival of the true America, as he called it.

"I got quiet after that. Neither of us ever brought it up again. I always chalked it up to the alcohol, but in the back of my mind, even now, I can't help but believe he meant what he said that night."

I think you're right about that, Rory thought, still jotting down notes furiously.

"As the years passed," Shaw continued, "I saw Elizabeth less and less out in public. She rarely spoke or even made eye contact, but she would at least accompany John out to dinner with Julie and myself every so often. Then, after she and John moved into the Holling mansion, I don't know if I ever saw her out of the house again. She'd fallen ill with some disease that left her in constant, excruciating pain. Could barely get out of bed to use the restroom, from what I understood. The times I'd go visit her, she'd be buried in this massive pink bed with just her fair, blonde head poking out from under the covers. Usually she'd be sleeping, but sometimes I'd come into the room to see her smiling at me ever so slightly.

"I can't remember exactly when it began, but sometime after Elizabeth's illness, John began making every excuse imaginable to go down to the diner over on Central, which his family had owned for decades. Ever since we'd moved out to Hollingford, he rarely set foot through the door of that diner, but suddenly he was stopping in there whenever he had the chance. Wanted to see how the manager was holding up. Double check the books. Eat breakfast, lunch, or dinner there, even if he was alone.

"I went with him once for breakfast, and suddenly knew why he'd been spending as much time there as he possibly could: it was to see a waitress named Annalisa. Very pretty young lady: dark, curly hair. Big, brown eyes. He never said anything to me about her, but he never had to either. I could tell from the way he talked to her, flirted with her, stared at her, that he was obsessed. For her part, she seemed nervous but flattered by the attention. This was one of the richest men in the state flirting with you—he owns the restaurant you work in. Hell, the town you work in is named after his family. Not sure what else you can do but be nervous and flattered.

"John's frequent visits to the diner went on for months, until one day they came to a sudden end. It wasn't a gradual tapering off: he went from visiting that diner several times a day, to not at all—didn't even mention it again. At first I just assumed he'd lost interest in Annalisa, or even better, started coming to his senses and realized that there was no way in hell he was going to be unfaithful to his sick wife.

"But then, a few weeks later, when I stopped in to the diner for a quick cup of coffee and a piece of pie, Annalisa was nowhere to be seen. I'm not sure why it gave me a funny feeling in my stomach, but it did. I asked another waitress where she was—did she just have the day off?—and she told me Annalisa had moved up to North Jersey to be with her father. He'd had a stroke, and she wanted to be there to take care of him.

"The explanation made sense to me. And it made me sad for John: he'd only stopped going to the diner because Annalisa was gone, not because his conscience had broken through the chains of temptation. Other than the ugly comment he'd made about the 'mingling of races' before his wedding with Elizabeth, it was the first time I felt serious disappointment in him. But it wouldn't be the last.

"When Ezekiel was born not long after that—"

Rory looked up from his notepad at the mention of Holling's son, the other person who'd eluded him in his internet searches.

"—the whispers started. See, no one, including myself, had seen Elizabeth pregnant. John told me about the pregnancy one day at work, almost in passing. When I stood up and shook his hand and congratulated him, he seemed more embarrassed than happy. I asked when I could visit her, and John quietly demurred, saying she was too sick for any visitors.

"So perhaps it was understandable that people started talking, speculating, when the birth announcement appeared in the *Hollingford Herald* a few months later. I'd overhear them gossiping about it at the supermarket and the coffee shop. Wondering how such a frail, sick woman could carry a baby to term with no complications. Hypothesizing that John must have stepped out of the marriage and was keeping it quiet. I never said anything to these people, but it made me angry. John was their neighbor, a community leader—actually, *the* community leader. Those people probably had jobs because of him. And he was my friend. He wasn't some scandal-ridden celebrity living out in Hollywood. How could they say such things about him?

"It made me so upset, I avoided going to the supermarket and coffee shop as much as I could. I'd drive all the way down to the Acme in Egg Harbor for groceries, make my coffee at home. And, eventually, as rumors do, they died down and I began to forget about them myself. Until I saw the baby.

"I can remember that moment like it was yesterday. Ezekiel was maybe six months old when John finally allowed me to see him—I'd been asking about it constantly ever since he was born, and John always had some sort of excuse for why I couldn't come over to meet him. I guess he'd finally run out of excuses, or realized I was going to see him eventually, so might as well get it out of the way.

"The housekeeper let me into the mansion on that cold, March afternoon. I heard the baby crying as soon as I came in. John was sitting on one end of an enormous living room, and Ezekiel was in his cradle on the other side. John barely looked up from the paper he was reading when I walked in.

"'Hello, John,' I said.

"'Henry.' His eyes looked especially piercing and cold from over the top of his newspaper.

"'Where's Elizabeth?' I asked. 'I'd love to congratulate her.'

"'She's still in bed. Not feeling up for any visitors today.'

"Meanwhile, the baby was crying and crying. And John was just sitting there, ignoring him.

"I went over to the cradle to see if I could help with the crying, and there was the baby: dark-haired and dark-eyed. In fact, his hair was rich and curly, just like Annalisa's, the waitress from the diner. And I instantly knew. I looked over my shoulder at John, but he was buried in the paper again.

"I picked the baby up to see if I could calm him down—my sister back in Toledo had children, so I had some experience with infants—and his diaper was soaking wet.

"'John, I think Ezekiel needs a change,' I said.

"He shrugged. 'Susan will get to it.' Susan was the housekeeper.

"I turned to the doorway, feeling bewildered. And there was Susan standing a few feet outside the living room, her eyes shimmering with tears; John had ordered her not to help the baby, and I knew it. I could feel a lump of rage forming in my throat.

"'I'm going to take care of it now,' I barked. 'Where are the diapers?'

"John seemed temporarily taken aback by my tone. But then the hard look reappeared, and he lifted a hand toward the hallway. 'The changing room is back there.'

"I practically ran down the hallway with the screaming baby in my arms and Susan right at my heels. We changed him and gave him a bottle, which he slurped down in seconds. He soon quieted down and even fell asleep in my arms.

"John barely acknowledged me again on my way out, and I was too angry to say much to him either. At the front door, I gave Susan my phone number and told her to call me if things got worse.

"'Sometimes I don't know what to do,' she told me. She was practically sobbing. 'Sometimes he's crying and crying, and Mr. Holling yells at me when I try to take care of him.'

"'Christ,' I muttered.

"'But most of the time, he doesn't seem to care what happens.' She wiped away a tear. 'I think I'll be ok. I think I can take care of him.'

"I left the mansion that afternoon more furious at John than I'd ever been before. And the image of the brown-eyed, black-haired baby, born to blue-eyed, blonde-haired parents, was seared in my memory."

There was a slight clank from the ice in Shaw's Coke as he lifted it to his lips for a sip. Other than that, the kitchen was silent. Rory had forgotten about his own soda; the ice cubes had melted down to tiny chips, and beads of condensation covered the sides of the glass like raindrops spattered on a window. Afraid he would miss part of Shaw's story, he'd also stopped taking notes and just listened.

"So you're sure Zeke is not Elizabeth's?" Rory asked.

"Positive," Shaw answered without hesitation. "I don't know where he put that waitress up while she was pregnant, or how much he gave her to keep her quiet, but I know that he did."

"Did John warm up to Zeke as he got older?"

Shaw shook his head sadly. "He was downright cruel to that boy. Would pick apart everything he said or did. Would call him stupid, ugly—tell him to shut up—right in front of me. See, Ezekiel was an embarrassment to John—an inescapable product of his shameful act. When John couldn't hide him away, he would berate and humiliate him, until he was old enough to send away to military school."

The Christian thing to do, Rory thought.

"And like I said before, it was right around then that John began changing to the point where I didn't recognize my old friend. He started going to that wackadoo church down at Crystal Lake. Tried to convince me to go with him at every possible turn, till I finally put my foot down and told him I wasn't comfortable talking about religion at work.

"He became more ruthless in his business practices, too—even criminal. He'd threaten and bully anyone who didn't comply with his wishes. One time, around '85 or '86, he had his eye set on this old family farm right off the business district on the White Horse Pike. He thought the property was worth millions, either as a housing development or as a location for a Wal-Mart or a Target. He was right, of course: that was prime real estate. When the family turned down his offer to buy the land, he used his friends on town council to stick them with tens of thousands of dollars in fines and fees. There were inspectors from the government going out there every other day, finding some new or unheard of regulation broken. He got the council to pass a massive property tax hike on privately owned land over a certain acreage: it was a direct, unabashed attack on this one family. They finally got so inundated with fines and taxes, they were forced to sell to us at a fraction of John's original offer.

"Now, John had always been an aggressive businessman, but this was new territory for him. Up until then, he'd always valued the community and the people of town. He was proud to see all the new jobs we'd helped create, all the opportunity we'd brought to Hollingford. I never thought I'd see him sink his teeth into regular, working people like that. I never thought I'd see him cannibalize his own community for the sake of profit. And yet, there he was. And it wasn't an isolated incident, either.

"I somehow managed to keep a decent working relationship with John going through this time, although our personal relationship had deteriorated to a shell of its former self. It wasn't until that one night, the night you came here to talk to me about, Mr. Callahan, that I decided I needed to exorcise John from my life completely. It was April 13th, 1992."

Although it was warm in the kitchen, Rory felt goose bumps pop up on his forearms. He picked up his pen again and was surprised to find that his hand was shaking; Shaw's sudden arrival at this crucial juncture left him unexpectedly nervous. He swallowed and asked, "So what happened that night?"

Shaw sighed, leaned back in his chair, and rubbed his hands anxiously. He looked down at Rory's notepad. "Please make sure you get this all down," he instructed. "If it helps right a wrong, please make sure you write down every last detail."

"I will," Rory promised.

"Even though, by 1992, John and I rarely to spoke to each other about anything other than work—and even that had become strained—he still had me over for dinner at the mansion once a month, primarily to discuss business matters. It was a tradition that started back when I first moved to Hollingford, and it had somehow survived all those years later. In the early days of our friendship, I would stay for hours; we would go through several bottles of wine and reminisce fondly about our time in Philadelphia, rant and rave about politics, crack each other up with dirty jokes. By 1992, all warmth and friendliness was gone from the monthly invitation. It felt more like an obligation that neither of us was happy to fulfill, but did anyway just for the sake of fulfilling it.

"On April 13th, we were finishing up dinner—I couldn't have been there for more than an hour and was already feeling eager to leave, which was typical by this point in our relationship—when someone started pounding on the front door. That pounding still echoes through my memory when I'm falling asleep at night: it was so desperate, urgent, frantic. John wiped his mouth with a napkin and excused himself to see who it was. He returned about five minutes later, with a look on his face that was somehow full of rage and utterly terrified at the same time. I'd never seen him like that before. Or since.

"'There's been an emergency,' he said. He was rattled, clearly, but was trying to sound calm. 'Please, take your time finishing up dinner, but I likely won't be back for several hours.'

"Before I could say or ask anything, he was gone. I did what he said and took my time finishing my meal. Oddly, I remember feeling relieved that John was gone, that I didn't have to sit through any more forced conversation or long, awkward silences with him. Dinner was far more enjoyable after he'd left.

"Eventually, I saw myself out and went home. I was curious about what the emergency was, where John had gone. The more I thought about it, the more worried I became. I kept imagining different scenarios, each one more horrible than the last. And who had it been, pounding on the door so frantically? What was so wrong that John had to leave immediately, and for several hours? I remember having a difficult time falling asleep that night.

"At around midnight, I got a phone call from John. It awoke me from an uneasy sleep.

"'Hello?' I mumbled.

"'Sorry to wake you, Henry,' John said quickly. His voice sounded strange. It was hoarse and had a sharp, bitter edge to it. 'I just wanted to apologize for leaving you so abruptly, but everything's ok.'

"'What happened?' I asked.

"'Ezekiel and some friends had stolen a bottle of gin from my liquor cabinet,' he explained. I had honestly forgotten Ezekiel was home from the military academy for spring break; John rarely talked about him, of course. 'They were drinking it down at the park, when one of his friends collapsed from alcohol poisoning. But I got him to the hospital, and he'll be fine. Everything is fine.'

"'Ok,' I said, confused about why he felt obligated to call me.

"'I'll see you at the office tomorrow morning.' He hung up after that. The next morning, John seemed tired, but essentially back to normal. He didn't mention one word about the previous night that day, or ever again.

"When news spread of the three missing boys, it made me sick to my stomach. I was worried for the boys themselves, of course, but I also couldn't shake everything that had happened the night before: the urgency of the pounding on the door, the look on John's face when he returned to the dining room, the edge in his voice when he'd called me at midnight. It wasn't sitting right with me for some reason. The idea, however absurd, however nonsensical, however unrealistic, popped into my head that John had something to do with the disappearances and, as much as I tried to convince myself of the madness of that thought, as much as I tried to laugh it off, I somehow couldn't. It started to haunt me.

"Wanting to rid myself of the absurd notion, I called the hospital to see how the young man with alcohol poisoning was faring. No one had been admitted for alcohol poisoning, the nurse told me. Desperate now, feeling a cold sweat break out on my back, I called every hospital in the area: no young men had been admitted for alcohol poisoning in the last twenty-four hours. John had lied to me, and I was becoming increasingly horrified as to why.

"A few days later, when it was clear something awful had happened to those boys, Chief McGarry paid me a visit at my house. Do you know him? Big fellow, very high-pitched voice. Kind of looks like a walrus."

Rory nodded wordlessly. He was transfixed by Shaw's story.

"Well, I'm sorry to hear that. He's a nasty, corrupt, arrogant man. John hand-picked him for chief of police, just like he did everyone on town council. So he was John's little sock puppet. Always has been, always will be."

So the whole visit—all the information about Jacob Neville—was just to throw me off the scent, Rory thought.

"Anyway, without warning, McGarry pays me a visit at home," Shaw went on. "I found that very strange. Very alarming. See, I'd never called him or asked to talk to him. I'd never bring that on myself voluntarily. But he sits me down, helps himself to my coffee, and in a very round-about way, tells me they already have a suspect: a violent child molester who lives in town with his mother. He tells me any theories or ideas I may otherwise have—for whatever reason imaginable—would only harm the reputation of the community and complicate the investigation into the obvious suspect, if I made them public.

"Very patronizingly, he asks me, 'And you wouldn't want to hurt the reputation of this town, or endanger its people, would you?'

"'Of course not,' I tell him. I know in my heart he means 'John's reputation,' though.

"'Good,' he says to me. 'Good.' He licks his lips like always does when he talks. 'You're not local, but you've done well here. Hate to see business suffer because Hollingford's reputation gets ruined.' And then he leaves without saying another word.

"I know the visit was meant to scare me, to keep me from saying anything about John's strange behavior the night those boys disappeared—and I know John sent the chief over to say those things to me. Which, in the end, only made me realize John did have something to hide. Something important. Why else would he send McGarry over to threaten me like that?

"You know what happens next, Mr. Callahan: they arrest and convict Randall Thompson, and everyone can sleep well again at night. And as for me—" He stopped, balled his bony hand into a fist, and gently hit his chest with it several times; it made an empty thud every time it landed. "I took the coward's way and actually listened to McGarry. I stood idly by and did nothing. Until tonight, I've told no one, besides Father George in Confession, about my reprehensible silence.

"There's no justification for keeping silent, but for a time, I was somehow able to accept it. I knew that John, as unethical as he'd become, was the lifeblood of Hollingford and that saying anything about my suspicions could ruin him, and maybe the town in turn, just like McGarry said." Shaw paused and scratched his head. He smiled sadly. "I guess that didn't make much of a difference in the end, given how badly the town is getting along these days."

"You did what you thought was right," Rory said.

"Maybe," Shaw acknowledged. "But I found other ways to rationalize it, too. When they did convict Thompson, when they found those video tapes in his bedroom, I thought maybe that night—the pounding at the door, that look on John's face, the lie about the alcohol poisoning—had meant nothing. Even if Thompson wasn't guilty, I told myself, he should be in jail anyway. Maybe he didn't kill those boys, but he could very well hurt other children if he were free.

"But as soon as that woman, Thompson's mother, began hanging flyers all over the place, talking to everyone is town, ringing doorbells, it was a reminder of my failure, my cowardice. Seeing her roaming the streets, dedicating her life to winning her son's innocence, made the guilt grow inside me like a cancer. I couldn't bear to see John's face anymore, hear his voice—every time I did, I thought of the look on his face that night, that mix of anger and fear. I remembered the hoarseness, the edginess in his voice from that phone call.

"I finally, pathetically, disgracefully even, retired, just to be done with John. I sold the old house—it was far too large for just myself—and moved in here. I'd considered moving back to Toledo, but everyone I once knew there was gone. My wife Julie had passed away in 1990. I had no one and nothing, and I didn't want anyone or anything except solitude—to be hidden away from the reminders of my inaction.

"So I never leave the house, except for Confession, and I never talk to anyone but Father George." Shaw sighed deeply, mournfully. "And yet, to this day, I believe my once-friend and business partner killed those three boys on April 13th, 1992. And I did nothing to bring him to justice."

Shaw's face, which had been so vibrant and lively earlier that evening, now looked drained and wan. He managed a small, lopsided smile. "And now," he whispered weakly, "it is out of my heart and into God's hands."

Twenty-Nine

But why? What's Holling's motive? Rory thought to himself over and over again on the drive home. *Could the rumors about Christ's Healing Touch really be true? Shaw said Holling changed around the time he got involved with them. Maybe the person pounding on the door that night was someone from the church summoning him to the ritual killing? That's insane, though. Right? Christ's Healing Touch is just creepy, not homicidal. As Daniels said, that's a pretty big difference.*

Rory pulled into the driveway and shut the engine off, but remained in the car for a few minutes as he processed everything Shaw had just told him. *Shaw's story makes Holling sound pretty fucking suspicious, but does it really mean anything? It doesn't provide any actual evidence, or even an account of actual evidence. It would be different if he saw Holling with a shovel or bloody clothes or something that night—but no, all he really knows is that Holling was acting strangely and then lied about where he was. For all we know he was in North Jersey paying a visit to Annalisa.* Rory sighed and hunched over, leaning his forehead against the steering wheel. *But why would Holling send the chief of police over to pressure Shaw into staying quiet if he didn't have anything to hide? And why would he lie about the kid with alcohol poisoning? But then, of course, it all comes back to motive. There's no fucking motive.*

Eventually he pulled his keys out of the ignition and went inside. The house was dark and quiet; Kathleen must have still been at the church concert. He flipped the foyer lights on and walked straight back to the kitchen for a beer, which he took into the living room. After turning the baseball game on for background noise, he sat down with his notepad and read over the pages of notes he'd taken while listening to Shaw.

An hour and three beers later, he was still no closer to understanding a possible motive for Holling. *Shaw seemed so intent, so confident, though—but besides the most ridiculous speculation, there's simply no reason for Holling to get up in the middle of dinner, drive down to the middle school, and viciously murder those children. It makes no fucking sense. If Holling actually did it, like Shaw thinks, there's still a huge piece missing. Who was knocking on the front door that night? Why did Holling have that horrified look on his face when he came back from answering the door? That's the missing piece right there, but fuck if I know how to find it.*

Frustrated and out of ideas, Rory drifted into the dark kitchen and stared out the window into the backyard, sipping his beer. *What do I actually have?* He sighed and glanced around the kitchen, before his eyes settled on the basement door. *Maybe.* He suddenly remembered something Daniels had said about the boxes, the ones filled with Nathaniel's and his grandmother's possessions, down in the basement: *"We have to look through them...there's so much we could learn."* With his beer in hand, he went over and opened the basement door, letting the cold mustiness fill his nostrils.

The stairs creaked as he slowly descended them, his shadow thrown against the concrete floor in wild distortions from the single light bulb hanging at the bottom of the steps. *Maybe I missed something the first time through*, he thought. *Not that I even know what I'm looking for.*

The boxes—given to Kathleen by Evelyn, Nathaniel Foster's grandmother, when she passed away—were still scattered in the pool of light at the bottom of the staircase, where Rory had pulled them to get a better look inside. He'd never put away the empty photo albums and picture frames, so the first thing he saw when he got to the bottom of the stairs was Nathaniel's First Communion picture: the neatly combed hair, the white suit, the shy smile. Rory felt a momentary jolt of panic, nearly spilling his beer, as he remembered his nightmare of the beach house—of Nathaniel Foster standing in the shadows of the back hallway, always just out of reach, always disappearing just as blood began seeping from the ceiling and running down the walls. He quickly regained his composure, but turned the photograph over so Nathaniel Foster's luminous green eyes would not be fixed on him as he searched through the boxes.

Rory found a cobwebby beach chair in the corner of the basement, its legs scaly with rust, and brought it over so he could sit comfortably amidst the collection of sixteen boxes. He dragged a box over, the closest one within reach, and carefully opened it. It was filled with books. He removed a stack of the books, releasing a plume of dust, and set them in his lap so he could browse through them. There was a wide assortment of titles within that single stack: everything from *Jane Eyre* and *Wuthering Heights* to 80s murder mysteries and Stephen King novels. Rory guessed that Evelyn's and Nathaniel's separate book collections had gotten mixed up and packed together after Evelyn had died. He lifted the front cover of the King book *Salem's Lot* and read the inscription on the title page:

To Nathaniel

Happy 12th Birthday!
Don't stay up too late reading this, or else you'll get nightmares.

I love you,
Grandma

After examining each and every book, Rory returned them to the box in the same order he had found them and folded the lid shut. He took a drink of beer and clapped the dust off his hands and lap before leaning forward to slide over the next box.

By the time Rory opened the box filled with neatly folded boy's clothes, he had already spent well over an hour pulling out and meticulously looking through even more books, bubble-wrapped ballerina figurines, superhero and *Star Wars* action figures, folders stuffed with Nathaniel's curled and yellowed school work, and VHS tapes of Disney cartoons and other family movies like *E.T.* and *Home Alone*.

"What the fuck am I even hoping to find?" he mumbled to himself.

When he'd popped open the lid, revealing a row of carefully folded, dust-covered, t-shirts, shorts, and jeans, he considered giving up and going back upstairs for another beer. But instead, because he had no idea what else he could do to satisfy his gnawing desire to discover something—anything—to help understand why Holling may have killed the three boys, he dug his hands into the box and held up each article of clothing to examine.

The t-shirts were all suitably tiny to fit Nathaniel's small body. Some featured solid colors while others were striped. There was one with a Phillies logo and another with a print of the Tasmanian Devil from *Looney Tunes*, his unnaturally long tongue unfurled, shedding droplets of saliva. The jeans and shorts were all designed for a boy with short legs and a skinny waist.

Rory set the shirts, jeans, and shorts aside and reached in, without looking, for the next piece of clothing. What he brought out of the box next surprised him: it was a small, green dress. *I guess some of Evelyn's clothes got mixed in with his*, he thought. He put the dress down and leaned over the edge of the box. There was another dress—a blue one—a skirt, and a red blouse that looked as if it would fit a young girl.

When Rory reached in to lift out the remaining layers of clothes, his hand bumped up against something cold, metallic, and wiry at the bottom of the box.

"What the hell?" he said.

He pulled out the object and held it up in the light: it was the spiral binding of a well-worn notebook. And on the badly creased, orange cover of the notebook was written, in black Sharpie, *Nathaniel's Journal PRIVATE!!!* Feeling a rush of excitement, Rory immediately flipped it open.

The first entry was dated March 3rd, 1991. *Dear Journal* it began, and went on to describe how much school sucks and how lucky he is to have a friend like Christopher. *Without Chris*, he wrote, *I would kill myself. No doubt about it.* His handwriting was big and loopy, but his spelling was impeccable, and his writing style was sophisticated.

Rory scanned the journal entries through the spring and summer of 1991. Nathaniel had been consistent both in the frequency of his entries—there was at least one every month—and in the range of topics they covered: the wide awake nightmare of middle school, the new video games he was looking forward to playing, the book he was reading at the time, how much fun he was having over summer break, how much he missed summer break once school started again in September. He often wrote about his friendship with Christopher; they seemed to do practically everything together. Ride bikes. Go to the movies. Play video games. Have sleepovers. It was clear from the journal that Christopher had truly been Nathaniel's only friend.

Then came an entry from September 23rd that initially caught Rory's attention because of its brevity.

Monday, September 23rd, 1991

Dear Journal,

I want to tell Chris what I'm feeling, but I'm not sure it even makes sense in my own head. I don't know how to describe it, journal…all I know is that when I look in the mirror, I…don't see myself. I wish I knew what that meant because it makes me feel empty and lonely every time I look at myself. It's been going on for so long, too…maybe even years. But recently, it's gotten so bad, I'm purposefully avoiding mirrors…I even hate catching my reflection in the car window. I'll let you know if I talk to Chris about it.

Sincerely,

Nathaniel

The entry from October was more typical: he wrote about feeling sad that he was getting too old to Trick or Treat, but that he and Christopher were going to order pizza and watch scary movies on Halloween. Rory turned the brittle notebook page to find a longer entry from November. It looked as if it had been written hastily.

November 16th, 1991

Dear Journal,

I can't believe I'm actually writing this…I guess I'm still in shock about last night, so it feels weird to be putting this into words. Chris was visiting his cousins in New York, so I was left to fend for myself on a Friday night. Grandma was playing cards with her friends, and I was home alone.

I watched TV for a while, then played Nintendo, but I eventually got bored without Chris there. Besides, I was pretty distracted. I kept thinking about that weird feeling I get whenever I look in the mirror (I told you about it earlier). Then, out of nowhere, I got this crazy idea that I thought might make me feel better. For some reason I thought it would make that bad feeling of being empty and lonely go away.

I checked the time to make sure grandma wouldn't be home soon…and, I know this is crazy, journal…I snuck up to her bedroom. She has this giant closet that smells kind of sour, like old perfume or something, but with lots and lots of clothes. I don't know why I thought I should go in there…but something told me it was ok. It would make me feel better.

I looked through her clothes till I found this old, blue dress. It was soft and very beautiful. My hands were shaking and my heart was pounding as I did it, but as quickly as I could, I slipped off my jeans and t-shirt and…I put the dress on.

With my hands still shaking, I went over to the drawer in grandma's bathroom, where she keeps all her makeup, and opened it. I must have watched her a million times put makeup on, but I kind of froze there, staring into the drawer. Then, with butterflies fluttering in my stomach, I opened a lipstick and put some on. I couldn't look at myself in the mirror. Not yet, at least. Then I put some blush on, and finally looked up in the mirror.

This is the weirdest part, journal. I didn't feel so empty when I saw myself in that dress and with the makeup on.

Then, I thought I heard grandma pull into the driveway, so I jumped out of the dress, hurried it back into the closet, and sprinted back to the bathroom to wash my face. Turns out it was just a car passing by, but I'm glad I was careful. Grandma would be furious at me if she knew what I did.

Should I tell Chris about it? I don't know…I need to talk to someone, journal (a human, that is…no offense!). I think he would understand, but I'm scared he'll think I'm some weirdo and that he'll never want to talk to me again. I have to be brave and make up my mind. Thanks for listening, journal.

Sincerely,

Nathaniel

Rory turned the page. The next entry was short and undated:

I want to be a girl. I know it's weird, but it's true. Putting it into words helped me realize how true it is. What's wrong with me, journal? I don't want to keep thinking about how good it felt to wear that dress, to put that makeup on, but it's all I can think about. I can't help it. What do I do?

Poor kid, Rory thought. *No one to talk to at all.* He turned the page and read the next entry.

Thursday, January 2rd, 1992

Dear Journal,

My New Year's Resolution was to tell Chris about…the thing. I needed to get it off my chest, to hear someone tell me I wasn't crazy. And Chris is my best friend. If anyone would understand, he would. So I told him yesterday when we were hanging out in his basement.

I think he was pretty confused at first. Heck, I don't blame him! I think he was even a little weirded out. But then I told him about the night I tried the dress on, and the makeup, and how I felt more…normal when I did.

I said I hoped he didn't think I was completely crazy, that I hope it wouldn't affect our friendship. I still wanted to go fishing with him and play video games and everything, but that I hadn't felt 100% myself for a long time, and I wanted him to know why.

He eventually smiled and said that if it felt right to me, then it was right. He said I should listen to my heart. When I got home later that afternoon, I went upstairs and cried…such a huge weight off my shoulders!

There were only two more entries left, leaving the vast majority of the notebook filled with blank pages. The next one was undated, but featured a faded Polaroid picture affixed, with several layers of Scotch tape, to the top of the page. The photograph was of the dresses Rory had just pulled out of the cardboard box; they looked as if they were laid across Nathaniel's bed. He had Superman sheets.

What do you think, journal??? I know, they're not much, but they were all I could afford at the thrift store downtown with my saved up allowance.

Chris actually helped me pick them out...I told him he could wait outside or go into the comic book shop while I looked if it made him feel weird, but he insisted on coming in with me. I'm so glad I told him about everything...we don't talk about it very much, but it's just nice knowing that he's ok with me still, that it doesn't bother him.

Oh, and also, I'm working on coming up with a new name for myself. I really like Alexandra. What do you think?

The very last entry was dated March 11th, 1992: over a year since the first entry and about a month before both Nathaniel and Christopher were both murdered. It was also the longest entry by far, filling the back and front of four full pages. Rory read every word carefully.

Dear Journal,

Things had been going pretty well...until two really bad things happened last week.

First, just to keep things a little balanced, let me tell you some good stuff. I guess the best thing in my life lately has been Grease rehearsal. My part is pretty small...actually, I don't even have a line. But I'm OK with that. It's really just fun to hang out with Chris. He's an amazing actor and singer. I love watching him rehearse. I know we're only in middle school, but I have no doubt he'll get into Julliard one day. I just hope he remembers me when he's famous.

Plus, I feel like telling Chris my secret has only made us better friends...if that makes any sense. My greatest fear was that he'd stop wanting to be my friend or, worst case scenario, tell everyone and make fun of me. But I know now it was stupid to think he'd do something like that. He doesn't judge me even though I know he doesn't completely understand what I'm going through and how I'm feeling. But he listens to me and just wants me to be happy. And that's all I need.

But...now for the not so great stuff. So last Sunday when grandma was doing something at church, Chris came over to hang out and I asked if it would be ok with him if I put one of the dresses from the thrift store on. He said yes, of course. So we were using his video camera to work on our movie (we're making a movie using my castle Lego set...not sure if I told you that) when I had the "brilliant" idea of going outside to film on the front lawn. It was such a nice day, I thought it would be fun.

But, of course, I forgot about my dress! As we were outside playing, an eighth grader rode by on his bike. I don't remember his name, but I know he lives down the street. He stopped and laughed at me. "I always knew you were a fag," he said. Chris told him to shut up, but I just felt my throat get really tight, and I tried not to cry. Ever since then when I see him in the hallway, he'll step on the backs of my shoes and whisper, "Fag," in my ear. My cheeks burn every time, and I hope no one notices.

I think he may have told other kids, too...I can't be sure, but it just seems like everyone is looking at me all the time like I'm some kind of freak. Whenever I hear someone laughing, I just assume it's about me. It's been horrible...I feel sick to my stomach every morning when I have to go to school.

To make things worse, being at home has become torture, too. Last night, I had my green dress on and was looking in the mirror, putting some makeup on that I'd borrowed from grandma, when I heard a knock at the door. My heart jumped...I really thought she'd gone to sleep! Before I had a chance to answer, she walked into the room, saying that she just wanted to check on me because she saw my light was still on.

It's hard to describe what happened next...the memory is kind of blurry. All I remember is the screaming. She screamed at me, ordered me to take the dress off. When I was going too slowly, she grabbed my wrist and yanked me toward my dresser. She practically ripped off my dress and started pulling my pajamas on me.

I was crying, trying to explain myself, just like I did to Chris in his basement...but every time I tried to speak, she would cut me off and start talking about God. I finally got so frustrated, and was already upset about the eighth grader at school, I screamed at her...told her that I hated her...and practically pushed her out of my room and locked the door. All night long, I could her hear crying downstairs.

So I just don't know what to do now, journal. This morning and tonight at dinner, she didn't say anything about it...she barely even looked at me. I got paranoid and hid all my dresses and my skirt deep in my drawers so she couldn't find them and throw them away. I don't know if she would do that, but she might...she might even take you away, journal, if she knew I was writing about this. I'd better be careful.

Anyway, writing this has made me start to cry all over again. I'll give you an update soon, and hopefully things will be better by then.

Sincerely,

Nathanial (aka Alexandra)

Rory held the open journal in his hands, sitting, motionless, in the cool, dark basement. In his head, the tragic words recorded in Nathaniel Foster's journal—of being forced to remain silent and afraid, of being bullied at school, or being upbraided by his own grandmother—intertwined with the ugly, homophobic remarks Holling had shouted that day in his office: *sodomites and perverts...what's next, a fag mayor?...go back to your homo-loving city.* Not only the words themselves, but their dichotomy—between Nathaniel's innocence and Holling's hatefulness—boomed inside his head on a seemingly endless loop, growing louder and louder each time.

"Holling knew," Rory whispered. The journal slid out of his hands and back into the box.

Somehow, through some channel, Holling must—he must—have heard about Nathaniel, he thought, working it out in his head. *It's a small town, after all: gossip travels. Maybe, somehow, he'd even heard from Evelyn herself? Regardless of how he'd heard about it, he definitely fucking heard about it. And he must have told his fellow members of Christ's Healing Touch. An abomination like that, sullying this community? Unacceptable in the eyes of God. They had to teach him a lesson. They had to teach him a lesson for the sake of his own soul and for the sake of this God-fearing town.*

"There is joy in suffering," he remembered Dana Gladwell, the business manager at the church, telling him.

He imagined Holling, Gladwell, the pastor of the church, and a dozen other wide-eyed, pale-faced figures emerging from Sattler's Woods to confront Nathaniel that night. He imagined the terror in Nathaniel's green eyes as they grabbed him by the arms, his repulsion as they exhaled sour breath on him during the struggle. And he imagined the satisfaction they felt as they picked up the heaviest logs and stones they could find and began beating that poor child with them. He imagined Christopher and Andrew, their mouths covered and their arms pinned behind them, watching helplessly while the church members smiled as they did God's work.

Rory grabbed his phone out of his pocket and texted Daniels: *I know who killed the boys, and I think I know why. Call me ASAP*

Thirty

As soon as the clock on the radio of his Ford turned from 8:59 AM to 9:00 AM, Rory shot out of the car and through the doors of the Holling Chevrolet Dealership.

"Welcome to Holling Chevrolet," Mike, the same man who'd sat hunched over the reception desk three days earlier, said in the same monotone voice. "How can I help—" When his dark brown eyes drifted from his computer screen over to Rory, he froze. "You?" he asked, sounding confused. "Mr. Callahan."

"Is your boss in?" Rory blurted out. Ever since his epiphany in the basement the night before, he had been savoring the opportunity to confront Holling. Rory longed to see the look on Holling's face as he told him about Shaw, about the journal at the bottom of the box of clothing.

"Boss? My boss?" Mike stuttered.

"Mr. Holling," Rory replied sternly. "Is he in?"

"He's—not. I'm sorry. Do you want to leave a message for him?"

"Sure." Rory leaned over the desk. "Tell him I know what he did twenty-two years ago. And tell him I know why he did it, too."

Mike's eyes became wide with concern before narrowing again. An odd, almost menacing smile crept across his face. "Is that it?" His voice was suddenly gruff.

"That's it." Rory turned and, in an instant, was outside in the humid morning air.

He checked his phone as soon as he got back in the car, hoping for a message or voicemail from Daniels, but there was nothing. If she'd been working a night shift, she'd probably be getting back to him any minute now, but he couldn't be sure. He drummed his fingers on the steering wheel.

That was rash. That was fucking rash, he thought. *I really should wait for her. But what if I push Holling just a little bit and he completely crumbles? Perhaps he's been waiting to confess for years and breaks down as soon as I mention Shaw? I might be able to bring her something really big—the whole fucking case—rather than a couple pieces of hearsay and circumstantial evidence.*

"Fuck it." He started the car and headed east down the White Horse Pike toward the Holling Mansion.

The sky beyond the sprawling mansion was a solid, impenetrable gray. Rory glanced up at it before returning his gaze to the sharp gables and immense turrets of the mansion as they rose up over the black, wrought-iron fence surrounding the property. The vine-choked forest on the opposite side of the road was completely still in the dead summer air.

Rory turned up the driveway and stopped at the gate, just as he had a few days earlier. He rolled down his window and pressed the button on the intercom, expecting to hear the same, crackly voice of the woman from before. He waited about a minute, but there was only silence. He pushed the button again, and again there was no answer.

Rory's grip on the steering wheel loosened, and his heart rate started to return to normal. He exhaled sharply. *Probably for the best: this was a pretty fucking stupid idea. I need to meet up with Daniels, fill her in on everything, and then figure out the next step before talking to Holling. Yes—this is definitely for the best.*

He was just about to put the car in reverse when, suddenly, a black Chevrolet pulled up directly behind him, blocking his exit. Before he had a chance to react, there was a man standing beside the driver side door, leaning into the open window. Rory looked up to see the dull brown eyes and tangled beard of Mike, the receptionist from the dealership.

"What are you—" Rory started to ask.

"Shut the fuck up," Mike snarled. "What did you say back at the dealership?"

"It was a message for Mr. Holling," Rory answered, startled and confused.

Mike reached around to his back and pulled out a .45 caliber Glock. "Tell me, again, what the message was." He rested the muzzle of the pistol gently on Rory's left temple. The steel felt cool against his flushed skin.

"I said—" Rory stuttered. "I said I know what he did twenty-two years ago, and I know why." He licked his suddenly dry lips and looked pleadingly into Mike's eyes. "Listen, I don't know what the hell this is about, but I promise we can work it out."

Mike stared—his eyes bereft of any kind of spark or emotion—and he slowly lowered the gun. "Yeah, you're right," he mumbled. "We can work this out."

Rory heard only an animalistic grunt bubble out from Mike's lips, and felt only a hot flash of lightening as the butt of the pistol struck him across the forehead. In his head, the windows of the beach house shattered, Kathleen screamed and begged for her life, while his hand drifted away from Marie's in bed and plunged into coldness—and then, he tumbled into black.

Thirty-One

The first thing Rory noticed when he came to was the smell: a combination of rotting wood, sodden paper, and dust. It wasn't pungent, but it was heavy and rich; he could feel it resting in his nostrils and swirling through his lungs every time he breathed. It was overpowering.

Then came the throbbing pain in his head: it would start in his forehead before, like forked lightning, radiating throughout his skull. He tried lifting a hand to his forehead to lightly touch the epicenter of the throbbing pain, only to find his hand unable to move. He tried the other hand, but it, too, refused to budge from behind his back. With all his strength, he tried raising both hands simultaneously, only to feel the sharp, prickly burn of a coarse rope pull taut against his wrists. He looked down to see rope wrapped, with a sadistic degree of tightness, around his ankles as well: he was tied, securely—no room to maneuver even a quarter inch—to an old, wooden chair.

As the room came into focus, Rory saw he was in the middle of a small library. Shelves of books lined the walls, while a leather chair, footrest, and reading lamp sat in a corner. A wide, wooden door with a yellow glass doorknob stood in the center of the wall directly in front of him. Thick shades over the windows were drawn, leaving the room bathed in a dim, cold, blue.

Although the room was quiet, Rory could sense he wasn't alone. He turned his head slowly—afraid any sudden movement would cause a bolt of pain to shoot through his skull—to see a thin figure propped up in a large, leather chair, identical to the one in the corner. In the weak light of the room, he had to squint to see that it was a woman—stick-like, ancient-looking, but smiling widely. She had no teeth, so her smile was purely gum: dark pink and splotched with patches of black. Her long hair was thin and pure white. Her eyes were sunken; her face resembled a skull covered with only the thinnest possible layer of rippled, pure white skin.

"Hello?" Rory said. His voice was hoarse.

The woman seemed to be staring at him—it was hard to tell in the dim light—but remained silent and smiling toothlessly.

"Why am I tied up?" His voice was slightly stronger. "Where the hell am I?"

There was no answer from the woman: she remained silent and completely motionless. Her hands rested on her lap. Her emaciated body was covered in a lacy, white nightgown.

"Who are you?" Rory asked.

Just then, the heavy, wooden door opened, and Mike was suddenly standing inches away from Rory. He still held the pistol in his right hand.

"Don't you dare talk to mommy," he hissed. "She doesn't care what you have to say." He began pacing back and forth in front of Rory, like a dangerous, caged animal. "I just brought her down here so she could see what I caught: the man trying to destroy our family. Daddy's going to be happy to see that I caught you, too."

Rory still felt dizzy and disoriented from being knocked unconscious. He gently shook his head to clear away the cobwebs. "Where the fuck am I? Why did you bring me here?"

Mike continued pacing: anxiously, aggressively. He grunted a single, guttural laugh. "You're in our house, of course. And you know why you're here."

Rory shook his head gently again. "No. I don't."

In the blink of an eye, Mike leaned over Rory and gripped the arms of the chair until his knuckles turned red, then white, beneath a thick layer of dark hair. "Daddy always said I was stupid." His breath was sharp and rotten. "But I'm not. So don't treat me like I am."

Rory didn't immediately feel the butt of the pistol as it smashed into his temple—just the realization that his neck was twisted around and he was suddenly looking into the hollow eyes of the old woman.

He thought he heard a soft, wheezy laugh escape the grinning woman's toothless mouth.

Mike's scarred, pockmarked face was now directly in front of Rory's, though it took a moment to come into focus as the explosion of pain in Rory's head gradually died down to a smoldering ache. "You're here because of what you told me. That you figured out what we—" He stopped and struck himself several times, violently, with a heavy fist, on the head. "—what I," he corrected himself, "did in 1992." He went back to pacing, faster, more frantic now. "I tried to warn you. I tried to warn you and your mother not to look in those boxes. I tried to warn you with my letters. But you must have looked anyway. You had to write that fucking article, and you had to look in those boxes. You had to find his dress."

As if for the first time, Rory noticed Mike's brown eyes, his dark, curly hair. "You're—" He whispered. "You're Zeke."

"Ezekiel!" he roared. "Not Zeke! I hate Zeke. And not Mike, either." His monotone voice was softer now, almost gentle. "Daddy gave me that name—Mike. And I've always hated it. I've always fucking hated it."

"And you," Rory said quietly, "killed those boys?"

"I didn't mean to!" he screamed. "I didn't mean to!" He grabbed a fistful of his curly hair with his free hand and pulled it viciously. "Andy told me they were fags—worse than fags. One of them wore a dress! I only wanted to rough them up a little, 'knock the fag out of them.' Daddy talked about doing that to homos all the time! I thought he'd be proud of me if I came home with raw knuckles from beating up a couple of little flamers.

"But now I know, I know I got carried away. I don't know what got into me." His voice was quiet again, and tears were running down his cheeks, hanging from the tip of his nose, soaking his wild beard. "I know I never should have pulled down his pants and done what I did with the stick. That's when he started really screaming—they both started screaming—and we couldn't get them to shut up. That's when I grabbed the rock."

As Rory listened, he tried to manipulate his hands to loosen the ropes binding them to the back of the chair even just a little. But it was to no avail: the rope was tied so tightly, he was beginning to lose sensation in his fingers. *None of this will matter if the next time I leave this room is with a bullet lodged in my brain*, he thought.

"And Andy," Ezekiel said. He covered his face with a hand and began sobbing uncontrollably. "Andy," he repeated. "He didn't even want to go. But I made him. Told him it meant he was a fag if he didn't help me. And then—daddy said we had to do it. We had to do it if we wanted to protect the family. Daddy knocked him to the ground with the shovel, but he made me—" He was choking on his tears. A rivulet of snot ran down from his nose and covered his lips, forming mucus stalagmites every time he opened his mouth. "He made me—"

"What have you done?" John Holling's voice was calm and controlled, with only the slightest hint of anger; it was more scolding than furious. "What in God's name have you done?" The second time, his voice was plaintive, defeated. The diminutive, silver haired man stepped into the room cautiously. He was wearing an expensive gray suit; he must have been at a business meeting when Ezekiel called him away with urgent news.

At the sight of his father, Ezekiel immediately regained his composure, wiping his eyes and nose with the back of his hand. "I told you I had a surprise, daddy," he said, a trace of cautious elation in his voice. "He figured everything out and was looking for you, but I caught him before he could tell anyone."

Holling eyed Rory wordlessly, but stayed several feet away, as if he were repulsed by Rory's presence. He looked over at the scarecrow of a woman propped up in the leather chair. "And what is she doing down here?"

"I wanted mommy to see what I've done," Ezekiel answered, smiling a shy, lopsided smile.

"And what, exactly, have you done, Ezekiel?"

"I, uh—" He stuttered while a single, thick eyebrow rose in confusion. "I, I—I saved the family. I saved us."

Holling smiled sadly. "No, Ezekiel. In your final act of brain-dead idiocy, you did just the opposite."

"What do you mean, daddy?"

"All the hard work I've done. All the strings I had to pull to make sure that pederast ended up with those horrid video tapes. All the money I spent sending you away to the mental hospitals. All the lucky breaks we got, all my prayers that were answered, when the jury swiftly convicted the pederast. All of that delicate planning and architecture comes crashing down now."

"I don't understand, daddy."

"Of course you don't. You were the product of sin, so God cursed you—and me—with a violent soul and the intellect of an insect."

"Daddy?"

Holling smiled again and reached out his hand. "Give me the gun, Ezekiel. Let me do it."

Ezekiel hesitated but did what he was told and handed the gun to his father. Holling looked down at the gun in his hand, then up at Rory. His cold, blue eyes were far away. "God, please forgive me." With a single motion, he raised the gun to his head and pulled the trigger. The blood and flecks of brain matter spattered over the dusty Oriental rug, onto the hardwood floor at the edge of room, and even onto the lowest row of books on the bookshelf.

Once his ears stopped ringing, Rory could swear he heard the slightest, nearly inaudible laugh creep out from Elizabeth's shriveled lips.

"Daddy?" Ezekiel screamed. He fell to his knees at Holling's side and shook his lifeless body. "Daddy!" he cried, over and over again. "Daddy!"

While Ezekiel wept over his father's body, Rory struggled desperately to free himself from the chair. He pulled on the rope until he could feel blood running down his palms and began thrashing his legs as hard as he could. The movement seemed to catch Ezekiel's attention, and he looked up at Rory with red, bloodshot eyes.

"You," he growled and grabbed the gun off the blood-soaked rug. "This is all your fault!" He pushed himself off the floor and staggered toward the middle of the room. "You killed daddy!" He pointed the gun squarely at Rory's head. "I'm going to blow your fucking head off, just like you did to him."

"Please, you don't have to—" The image of a roof being torn off its rafters and flung into an endless, black abyss flashed through Rory's mind.

"Police! Put the gun down!" a voice suddenly thundered through the library. It was Daniels.

Ezekiel held the gun out in front of him and turned slowly to face Daniels in the doorway. "What do you want?" he said, fighting back tears. "You've already taken everything away from me." He was weeping when he swiftly raised the gun and pointed it at Daniels.

Two shots rang out, and Ezekiel instantly crumpled to the floor. Daniels rushed over to him and grabbed the pistol that had fallen from his hand.

"Fuck me," Ezekiel groaned as he held his bloody knees. "Please. Just kill me. Please. Shoot me. Please." The words sputtered from his bloody lips.

Daniels flipped him over gently and handcuffed him without any trouble. Then, she looked slowly around the room. She gasped and recoiled slightly when she saw Holling's corpse and the blood spatter radiating across the floor from his head, as well as the skeletal figure still sitting, and smiling with pink and black gums, in the chair across the room.

"Thank you," Rory said to get her attention.

Her distant look suddenly snapped back. "Oh my God," she said, and she immediately knelt down at the chair to begin untying him.

"How'd you know I was here?"

"I stopped by your mom's house when I got your message," she answered. She was doing her best with the ropes, but her hands were shaking badly. "She told me you went to the dealership. When you weren't there, I figured you might have driven out to this place."

"Nicely done, Officer Daniels."

"You, too, Mr. Callahan."

Ezekiel had stopped writhing on the floor and only whimpered now. He occasionally mumbled, between violent sobs, the same word over and over again: "Daddy."

Thirty-Two

It was five weeks later when Rory and Daniels spoke again. They met at The Oasis for a beer after Daniels's shift. As always, the bar was quiet and lightly patronized, but they sat in a corner booth for privacy anyway.

"How've you been?" Daniels asked after taking a long swig of a Victory IPA. Her usually bright brown eyes were flat and tired-looking.

"All right," Rory answered. "My son flew in a few weeks back, after he'd heard about—" He didn't complete the sentence. "Got to see him and my wife for a few days back in the city."

"How was that?"

Rory shrugged. "It was nice. Awkward, I guess, but nice." He smiled slightly. "Now I know if I want my son to fly home to visit, all I have to do is nearly get myself killed."

Daniels laughed politely, but her mind seemed elsewhere. "Whatever works," she joked.

"How about you?" Rory asked, sipping his Guinness. "Investigation coming along?"

Daniels nodded. "Things are moving quickly. Zeke broke down and confessed everything, so Thompson may get released as early as September."

Rory winced. *Exactly what he didn't want, and I brought it on him.*

"They have Elizabeth down at AtlantiCare," Daniels continued. "They said she was so malnourished, it was a miracle she wasn't dead when they found her. Holling had hired a nurse to take care of her during the day, but apparently she didn't do shit—and, apparently, Holling didn't care. They think her mental state deteriorated from decades of being bedridden."

"Jesus Christ," was all Rory could muster.

"On the bright side, Ezekiel also opened up about the Church of Christ's Healing Touch. He said parents forced their children to use those 'Purity Bands' all the time. Holling made him use them, not surprisingly. We've already brought Mark Forsythe, the pastor, in for questioning, and may be able to make an arrest within the month."

"Glad to hear something good will come of all this."

"And the department is a complete clusterfuck. McGarry, a bunch of other officers—maybe even the D.A.—are all being indicted for obstruction of justice."

"Good," Rory said. "Any of them resign yet?"

"McGarry already has, and I'm sure the others will follow suit once the state's investigation into the department really heats up."

"You weren't kidding about that clusterfuck comment."

Daniels sighed. "Complete shit show."

For several moments, they were both silent. They looked down into their beers, at the reflection of the Phillies game on the TV above the bar in the dark window, at the table, but they purposefully avoided each other's eyes.

"I keep having this dream," Daniels said after a time. "I'm wandering through that mansion again, looking for you. I follow the sound of the gunshot, but when I get to the library, he's already killed you." Her lips started to tremble, and her eyes dropped to her lap. "Your head has fallen back at an angle, and blood is falling from the hole at your temple in a steady drip. I can't move when I see you—I'm in complete shock that I failed, that I showed up too late. And as I'm standing there, someone comes up from behind and grabs me, puts his rough hand over my mouth so I can't make a sound. And—that's when I always wake up. Sweating, my heart pounding. I was screaming once, and woke Derek."

She looked up at Rory, and the two of them made eye contact for the first time in minutes. But again, they felt silent, as neither one of them knew what to say to help heal the wounds they had, in a way, inflicted upon themselves.

"There's a nightmare I keep having, too," Rory finally said. He told her about the little beach house and the sound of the storm winds—of his family huddled and frightened in the living room, of Nathaniel Foster standing in the shadows dressed in his First Communion suit. "I started having it after I lost my job, let my marriage go to shit. For some reason, I thought figuring out this case would make it stop. But I've been having it just as often as I did before the—" Once again, he didn't complete the sentence.

Daniels took another long drink of her beer and wiped her lips with the back of her hand. "So what are you going to do now?"

Rory thought about it for a moment. "I don't know," he answered. "I guess I'll write the article about—everything. When I feel ready, but I don't know when that will be." He lifted his glass and drained his Guinness. "What about you?"

Daniels smiled genuinely for the first time that evening. "There are a bunch of high-ranking positions about to open up," she answered. "And I think I'm due for a promotion."

When she got back to her apartment later that night, Daniels carefully laid her keys on the counter and quietly removed her holster so as not to wake up Derek. She undressed in the dark and slid into bed next to him without making a sound.

As she lay in the dark, the image of her mother's face from across the kitchen table that one summer morning—from years ago, before senior year—drifted to the forefront of her mind: the dark brown hair pulled back in a bun, the freckles, the warm smile. How it was like looking into a mirror. And the scars were there, too: the one snaking along her hairline, the other a clover-shaped pucker off the corner of her right eye.

Daniels suddenly felt a welling sense of comfort and peace rise from deep within her, and she soon fell into a sound, dreamless sleep.